Praise for *Below the Tree Line*

"A woman with healing hands and a rescued dog trap a killer in Susan Oleksiw's engaging *Below the Tree Line*."

—Hallie Ephron, *New York Times* bestselling
author of *You'll Never Know, Dear*

"Oleksiw crafts a classic small-town mystery, set in a near-forgotten corner of Massachusetts, where a closely knit cast of characters are forced to wrestle with the unwanted intrusion of the modern world that threatens long-standing traditions."

—Sheila Connolly, *New York Times* bestselling author of the
County Cork, Victorian Village, and Orchard Mystery series

BELOW
THE
TREE LINE

SUSAN OLEKSIW

BELOW
THE
TREE LINE

A PIONEER VALLEY MYSTERY

MIDNIGHT INK
WOODBURY, MINNESOTA

FIRST EDITION
First Printing, 2018

Book format by Bob Gaul
Cover design by Shira Atakpu

Midnight Ink, an imprint of Llewellyn Worldwide Ltd.

Library of Congress Cataloging-in-Publication Data
Names: Oleksiw, Susan, author.
Title: Below the tree line / Susan Oleksiw.
Description: First edition. | Woodbury, Minnesota: Midnight Ink, [2018] |
    Series: A pioneer valley mystery; #1
Identifiers: LCCN 2018016325 (print) | LCCN 2018020034 (ebook) | ISBN
    9780738759272 (ebook) | ISBN 9780738758916 (alk. paper)
Subjects: | GSAFD: Mystery fiction.
Classification: LCC PS3565.L42 (ebook) | LCC PS3565.L42 B45 2018 (print) |
    DDC 813/.54—dc23
LC record available at https://lccn.loc.gov/2018016325

Midnight Ink
Llewellyn Worldwide Ltd.
2143 Wooddale Drive
Woodbury, MN 55125-2989
www.midnightinkbooks.com

Printed in the United States of America

For my parents

One

On the third night Felicity lifted the shotgun from its place in the cabinet, and this time she loaded it. Uncertain if she'd heard anything on the first night, she'd come down the stairs of the old farmhouse one step at a time and walked carefully through the front room and on into the kitchen, listening and wondering if she'd imagined the sound of activity outside. At first she'd told herself it was nothing, just animals scratching around, perhaps a skunk, or mice fleeing an owl. Perhaps it was just a gust of wintery air rattling an old sash window. She'd peered through the glass panes, scanning the side yard by the kitchen. It was too early in the year for a curious bear, and she'd never known moose to wander so close to the house. Perhaps it was nothing more than raccoons trying to get into the storage shed, or coyotes circling the barn where the sheep dozed. It might even be a dog enjoying a night off-leash.

But she knew sounds and smells, and something had told her this was different. By the second night she'd been sure of it, for two reasons. The persistence of the noise, for one thing. And the consistency of the hour, for another. It might only be reckless kids, but she didn't dare ignore whatever it was. On the third night, she set aside her doubts and slept fitfully in a chair in the living room, dozing and waking. If there was something to discover, she would do so tonight.

And then, just before two o'clock, she heard the noise she'd been waiting for and hoping wouldn't come. She slipped in the shotgun shells, hearing the familiar clicking sound like cutlery sliding into a drawer or a screwdriver tapping on a car engine. She locked the cabinet and eased open the front door.

The porch ran the length of the small house. From her spot in the dark doorway she could see well enough by moonlight to study the ground immediately in front of her. She'd left her gloves inside, but she felt warm with her boots and flannel shirt and jeans. She scanned the ragged lawn for footprints in the hoar frost. Across the dirt driveway and beyond the fencing lay a field open to the night sky. She waited for a shadow to separate from a fence post, or rise up from the covering on the vegetable garden. But when all remained still, she stepped off the porch. She turned to her left, toward the barn. Not a sound of distress reached her. Whatever it was hadn't alarmed the sheep. If it had been a predator, she would have heard them stamping and bumping each other, and whining, frightened by the smell. But they slept, quiet and still.

She walked to the corner of the house, where she strained for a sound to guide her. A tree branch rustled in a windless moment and she lifted the shotgun and stepped along the side of the house. She took each step consciously, waiting and listening. As she passed in front of a window, she placed her foot on the ground. Here it was soft, partly thawed where she had cleared away debris, exposing the stone foundation to the heat of the sun. She'd forgotten about the rake she had left leaning against the shingles earlier in the day. Her foot on the softened earth was enough to sink the soil and jostle the rake; it clattered along the shingles as it slid down. She held her breath. The birds fell silent.

From behind the house came the rustling and tearing of branches. She bolted the few steps into the back yard, lifted the shotgun, and fired into the air, shooting over the twisted black branches of the old, abandoned apple trees. She didn't want to hit an unknown creature or person but she did want to scare off whatever or whoever it was.

Gradually the silence returned. The ground around one pole for the laundry line looked freshly torn up, as though two people had scuffled there, close to the old foundation. Felicity felt a rush of adrenaline. She'd thought of one person, never more than one. She tamped down a flash of fear and walked deeper into the orchard. In the dim moonlight draping the old fruit trees she traced a path through trampled ground leading away from the back of the house and into the woods. Ahead she could hear the indistinct sound of motion among trees, and then the night was still. She thought about following but she didn't have enough light for tracking at this hour. And she wasn't sure what she'd do if she caught whoever or whatever it was either. She'd have to leave that to Kevin Algren, the chief of police. She'd call him in the morning.

The little she could see told her whoever it was had been working along the back of the house. She headed to the side and inspected the ground around the bulkhead near the kitchen door. If someone was trying to get into the house, coming in through the cellar would make sense. But the area looked undisturbed. She returned to the other side of the house and picked up the rake. She kicked herself for not putting it away earlier. That tiny sound had given her away.

She walked over to the shed, which was in fact an old tack room added to the barn in her grandfather's day. He'd kept a few horses and wanted a place for saddles and bridles. Most of that was gone now, and Felicity used it for tools. If the intruder had gone for the tool shed, that would have made sense. She kept some of her better tools out here in warmer weather and moved them indoors when it got cold. She checked the latch on the shed, pulled. She shone her flashlight on the ground. But there was no sign anyone had tried to get in.

Maybe it was kids after all, too young to know that tools in the shed were valuable and could be pawned, the bulkhead had almost no security, and trying to dig through a crumbling foundation would never work. But anyone who knew anything about Tall Tree Farm knew she didn't have anything worth stealing except the tools. Neither did anyone else in West Woodbury. This part of Pioneer Valley might be beautiful, but it was a forgotten corner of rural America, a land prosperity had abandoned, choosing instead to follow the turnpike farther south.

Felicity walked back to the front of the house, making a mental list of what she'd have to do to put up motion detector lights on the back. She had them for the barn, but not the house, and that would have to change. She turned for one last look at the back yard and the old orchard.

"Next time," she whispered into the night, "you won't be so lucky."

Two

Felicity swung the pitchfork up and over her shoulder and heard the satisfying thump of soiled straw hitting the wheelbarrow behind her. It rocked on its rusty legs. She finished mucking out the stall and laid down a fresh bed of straw. When she'd first agreed to take on the three Merino sheep for local fiber artists, she hadn't given much thought to the extra work. She was used to work. But she hadn't cared for animals for a number of years, not since her dad had given in to medical problems and sold or gave away the few they had. And once he'd moved to the Pasquanata Community Home, she was too busy focusing on timbering and the vegetable garden to think about acquiring any animals.

She'd quickly adapted her life to caring for the sheep, and she'd begun to enjoy them. They nibbled

at her shoes and rubbed their noses against her jeans, and their growing coats made them look like tubby toys. She stabbed the pitchfork
into the fresh straw, breaking it up and spreading it around. Through
the cracks in the old barn wall, light washed over the new bedding and
lit up the dust rising into the air. She sneezed.

"Gesundheit."

Felicity backed out of the stall and turned to the barn door. "I
didn't hear you drive up. How long have you been there?"

"Just got here."

She tossed the last of the soiled straw into the wheelbarrow, hung
up the pitchfork, and maneuvered the wheelbarrow through the barn
door and around the back. A moment later she returned to the front,
where Jeremy Colson leaned against his truck, his arms resting on the
hood and his feet crossed at the ankles. The morning sun glinted on
his brown hair, turning it golden, and Felicity noted that in this light
she couldn't see the gray hairs growing in at his temple.

"I love watching you work," he said. "Especially when you sing to
yourself."

Felicity had known Jeremy her entire life, and they'd been partners
since his marriage fell apart, when his wife ran off with another man,
leaving him to raise his little girl alone. That was over fifteen years ago.

"So? I can enjoy myself, can't I?"

"I still can't believe you took them on." His blue eyes twinkled
with amusement.

Felicity followed his glance to the sheep in a small fenced field. "I
think they're kinda cute." She laughed. "Besides, you know I only say
that because they're not mine. If anything happens to any of them, I
just get on that phone and I call the artists' co-op and I say heya, folks,
your sheep need to see the vet. And they come running over like someone sighted Michael Jackson in the apple orchard." She rested her hands

on her hips and smiled. She was tall and slim, and wisps of dark brown hair loosened from her ponytail floated around her cheeks.

"Speaking of your orchard," Jeremy said.

"What about it?"

"You called Kevin Algren at five thirty this morning. What's this about someone trying to get into the house last night? Or maybe early this morning?"

"I was wondering why you were over here so early. You're working over near the Durston line, aren't you?" Jeremy owned a construction company, building new homes or other small or mid-sized projects. "Come on." Felicity waved to him to follow her. "I'll show you." She led the way around the barn to the back of the house. The morning sun had warmed the earth and any sign of frost had evaporated, but the ground was still torn up around the laundry pole. "It looks like people were fighting here."

Jeremy knelt down, looking along the old stone foundation and around the yard. "Well, the ground sure is churned up." He stood. "Interesting how much it's thawed, and so early. Kevin said you took a shot at someone, maybe two people."

"I shot high, over the trees in the orchard. I could hear something moving but I couldn't see clearly." She stepped toward the crumbling stone wall that once encircled the old orchard and pointed to the flattened grass. She cut the grass in the area only twice a year, once in the early spring and again in the late fall. Otherwise it grew as it wanted. She brought the sheep here once in a while and they seemed to keep it mostly in trim.

"You said it might have been one or two."

"I don't know how many, if it was just one or two. I'm not even sure it was a person."

"But you think it was."

Felicity rested her hands on her hips and gazed into the woods. "I do." She turned to look directly at him. "And so does Kevin or he wouldn't have called you. Did he call you as a friend or as an auxiliary cop?"

Jeremy shrugged. "He didn't say."

He walked into the orchard, following the path made just a few hours earlier, the matted grass slow to spring back in the late winter chill. Even though it had been an unseasonably warm winter, the earth resisted being hurried into spring. He held up a branch as he stepped into the woods, onto ground covered in debris instead of trampled grass.

"Lots of broken twigs," Felicity said, coming up behind him, "but nothing useful like a snagged scarf or a pair of gloves. I tried to follow the trail, such as it is, but I couldn't tell which way they went."

"You didn't find any tools they left behind?"

Felicity laughed. "It's not funny, I know. They do seem incompetent. Three tries and nothing to show for it." She grew serious. "The persistence alone is troubling, but it wouldn't take much to get into the house. The locks are old and I probably didn't even lock the kitchen door the first couple of nights. But what could they want?" She led the way back to the yard.

"It looks like they thought you had a cellar they could get into." Jeremy walked over to his truck.

"Then why didn't they go to the bulkhead, at the side?"

"Can't tell you that, Lissie. But Mom sent you something."

"Loretta?" Felicity frowned, her gray eyes shedding their sparkle. She liked Jeremy's mom, a lot. Never afraid to say what she thought, Loretta showed no signs of aging gracefully, or at all.

"The last time she went over to the shelter to volunteer, a few days ago, she came home with a dog to foster. And she thinks this one would be right for you. I told her you have a cat."

"Miss Anthropy can handle any dog of any size." As if in response to her name, a calico cat curled up on the porch lifted her head, flicked her tail, and resettled herself. Felicity looked into the cab of the truck. "So even though Kevin thinks this is nothing serious to worry about, just the random animal digging in my yard, he called you and you called Loretta and she suggested a dog?"

"Something like that."

"You're feeling guilty, aren't you? Like you should have been here."

Jeremy rested his hands on his hips, then put an arm around her and kissed her. "We've talked about this six ways to Sunday. Someday we'll have to make a decision."

Felicity nodded and ran her hand over his back before turning to the truck. "Is it the little Lab that Loretta was thinking of giving your daughter when she graduates from college next year?"

"Mom told me she thought you should have a dog right now— after she gave me a piece of her mind for leaving you alone out here."

Felicity looked back at the house, then at the sheep in the paddock beyond the barn. "I kept telling myself it was nothing, but I was watching myself take down the shotgun and load it, all the while thinking it's nothing, just an animal. But it wasn't. I know it wasn't. I just can't figure out what they—he or she or whoever—wanted."

"You may have scared them off with firing at them." Jeremy walked to the back of the truck and dropped the tailgate. He drove a white Ford F-150, which he traded in every two years. His construction business was hard on vehicles, he said, but Felicity knew he hated driving around in old rattletrap trucks, as he had for years when he was younger. And as she did now. Her Toyota always looked pathetic next to his Ford. He kept it clean and shiny, the better to highlight his company name, *Colson Construction*. He pulled the dog crate closer to the edge.

9

"Is there anything special I should know about the animal?"

Jeremy shook his head. "Forty pounds of love and affection."

"So where is this dog?"

"He's in there somewhere." Jeremy unlatched the crate door. Instead of jumping down and rushing to freedom, the small black Lab stared at him with worried eyes.

"Oh dear." Felicity peered in at the animal. "Why me?"

"Loretta says you're patient and the dog needs patience. Besides, this is what she had and she doesn't trust you to go get one even though it would be a good idea."

"So then I'd have two dogs."

"Not a bad idea."

Felicity and Jeremy continued to look in at the animal, which seemed to retreat deeper into the crate.

"What's his name?"

"Shadow."

"Hmm. What happened to him?" Felicity bent over to get a better look at his floppy but slashed ears.

"Not sure, but it looks like he was meant for dog fighting." Jeremy didn't try to hide the disgust he felt about this. He'd helped his dad with the dairy farm from an early age, and Felicity knew he was exceedingly gentle with animals. After his father died, Jeremy let the dairy business go, but he kept a small herd of dry cows because he liked having them around.

"Oh, I dunno, Jeremy." Felicity stepped back, shaking her head. "Dogs that have been used for that require far more know-how than I have."

"He didn't fight. He's what they call born cold. Such dogs won't fight, even if put in the ring with another dog going after them. They just lie on their backs and let the other animal tear them to bits."

"Jeremy, you're making me sick." She pressed her hand against her stomach.

"The rescue group got to Shadow first. He was in a holding place, with about fifty other animals. It doesn't look like he'd been held for very long, but that's only a guess."

Felicity peered in at the little dog. "He doesn't look like anything anyone would pick for fighting."

"That may be what saved him. But when he's upset, if someone comes to Loretta's house, he goes wild."

"So you think he'd be a good guard dog?" She stepped back to focus on Jeremy.

"Loretta does." Jeremy pulled the dog out of the crate and gently placed him on the ground. The four black legs trembled and almost collapsed. Felicity bent over and began petting Shadow, running her hands along his back and down his legs and over his stomach. And then she held her hands still, right along his sides. She closed her eyes and pressed her fingers deep into the dog's coat. The spindly, wobbling legs stilled, his breathing slowed, and the animal grew calm. After a moment, she opened her eyes and took a deep breath.

Through it all, Jeremy watched, his brow furrowing. "Well?"

"He's healthy. I guess it's okay."

"I've never seen you lay hands on a farm animal before." His smile was both affectionate and skeptical.

Felicity looked up at him, her hands resting on the dog's back. She looked down at them and turned them over, palms up. "Yes, I can tell. They heat up when I sense illness. Anyway, he's fine." She stood up and leaned over to rub the dog's head.

Shadow sat between them, looking from one to the other and then along the driveway. Felicity couldn't tell if the smells from the barn and sheep were new to him or if the dog was merely absorbed in figuring out the new humans. Jeremy lifted the carrier and deposited the plastic and metal crate in the back of her blue Toyota Tacoma pickup, then clipped a leash to Shadow's collar and handed it to Felicity.

She gave a gentle tug and took a few steps. "Let's see how he is on this thing, since he's probably going to have to be on one for a while." They walked down the driveway toward the road, the dog trotting between them, looking both alert and doubtful. They could hear cars in the distance. At this early hour, barely seven o'clock in the morning, the only traffic was a few commuters taking a shortcut to the old highway. The rhythm of life slowed considerably in this part of the world.

Felicity watched the dog sniffing his way ahead, not sure if he should be interested in the squirrels watching him with a bored look or the rustling near the stone wall. He seemed too timid to chase anything and she let her attention relax. She was relieved that he was as calm as he seemed, so far.

"Looks like you're getting a visitor." Jeremy nodded toward the small gray sedan turning toward Felicity's driveway, but instead of making the turn, it swung wide along the entrance and veered back into the center of the road. The sedan crossed back and forth along an invisible center line, slowing down and speeding up again.

"Who is that?" Felicity asked.

"It looks like Clarissa Jenkins's car. She runs the shelter where Loretta volunteers. Why is she coming to see you? Do you know her?"

"I don't think so. Maybe Loretta told her I was getting Shadow today."

"You sure are popular right now. First someone tries to break in, and now you have strangers coming by first thing in the morning." Jeremy watched the car swerve again. "Whatever she wants, she shouldn't be driving." He pulled out his cell as the car disappeared down the road. Felicity listened to his call into the police department.

Before he could finish, however, they heard what sounded like a car smashing through trees. They glanced at each other, and both took off running.

———

Jeremy reached the car first, folds of steel crushed between two trees, the hood popped, the undercarriage caught on boulders. The woman driver's body rested against a deployed airbag, with her face turned to the window. Blood ran from her temple down the side of her head.

"She veered off to miss a raccoon or a squirrel. I couldn't see." A young boy stood on the opposite shoulder, looking stunned. His bicycle lay on its side, the back wheel still spinning.

"Just stay over there," Jeremy called out to him. He reached in through the open driver's side window and grabbed the steering wheel. For a moment he lost his balance, but he recovered and leaned through the window. He laid his fingertips on the woman's neck and then turned his head so his ear was close to her mouth. After a moment he turned to Felicity and shook his head.

Felicity felt the leash tugging on her wrist. The little dog jumped from one spot to another, whining and struggling as he sank into the leaves or a rotten tree limb broke under his sudden weight. Felicity reached for him and pulled him away from the car, but the whining continued.

"He recognizes her, Jeremy, and it's making him crazy." She knelt down and tried to soothe the dog. He rested his muzzle on her shoulder, but his gaze was fixed on the body in the car, and the whining, though softer, filled her ears.

Jeremy stepped back and stared at the car. "The police should be here soon." He looked across the road. "Is that boy all right?"

Felicity turned to the boy still squatting on the shoulder by his bicycle. "I'd better make sure he's okay." She had to struggle to get the dog away from the car and across the street, and immediately the boy knelt down to hug Shadow. She heard the sound of a siren in the distance.

"Are you okay?" Felicity asked. "Were you hit?" She looked him over quickly but saw no sign that he'd been struck. His bike was on the ground but looked undamaged. "Do you need the ambulance?"

The boy, not yet a teenager, shook his head. For all his trendy appearance, with a Mohawk haircut and ripped jeans, he was a scared child. He pulled the dog closer, and when Shadow nuzzled him, both grew calmer. "She just came over the hill at me and then she swerved into the trees." The boy looked across the road, and then quickly looked up at Felicity. "Is she okay?"

"I'm more worried about you," Felicity said. "You're Pat Holyoake's boy, Nathan."

The boy nodded. Hearing his name seemed to draw him back into himself. He wrapped his arms around the dog and hugged tighter. Shadow whimpered and rested against him. She felt a rush of gratitude for the dog's unexpected appearance in her life, just when she needed him. She had no way to tell young Nathan that Clarissa Jenkins couldn't possibly have survived, not with the injuries she could see, to say nothing of those she couldn't.

Three

The day after the accident, Felicity was still unsettled. She'd watched the EMTs carry off Clarissa Jenkins and made her statement to the police. Chief Algren thanked her and Jeremy and sent them on their way. But the experience left her feeling strangely unnerved, and she kept hoping the young boy was faring better. She turned to work for comfort.

She spent Tuesday morning inspecting the back part of the farmhouse. If an intruder really did think he (or she) could find a way in, the least obvious site was the rear wall, where an old porch had been winterized years ago and then turned into a storeroom over a cold room off the cellar. This was the least-used part of the house. But it was where she'd found evidence of activity, near the laundry pole, so it was where she went to work. She cleared away twigs and leaves near the foundation, reattached some of the storm windows, and fixed the lock on the kitchen door, aligning the hasp and tightening screws. She dug into the deteriorating stonework and added a bag of cement to her list of items for the hardware store. Despite the poor condition of the foundation, she found it hard to believe anyone thought he could pull out stonework and tunnel a way in. Still, that's what it looked like. As an extra precaution, she cleared away some of the plantings she'd allowed to grow out of control, just so no one had a place to hide. Perhaps if the house looked like someone was resisting, the attacker would go away.

The extra work put her behind schedule, so she postponed a training lesson for Shadow and decided to take the dog along on her errands. She lined the cab floor with an old army blanket for him and loaded the empty crate into the back of the truck, just in case. She wasn't really afraid the dog would figure out how to escape the carrier, jump out, and bolt, more that he'd fall out and run off in terror. Before she could get the dog into the front seat, however, a small yellow sedan pulled into the driveway and parked behind her pickup. A woman climbed out. Shadow stared at her, his ears up and his nose quivering.

"Felicity O'Brien?" The woman introduced herself as Sasha Glover. Perhaps in her mid-twenties, she was a pretty blonde in stone-washed jeans and a striped red-and-white boatneck jersey under a quilted red jacket. Her eyes were red-rimmed.

Felicity smiled as she extended her hand.

"I wanted to thank you." Sasha was polite and formal, but her chin quivered as she spoke. "For being there at the end with Clarissa." She paused, but when Felicity looked confused, she continued. "She was a second cousin. Actually, my mom's cousin, but we were pretty close."

Felicity never wanted to take credit for something she hadn't done, but she held her tongue as she listened to the words of gratitude. She hoped no one would ever tell Sasha that the cousin she was so fond of died alone. She should never lose that tiny bit of comfort. Felicity looked for a way to move on to something less painful. "We thought Clarissa might be coming to see me."

"We?"

"My friend Jeremy Colson was here. He'd just brought me a dog to foster."

"Is that the dog?" Sasha leaned forward to get a better look. "That looks like one of Clarissa's shelter dogs. Is it Shadow?" Through the window the two women could see the animal, with his snout resting on the back of the driver's side seat, staring at them, looking mournful as only a Lab can look.

"That's him. He's adorable but still very frightened." Felicity turned back to Sasha. "Loretta probably told her I had the dog. Perhaps that was why she was coming here to my place."

"She told you she was coming?" Sasha looked hopeful and took a step toward her, as if Felicity had solved a problem.

"No, but she started to turn into my driveway, and then it looked like she changed her mind. Do you know why she might have come here?"

"No, but I knew she meant to." Sasha looked lost, as if Felicity had given the wrong answer to an important question. "She told me she wanted to talk to you first, and then she said we'd talk." Sasha seemed doubly disappointed. "She had something to tell me but she was waiting till she talked to you. Now I guess I'll never know."

Felicity gave her head a quick shake. "I can't think of anything either." Every time she looked at Sasha, she heard the sound of the crash and saw Clarissa's blood-soaked hair matted to the side of her head. She shut her eyes to dispel the unwelcome image. When she opened them and looked at Sasha again, Felicity felt a surge of compassion for the young cousin. "I heard she'd just gotten engaged. Jeremy mentioned it."

"Yeah," Sasha began. "We knew she was seeing someone, but she didn't tell me who it was." She frowned and pursed her lips.

"The police will want to notify him also." Felicity waited for Sasha to say something, but instead the woman gazed around at the fencing and barn. "Was the relationship not working out?"

Sasha turned back to her. "I'm not sure. We'd planned on getting together later this week. She said she had a couple things to tell me." She perked up at this memory. "We were wicked close." Then she relaxed and continued looking around the farm. "You have a nice place."

"Thank you." Felicity was surprised at the change in the conversation. "Would you like to see the sheep?"

"I have to get to work, but I'd love to sometime. Clarissa said you inherited your place. She knew all about the old farms around here. Your family has had this place for generations. Lots of trees and vegetables." Sasha scanned the fields ahead, the paddock with the sheep, the barn with its wide-open doors, as though checking items off on a mental list. "I know nothing about farming."

"You don't have to unless you're planning on taking it up. Are you?" Felicity was surprised at the young woman's comments about Tall Tree Farm, but she understood grief. After losing her mother when she was barely an adult, she had struggled to understand her place in the world, and she'd learned the hard way that life in a city apartment was not for her. That was almost twenty years ago, but the memory was still vivid. She felt it again as she studied Sasha, who in her heels and beringed fingers surely viewed life differently. She'd definitely fit in an urban world.

Sasha gave her a startled look and grinned. "Me? Farming?" She shook her head. "Oh, no. But Clarissa told me you're doing that CSA gardening. What is that?"

"CSA is community supported agriculture. It's a fancy term for buying produce from your local farmer."

"That's good flow. I like that." Sasha nodded, a smile warming her expression. "Clarissa and I used to talk about how the old farms grew and then were cut up, but not here so much, and how it's been pretty quiet here all the time. She wanted me to know that."

"She wanted you to know about the history of farms in this area?"

Sasha nodded, her initial reticence fading. "She said there's a history here, a special value, that no one knows about. The land around here has been spared what happens when people find out about a small town with land." Sasha glanced at Felicity and then looked away, as though she'd said too much. "That's one of the things Clarissa liked to talk about."

"It's nice to hear our area is being appreciated." Felicity felt deeply touched to hear this young stranger talk about the values her cousin had passed on. "This area has always been mostly poor. We had the period of the mills, but we were never as large as other towns and the population here never grew much. The farms pretty much remained intact, even if they were small. This is the most rural part of the state."

Sasha began to chew her lower lip. "Clarissa thought it was important to understand the land. She talked about that a lot. I drive by farms all the time but I never gave it any thought until Clarissa started talking about it. She wanted me to understand how she felt about things."

"You'll miss her," Felicity said.

"Yeah." Sasha rested her hand on the fender of the blue pickup and studied the mournful dog in the window as she steadied her feelings. She watched the sheep in the distance and took in the pile of kindling and the wood-splitting tools left near the side of the house. She seemed to be working something out for herself. A passing car tore the silence and broke the spell.

Felicity ran her finger over her watch crystal, rubbing the flat surface. If she delayed much longer, her father would be going into lunch and then she wouldn't have a chance to talk to him in private, when he was more likely to reminisce. But she liked Sasha, and liked hearing her talk. The woman had forged a bond with a cousin very different from her, and now it was broken. She'd feel the loss acutely. There was nothing Felicity could say that would lessen the pain, but perhaps there was something she could do.

"Have you got a minute?" she asked. "Come with me. I want to show you something special. You've got a minute, haven't you?"

"Well, I guess ... "

Felicity led the way past the house and into the woods. The air cooled in the shade of the pine trees, then warmed when they passed through a patch of sunshine. "The winter has been so mild and the spring started so early that a lot of the wildflowers are coming up much sooner than normal. But this one regularly comes up in April. I always feel better about life when I see it." The two women crouched to walk beneath branches and through the undergrowth. "Watch where you step, Sasha." And then she knelt down and pointed.

Sasha stood behind her and leaned over. "Omigod, what is it?"

"It's a lady's slipper. Pink."

"What's it doing here?" Sasha slowly knelt down and leaned on her hand, to get closer.

"It's a wildflower, a kind of orchid," Felicity said. "Haven't you seen one before?"

Sasha shook her head. In the silence the two women admired the softly rounded pink-and-white flower dangling on its stem. The bird chatter picked up again and the wind continued its path, carrying the fragrance of pine trees.

"Not many people know they're here. But when you do, you have to be careful because it's so easy to step on them. When I was a little girl my parents used to bring me out here to show me when they first came up. My mom used to tell me a story about them. According to folklore, these flowers represent the footprints of an Indian woman who ran through the snow looking for medicine to save her tribe. She ran until she collapsed and died, her feet bloody and frozen. The lady's slippers grew where her feet touched the ground."

"Oh, that's so sad." Sasha screwed up her face in sympathy. "And so beautiful."

"My parents always warned me to step carefully. I used to walk past them on tiptoe, afraid even my tiny feet might damage the ground where they grew. Whenever I come here I feel just like I did as a little girl."

"I never even knew they existed." Sasha leaned back, still admiring. "If I had some of those in my yard, I'd bring them in and keep them on the windowsill."

Felicity laughed. "Where they would die."

"They don't like sun?" Sasha looked up at the thick canopy.

"They don't like leaving their natural home. They're very hard to clone. The real ones usually die if they're dug up. They need a particular kind of fungus to grow, and they take forever to grow from seed to something like this. Fifteen years or so." She reached out to run her index finger along the curve of the flower. "They used to be scattered through the woods, but over the years they've been crushed and their environment pretty much ruined. This is probably one of the last few around here. There might be others, but no one cares as much anymore."

"And you come out here every spring to see them?"

21

"I keep quiet about it because they'd be trampled if too many people came by. But you're welcome to come any time."

Sasha studied her, a warmth of affection spreading across her face.

"I'm sorry about Clarissa," Felicity said. "From what you've told me, she would have enjoyed something like this."

"She would have loved it." Sasha touched her index finger to the flower's tip. "And she would have understood it the same way you do."

———

Later that morning, soon after Sasha drove away, Felicity stopped into the West Woodbury Police Department. Even though West Woodbury was a very small town, with a population under five thousand souls, there were usually three officers on duty throughout the day. To her surprise, Felicity didn't see even Padma Mantell, the department administrative assistant, when she walked in.

The department was located on the first floor, which was really the basement level, of Town Hall. Built into the side of a hill at the end of the nineteenth century, Town Hall creaked and occasionally shifted an infinitesimal amount but was never less than the sturdy remnant of times gone by, an imposing Victorian building reminding the residents of their duty. The police department enjoyed the advantage of being the only cool spot in the building during the summer heat, and the least pleasant place in the winter. In the spring, every person's temperature fluctuated, perhaps in accordance with the weather or the upcoming town meeting.

"Hey there," Padma said a few minutes later. She dropped a paper sack on her desk and slid into her chair, letting it roll back to the wall, where it bumped gently before she walked it forward to the desk.

"No one was here when I came in," Felicity said.

"So did you steal anything?" Padma grinned. "Sneak into any files?" With her varied-colored hair—today it was green—Padma was a reminder of the larger world and its trends. She sported a spiked hairstyle, nose rings, tattoos, and rows of tiny silver bracelets, all in contrast to the conservative clothes Chief Kevin Algren insisted on. She could wear colored tights to match her hair, but she was otherwise to be covered in such a way that his grandmother would feel comfortable walking into the office. But Kevin had learned to spell her new name, which she'd adopted after her first yoga class.

"I wanted to know if Kevin had come across any reason why Clarissa Jenkins might have been on her way to see me," Felicity said.

"Was she?" Padma asked, her heavily made-up eyes widening.

"Jeremy and I were out walking, and we saw her coming down the road. It looked like she was about to turn into my driveway but then changed her mind." Felicity glanced around. "She was driving very erratically."

"That's what Jeremy said when he came in yesterday. But I haven't heard anything."

"Where is the chief?"

Padma turned toward an inside door. "Coming down the stairs. With the head selectman, it sounds like." And, of course, she was right. Kevin came through the door first, nodded to Felicity, and headed into his office. The head selectman followed. When the two men finished their conversation, Dingel Mantell, Padma's dad, came over to his daughter's desk.

In addition to his role as head selectman, Dingel ran a small sawmill a few miles down an old side road. He was one of the few people not entirely unhappy at the sight of new homes sprouting in old pastures. More than halfway through his fifties and the survivor of numerous industrial accidents, Dingel was still the first one to be called when fine work was needed. Felicity inhaled the comforting aroma of fresh sawdust emanating from his denim overalls, which he wore belted at the waist. The sleeves of his plaid flannel shirt were rolled up to his elbows, and shavings stuck out of the cuff-made pocket.

"I stopped in to see Kevin," Felicity began, "but I can do two things now. I'm getting ready to file the next cutting plan I've been working up with my logger, Lance Gauthier, so you should be hearing from him."

Dingel, always a man of few words, nodded and tipped two fingers to his temple in acknowledgment. "You tell your dad I said hello. Miss him when I see that rod and reel."

"I'll tell him." Felicity knew how much the two men had loved fishing together. Nothing was allowed to interfere with that sacred time. With another salute and a few words with his daughter, Dingel was gone. Felicity poked her head into Kevin's office. "Got a minute?"

Kevin waved her in. "Real sad business." He swiveled in his chair and inspected the half pastry Padma had placed on his desk.

"She was a friend of Loretta Colson's," Felicity said.

"So Jeremy said. What's this about her driving erratically down your road?"

"It looked like she was turning into my driveway but then she changed her mind. I wondered if you'd found anything in the car to explain that. I didn't know Clarissa, but she told a relative of hers she was coming to see me. It sounds like she had something to tell me." Felicity briefly described Sasha's visit.

Kevin swiveled in his chair and pulled open a desk drawer. He opened a file and scanned the contents. "This is all on the computer, but our WiFi, or whatever it is, is down."

"I thought the town was fixing that."

He looked at her over the file with an expression that said, *In your dreams*. "The phone company told us we weren't important enough for them to bother with, so we'll have to put up with the service we have."

"They didn't say that."

"In so many words, they did." Kevin returned to the file. "So, as to your question, the answer is yes. She had an old envelope addressed to her that had your name and address scribbled on it, so maybe she was coming to see you."

"What was in the envelope?"

"Electric bill."

"Anything else? A note, initials?"

"You think she was interested in the CSA garden?"

"You know about that?"

"Everyone knows about that, Felicity."

"Sometimes I forget how small West Woodbury is." Felicity gazed out the window at the steep side street and the small parking lot beyond. "May I ask a question here?"

"Would it do me any good to say no?"

Felicity laughed. "Was there any problem? I mean ... "

"You mean was she drinking at seven o'clock in the morning or smoking something or on pills?"

"Yes. I wondered if you'd noticed anything." Felicity licked her lips and took a deep breath. "Her driving was pretty erratic."

Kevin shifted in his chair, trying to get comfortable. "The answer to that is no, I didn't smell anything on her, and she didn't show any outward signs of being impaired. But the ME will have to decide on that one."

"It's frustrating."

"I know you talked to the young fellow on the bicycle." Kevin didn't wait for her to comment. "Saw her swerve, to miss an animal in the road, he thought. He's pretty shook up."

"Nathan Holyoake? My dog calmed him down while we waited for the ambulance."

"We found a repair bill in her purse." Kevin eyed the pastry again. "She'd just picked up her car at the Flat Road Automotive."

"That's where I go." Felicity recalled Jeremy commenting about the loose steering wheel and the absence of skid marks. Before she could ask about the car, however, Kevin pulled an envelope out of the file and shook out a small plastic sleeve holding a photograph.

"So I have a question for you." He held it out to her. "Recognize this?"

Felicity peered at the picture. A man and a woman stood together, with the woman smiling directly at the camera and the man looking over her shoulder, away from the camera, as though something behind them had caught his attention. "Is that the Grange building in Finerton?"

"It is."

"Who are the people?"

"That's Clarissa Jenkins and a man we can't identify." Kevin put the photograph away. "The family doesn't know who he is, but he could be the fiancé. We'll find him." He slid the envelope back into the file.

"Sad for something to happen now, when she was on the verge of a new life."

"It's sad whenever it happens." Kevin gave the pastry one last look and pushed it away. "Okay, Felicity. Let's talk about something else." He shifted in his chair, as though gearing up for a difficult task. "You didn't come in to talk about Clarissa Jenkins. Enough stalling. What's this about an intruder? And why didn't you come in yesterday about it?" He returned to the pastry, tugging at the corner of the napkin it sat on. Every time he turned his head, he seemed to catch a glimpse of it and the pastry moved another two inches to the left. Felicity watched it heading toward the edge of the desk. "Well?"

"I think I handled it okay."

He wiggled his fingers at her. "Come on. Details. Let's hear it."

"I thought I heard something."

"That's what you said at five thirty in the morning when you called me." Kevin struggled to get comfortable in his chair. "The town paid god knows how much for this damn ergonomic chair." Felicity gathered up the pastry and took it out to Padma.

"Okay, about the intruder," she said when she came back. "I thought I heard something for a couple of nights, and on the third night I was sure of it. So I went out with a shotgun but whoever or whatever it was bolted before I could get to it. Really, Kevin, why do you always do that when I tell you something?"

"Do what?" Kevin rested his elbow on the chair arm and his forehead in his hand, and then rubbed his hand over his face.

"Do that. Cover your whole face with your hand."

"You went outside with a shotgun."

"I told you that."

"And it was loaded."

"The third time, yes. I told you that."

"And you took a shot at someone, or maybe two someones."

Felicity pressed her lips together. "Three nights in a row, Kevin." She looked away. "I shot over their head."

"Felicity, the trouble with that is the shot has to come down somewhere."

"Three nights, Kevin."

"Jeremy told me he looked over the area with you and he can't tell if it was a person or an animal, but it looked like the ground was torn up." He clasped his hands in front of his stomach, his fingers looking for the belt buckle that used to be right there whenever he folded his hands over his middle, but in the last few years it had gone missing. He stopped searching.

"So?"

"Did your family ever bury scraps?"

"Kevin!" She tried to glare at him. "You've heard about composting?"

"You never know what could be enticing animals." He sighed and swung around to glance out the window at the street and parking lot beyond. "Anything last night?"

"Nothing."

"Taking precautions?"

"Cleaning up the area, tightening windows and locks, patching the foundation. And I have the dog now, too."

"That should do it." He bounced forward in his chair. "I'll make a note, so if something happens again we can compare it."

"You're not worried?"

"Not unless you are."

Felicity stood up. "I'm more worried about what happened to Clarissa Jenkins. I want to know why she was coming to see me."

Four

By the middle of the week, Felicity had taken Shadow twice to the Pasquanata Community Home for visits with her dad. Six months ago she had accepted the inevitable and moved her dad to the home, but it had taken her almost two years after finding him gasping for breath on the barn floor or falling silent on the phone when she asked him where he was calling from. Not dementia, his doctor told her, heart disease—heart attacks, strokes, heart failure. He kept bouncing back, but each time the bounce wasn't quite as high as before.

Shadow considered the visits a treat. When she snapped on the leash and headed for the home's front entrance, the dog perked up and trotted smartly to the door, where he was greeted by a row of elderly men and women enjoying the sunshine. Her first few minutes were given over to answering questions about how Shadow was faring, what he ate, and where he slept. The nurses tried to persuade the residents to stay on the concrete apron while one of the women headed into the great unknown of the straw-covered garden before quickly being redirected. Today, as usual, Felicity's father pushed his way to the front of the pack.

"You tell Loretta not to take those big ones," Walter O'Brien said, looking around the yard as though he might see other dogs. "They eat more than people." Today he wore a blue-and-white-striped cotton shirt, chinos, and a bright green sweater. He insisted on dressing properly, as he called it, if he was going to be around other people all day. It was a change after wearing only barn clothes and boots for almost eighty years, and Felicity wasn't quite sure what to make of this new version of her dad.

"I'll be sure to let her know. Only the little ones."

Walter insisted he wasn't cold and didn't want to go inside, so Felicity held on to the leash while her dad checked over the animal. He was remarkably supple and strong for his age and health conditions. He knelt down while he examined Shadow. "Hmm. Seems okay."

"He's been to the vet and I have his papers."

Walter got to his feet. "And the sheep?" He gazed at her.

"The sheep are fine, Dad. I have them in the paddock today and I move them every day." The little dog nuzzled her leg and stared up at Walter, perhaps unsure why he was no longer the center of attention. "They love the wildflowers. Those are three very happy sheep. They'll be even happier when the dandelions come up. Which is probably next week."

"They're stupid sometimes."

Felicity laughed. "But they're not mine, so I don't have to worry about that."

"Don't let him bother them." Her dad looked at Shadow. He pulled a chair out into the sun and sat down, keeping a watch on the dog. Most of the other residents had gone back into the building; two men sat along a brick wall, soaking up the sun. Felicity caught the smell of a smoldering cigarette and saw the man cupping his hand behind the chair. "Gotta watch new dogs all the time."

"Shadow's well trained," Felicity said. "Loretta Colson got him from Clarissa Jenkins. I think I told you that. Did you know her? She was from around here but I didn't know her. She was a Bodrun on her mother's side, according to Loretta."

"Oh, no, Lissie, you mustn't go visiting that family," Walter said. His breath quickened and he reached out his gnarled fingers to grasp her wrist. He could squeeze tight enough to hurt. "Now, you mustn't. Promise me. No, you mustn't go visit that family. Mustn't do that."

Confused by the sudden change in her father, Felicity took the easy route and agreed with him. "Don't worry, Dad. I won't." Surprised at his distrust of the family, she tried to recall anything she'd heard about them to justify her dad's feelings. "I thought you liked the Bodruns. Weren't you friends with Ezekial Bodrun?"

Her father reared back, his eyes widening, and then bolted to his feet. "Come on. I'll put a stop to this. I'm not dead yet."

Shoulders hunched and fists clenched, his bright green sweater almost glowing in the bright sun, Walter O'Brien headed down the cement walk to the parking lot. Felicity untied Shadow's leash and ran after her dad, dragging the dog, who seemed to think this was a waste of energy.

"Dad! Dad!" Felicity was startled at how fast her father could move even now. He hadn't shown such energy and determination in months, but he was halfway across the parking lot before she caught up with him.

"Not that way." He bolted away from her and headed across the narrow road into an old field, an abandoned pasture turning into a meadow.

Unable to stop him as he stumbled forward, Felicity ran back to the home and banged on the emergency exit, keeping her dad in view. An orderly opened the door, took one look at her and then Walter crossing the field, and raced after him.

"Dad!" Felicity and Shadow and the orderly caught up with her father and walked with him until he slowed down.

Walter scanned the horizon, then turned and looked back the way he had come. "There's a way in here." He stumbled back toward the road, and Felicity followed him. "I'll tell them," Walter said. "They'll have to listen to me."

Felicity and the orderly led him back to the front entrance, but there he balked. He looked around, confused but steady on his feet, and turned back to the view of the woods.

"It's okay, Dad. You don't have to worry." Felicity wasn't sure what he was worried about but figured reassurance was always good. "I have a guard dog now, so you don't have to worry."

Walter looked down at the dog and then bent over to look more closely. He pulled up a chair and sat down, then rested his hand on the animal's head. "He's a good guard dog. That's what they say about Labs. Good guard dogs."

"He's a good guard dog, yes." Felicity sighed with relief. Shadow was turning out to be a terrible guard dog. If someone approached the house or barn, he certainly knew right away, but he was as likely to hide under the bed as bark a warning. He was leery, wary, timid, and still uncertain about his place on Felicity's farm. And being small didn't help. Miss Anthropy was surprisingly tolerant of him, and, if she were human, one might even say she was kind. But then, Felicity worried the cat was just biding her time until she could teach the interloper a lesson.

"Don't go visiting strangers, Felicity."

"I won't, Dad."

"You haven't met that family. You don't know them, so don't go visiting them."

She guessed he had to be talking about the Bodruns and Clarissa Jenkins, and answered accordingly. "Clarissa's dead, Dad. So you don't have to worry."

But he would not be comforted. "You have enough friends and relatives as it is." He licked his lips several times and began rocking in his chair, back and forth, his hand pulling the dog's head closer and then back. The dog watched him but didn't protest. The animal seemed to understand Walter.

"I have plenty of friends, yes. And I seem to be getting a full barn."

Her father blinked, confused, and then broke into a smile. "Sheep." He nodded. "Chickens. Get some chickens. Keep them with the sheep."

"Why would I do that?"

"They clean up after the sheep, break up the scat and turn up the soil." He seemed very pleased with this information and bobbed his head, smiling and petting Shadow. "Save you some work." He seemed lost in thought. "Chickens and sheep. Small farming, but good."

"Did you and Mom start out with sheep and chickens?"

"Don't let them wander," he said. "You'll be chasing them. Keep them out of the woods." He looked down at the dog. "Don't let him wander either. No telling where he might end up."

"I'll keep an eye on him," Felicity said.

"No wandering, Lissie. You go chasing him, and he could go anywhere and then everyone would be chasing him. No telling where that might lead. Promise me, Lissie." He grabbed her wrist again, and so vehement was his demand that she promised and repeatedly reassured him. But by the time she left, he had grown agitated again, and she worried that talking about the farm had been a mistake.

———

The mild winter was turning into a mixed blessing for Felicity and her neighbors. The lack of snow melt meant they could be heading into a period of drought, but the lingering cool weather meant the trees had not yet fully leafed out. That made it easier for Felicity to review plans for a cutting with her logger, and she happily set out with him along the northeastern edge of her property, along an old dirt road.

Lance Gauthier had inherited his father's plumbing business and surprised everyone by preferring to work as a logger. A few years younger than Felicity, he'd repeatedly asked her about hiking and camping on her parents' farm, so his decision hadn't surprised her as much. After barely ten years, it was generally conceded that he probably knew more about the land in the central counties of the state than any other person living or dead. He was stocky through the shoulders and torso, with short muscular legs and thick light sandy hair. He had brown eyes that softened when he peered into the woods and sharpened when he was reading a cutting plan. Lance led the way, following a deer track, and listened to her comments as they went.

"We're lucky out here," he remarked. "Poverty has its advantages, Felicity."

Sitting comfortably at home in her farmhouse, in front of a fire with a cat on her lap, she might agree with him. But lately stacks of seed catalogues, garden plans, old seed envelopes, bills and estimates, and meeting notices covered the kitchen table, and Felicity couldn't remember the last time she'd settled in front of the fire for a nap or a good read. In the evenings now, if Miss Anthropy worked her way onto Felicity's lap at the kitchen table, the cat barely had enough time to fall asleep again before her owner was getting up for another project. "You mean the land is poor and the people are poor, so no one bothered with this area."

"There's a developer over the state line talking about gated communities with helipads," Lance said.

"Helipads?" That got her attention. "Where are they planning on going? To visit friends at the next gated community?"

"They don't appreciate the land, Felicity. They don't." Lance's eyes grew intense. She couldn't remember him sounding so obsessed before. "We have to save it, protect it."

"Hmm, just before I cut it down to sell for timber." She propped her hands on her hips and looked at the trees: white pine and hemlock, but also black birch, yellow birch, red oak, and red maple. They weren't exactly shaped like dollar signs but she was pretty sure the money was there.

"I was cruising another property," he began, using the term for assessing the value of an area for timbering, "and yours are much better. Not as good as out in the Berkshires, but still good."

"That's good news."

"We can start next week."

Felicity nodded and looked straight up. "They're good trees."

Lance glanced at Shadow, now leaning against Felicity's leg. "Have you let him off the leash yet?"

"A few times. He never goes far. But he doesn't seem to want to be off-leash." She knelt down and unhooked the lead. She wondered if taking an animal off lead was a sign in dog fighting that a fight was imminent. If so, it would explain why Shadow never minded being pulled along. He blinked at her and looked woefully about him.

Lance watched the animal. "Do you know him well enough to know how he'll behave if he meets another dog? I mean, you wouldn't want any surprises. What information did you get about him?"

"Almost nothing. He's under forty pounds but about full size. Healthy though he's been through a lot. He's just a timid little thing." As if to prove her point, Shadow snuffled nearby, looked about, and sat down.

"I've heard about those greyhounds from race tracks," Lance said. "They can take years to come back. They don't know what kindness is or how to play."

Felicity winced. "I hope he's not that bad."

Lance turned to his own concerns, pointing out a particularly good specimen. But whatever he was going to say was lost in the sudden change in Shadow. He jumped to his feet, looked about, put his nose to the ground, and began searching.

"Well, that's different." Felicity watched for a moment before she realized the dog might get away from her. "Oh, damn." She hurried after him. She and Lance tracked Shadow while he tracked something else. When he disappeared from view, they followed the noise he was making digging through the brush. They came upon him at the foot of a stone outcropping, where he paced back and forth, looking up and whining before twirling in a circle and backing away from the higher ground. Felicity took the opportunity to snap on the leash.

"Hey, he's not a total loss after all." Lance knelt down and brushed away leaves and other debris. It was late morning and a strong sun scattered light across the ground. "He's a tracker."

"What did he find? A coyote den?" Felicity didn't think that was much of a feat. Coyotes were ubiquitous in the area, and mostly predictable. She brought the sheep in every evening and avoided letting Miss Anthropy out after dark, despite her complaints. If she let her out, she was likely to find the cat sitting quietly on the rafters of the barn while coyotes whined below. But now that she had sheep to care for, she never left the barn open. Miss Anthropy was miffed.

"Not a coyote," Lance said, looking up at her with a grin. "Bobcat. Take a look."

Felicity knelt beside him and studied the outline of four toes pressed into the softening ground. The print might have been mistaken for that of a house cat except for the size, and she guessed the animal was about three times larger than Miss Anthropy.

"I'd heard bobcats had been seen in the area but I never thought I'd find one on my property," she said, standing up.

"This is the perfect place for it," Lance said. "That ledge, the distance from humans, access to small animals like squirrels and mice and maybe skunks and some birds, and water—it's perfect. And you'd never know the animal was here if you didn't do timbering. This is a very isolated spot."

"How worrisome is a bobcat for a dog like Shadow?"

Lance shook his head. "I'd be more worried about a pack of coyotes at night. Not a bobcat. Bobcats don't usually get bigger than twenty pounds. Shadow's bigger and heavier, so not in danger. At least not when there's other food around and he's not bothering the animal."

"Are you sure we should timber in here?" Felicity stepped back and looked up at the presumed den on the ledge. "This area is pretty quiet and remote. I sort of like the idea of keeping it this way."

"It hasn't been logged in probably forty years or more," Lance said, his voice dropping. He sounded like a lecturer now, strict and formal, almost officious.

"At least that long." Felicity tried to remember what she'd learned recently. "I did some checking, and there's part of the forest that my parents never timbered. The edge of this section here was included in the last two plans, so I figured I'd keep it up. But I don't know about going beyond this area."

"Timbering is important for giving the land the opportunity to replenish," Lance said. "It clears out full-grown specimens and opens things up for new growth."

"I know all that, but still … " Felicity didn't like being lectured. She tried to ignore his scolding tone.

"My suggested work conforms to the goals stated in the earlier plans you filed under Chapter 61 with the state." Lance stepped away and began to scrutinize the stands. "The DRC is paying closer attention these days."

"Really?" She didn't recall hearing anyone else complaining about the Department of Conservation and Recreation. "I haven't heard that."

Lance shifted his feet, resting one on a rock as he scanned the area. "Since it hasn't been done, it should be. You won't get away with ignoring it."

But Felicity wasn't convinced. She'd occasionally wondered about parts of the forest left untended but never thought much about it. After all, her family had plenty to deal with elsewhere. She tried to remember what her dad had told her about the older sections. Somewhere in the back of her mind she vaguely recalled that something was different there, but she couldn't quite get at what that was. She walked past the outcropping and ledge, where the ground began to level out. "Maybe we can work around this."

"You can rework the plan," Lance said. "But you should think about it. I can get in here and bring everything up to date. You'll be glad you did."

"You really think it's necessary?" Again, Felicity tried to ignore the man's hectoring tone. She had followed him through reasoning, lecturing, scolding, mild defensiveness, and now reluctant agreement. And it all left her uneasy.

"I do." He turned to look more closely at the trees.

Felicity watched him, curious at how intense he'd become. Lance had always done a good job, agreeing with her and her dad on where to clear and what to leave, and offering fair prices. But she'd never seen him like this, and she'd never felt pressured before. She dropped down to where Shadow sat watching them.

"So, you're a tracker?" She ran her hands over the dog. "I like that. I can't wait to tell Jeremy and Loretta."

Shadow seemed to take Felicity's gentle speech as encouragement. He bolted, the leash flapping behind him as he charged ahead. Felicity shouted and hurried after him, but the dog had found his world and gleefully romped through it.

"Not so timid now," Lance said after failing to grab him.

Felicity knew she should send Lance on his way, but she appreciated his efforts to help her capture the wayward animal. Shadow continued to dodge and lunge, and Felicity to scoop and grab, but the dog slipped past every time.

"I may have to give this dog back to Loretta." Felicity stopped to catch her breath. Running over uneven ground never meant for humans to walk through took its toll, and she was sweating. "Fostering rescue dogs is not for me."

"Loretta Colson gave him to you?"

"You sound surprised."

Lance shrugged. "I didn't know she was into rescue dogs." He glanced around, but Shadow had disappeared. "Maybe I should head back."

"Of course." Felicity felt guilty for having dragged the logger into her canine fiasco. "I'll get him. The leash is sure to get snagged on a rock or log, and then he'll start barking. At least I hope he will. He's not the sharpest tool in the shed, but I think at least he knows to do that much."

And he did. They heard Shadow barking in the distance. With a brief backward glance in the direction of the road, Lance fell in behind Felicity as she stumbled forward. They jumped from mound to mound along the deer paths before the trail veered away over a hill. She came around the slope first and spotted Shadow lying on his belly with his muzzle resting on the leg of a young woman. She seemed to be napping, her legs stretched out and her hands in her lap. She wore jeans stained at the knees and a quilted red jacket that had collected a number of twigs and dead leaves.

"Oh!" Felicity stalled a second and then hurried closer.

The young woman was sitting upright, her back resting against a sapling. But when Felicity touched her shoulder, she leaned to the side and collapsed onto the ground. Her body fell loose, as though her limbs were held together only by the covering of skin. Lance came up behind them.

"What happened?"

"I don't know." Felicity knelt down and lightly touched her fingertips to the woman's bare hand. After a moment, she snatched it away. She pulled a baseball cap away from the woman's face so she could get a better look. She gasped.

"What is it?" Lance leaned over her.

"Look at her skin." Felicity swallowed hard.

"What happened?"

"I'm not sure. Her name's Sasha Glover. I just met her yesterday. She came to the farm to thank me for being with Clarissa Jenkins when she died in that car accident. She was fine—" She started to say more but thought better of it.

"But what?"

"Nothing," Felicity said quickly. "Nothing. Just that." She stood up and pulled out her cell phone. When no bars came up she shook it. "Damn."

Lance pulled out his phone. "No reception in here. I'll walk back to the road and call the police." He looked again at Sasha. "We probably shouldn't leave her here, even if she's been here for a while, from the looks of it. Do you mind waiting with her?"

"Take the GPS coordinates so you can find your way back with the police. Call Kevin, Chief Algren. This is his territory."

Lance nodded and headed back through the woods. After a few minutes Felicity no longer heard his footsteps crunching over the ground. Instead of moving away to find a boulder to sit on, she knelt in front of the woman and looked closely at each limb, then leaned in to seek out an odor that might tell her something and walked around to the other side. She didn't want to disturb the body or the scene, but she was curious. She saw no sign of blood or other injury, no weapon thrown into the debris nearby, no signs of attack. Sasha had merely been sitting in the woods, leaning against a tree.

Felicity was glad of the chance to be alone with Sasha, but still she hesitated as she lifted her hands and held them over the young woman. The power of healing she carried in her hands was a family gift, one not meant to be shared carelessly or for gain. But she couldn't ignore the need in front of her. If there was a flicker of life, she had to try to nurture it. She pushed her sleeves back and rested her hands, palms down, on the young woman's torso, closing her eyes and breathing deeply.

She waited for the familiar warmth to come, but her hands remained cool, chilled by the late winter air. She tried to go deeper, but all she sensed was a single sharp pain piercing her right palm, and then it was gone. She opened her eyes and leaned back. Resting her fingers on Sasha's neck, she waited for a pulse, then sat back on her heels. She closed her eyes against the sting of tears. It was too late for her to do anything for Sasha.

Felicity had barely known the woman, but for some reason, Sasha had come to her and tried to tell her how upset she was, perhaps over Clarissa's death but perhaps over something else. She had wanted to talk but hadn't known how to say what worried her. And Felicity hadn't been able to draw her out.

Shadow continued to rest his muzzle on Sasha's leg, but tipped his head to peer at Felicity.

"There's nothing I can do, puppy." She ran her hand over his head and scratched behind his ears. He closed his eyes and sighed.

Felicity inhaled the scent of the forest, the rotting leaves, the carelessly upturned dirt, scat from passing animals. She sniffed, glanced at the dog, and wondered.

Above her, in the trees, a Cooper's hawk came to rest and glared at her. The leaves behind her ruffled and a small mouse skittered away into a moss-covered log. She knew it would be a while before the police arrived, and she would hear them coming, trekking through the woods.

She leaned toward the dead woman, taking in her neatly pressed jeans now stained with dirt, her red-and-white striped jersey pulled askew across her torso, her hair entangled with leaves. It was the outfit Sasha had been wearing on her visit to Tall Tree Farm just yesterday. "I wish Clarissa had told you what she wanted to tell me. But she's dead and now you're dead." Felicity studied the young woman's body, from the mass of hair to her dirt-covered, low-heeled black shoes. "I can't even tell how you died."

Five

Shadow turned into a docile and even dutiful dog the minute the EMTs lifted the plastic body bag. The Lab stood and waited, alert, nose up and tail straight. As the men began the arduous walk back to the road, the dog followed. Lance led the way.

Felicity spotted the ambulance through the trees, its shiny red-and-white markings a striking contrast to the muted colors of the woods. But just beyond it, pulled onto a rare patch of clear ground, sat a dark blue car, which Felicity recognized as one of the new unmarked vehicles the West Woodbury Police Department had recently purchased. Chief Kevin Algren waited behind the ambulance, but instead of approaching the EMTs, he walked around them to Felicity.

"I figured you'd be coming along with them instead of walking back to your place," the chief said.

"Lance and I were taking a walk-through," Felicity said. "And there she was, just leaning up against a tree." She was about to say something more but stopped when she saw he was barely listening to her. "You're upset. What's wrong?"

Kevin took her by the elbow and led her a few feet away from the ambulance, where the men were arranging the stretcher and safety belts inside. "I was slow getting here because they had a problem at Pasquanata."

Felicity's stomach seized. "Tell me."

"We think it's nothing to worry about, just something that takes time. The nurses said your dad was kind of agitated this morning and kept talking to himself after you left." Kevin paused to rest his hands on his hips. "They couldn't tell me much."

"He tried to run off into the field across the street this morning while I was there," she said, "but the orderly and I brought him back. Kevin, what happened? You didn't come all this way out here to tell me about my dad getting agitated."

"They said he wasn't making any sense." He stopped to watch the EMTs for a brief moment. "The nurses and the aides weren't much better."

"Kevin!" Felicity grabbed his forearm and shook him. "What?"

"Now, there's no reason for you to get upset too," the chief said. "Something upset your dad and he got out of the home and took off. One of the other residents said he went off to tell someone he wasn't dead yet." Kevin lifted his regulation hat and ran his hand over his still-thick hair. "Whatever that's supposed to mean. Anyway, we have men out looking for him."

"That's what he said this morning." Felicity frowned, recalling bits of the conversation and wishing she'd asked her dad what he was talking about when she'd had the chance.

"I came out here to tell you because I don't want you to worry."

"Not worry? Of course I'm going to worry."

"We'll find him." Kevin took a deep breath, as though he'd been climbing mountains in the search and had just stopped to rest.

Felicity tried to think. "Where would he have gone?"

"That's what I was going to ask you. Did he have favorite spots?"

"Loads of them."

"Where was he heading this morning?"

"He didn't say. He just took off and I'm not sure even he knew."

"We had a sighting out on the old road to Heaven's Lake."

"Heaven's Lake?" Felicity took a step back. "How would he get out there?"

"Hitch a ride with someone. He always looks presentable. He doesn't look like someone living in a retirement home."

"Don't describe him like that, Kevin."

Kevin put his arm around her shoulder and drew her toward the patrol car. "I've got everyone out looking for him, and we have plenty of volunteers including Padma and her dad. We'll find him. Tell me what you were talking about this morning, anything that might help us."

"I told him about Clarissa Jenkins, and we started talking about the Bodrun family. He knew Zeke, her grandfather, but he's been dead for years."

Kevin led her to the car as they talked. "I'll give you a ride back to your place. Sorry you have to ride in the back, but at least it's new and we haven't had that many people in it. Some people get in the car and they tell me they're being tormented by evil spirits. If they just said it smelled bad or had bad vibes I'd be okay, but … " He held open the door for her and she slid into the back seat.

"Oh! The dog." She leaned out of the car. "I almost forgot about him."

"Here he is." One of the EMTs walked around the car, dragging Shadow along behind him. The dog balked at the door, so the EMT pushed him into the back of the car. "He wants to come with us, but that's not on." Shadow climbed over the hump and into the other well and at once began whining and trembling.

"Poor thing. Too much has happened in a short time." Felicity rested her hand on his neck and scratched behind his ears, trying to soothe him.

"Maybe he can help you track your dad." Kevin was about to slam the door when Lance grabbed the handle and leaned into the back seat.

"Don't worry about the new cutting plan, Felicity. I'll go over it again, just to make sure it's what you want, and we'll avoid the bobcat den."

"I forgot all about that, Lance. Thanks. Just leave it in my mailbox and I'll get back to you." She could barely remember what they'd talked about. She tried to ignore the sensation that parts of her life were spinning out of control.

"Don't worry about it. We have plenty of time." He continued to reassure her, but she sensed his tension over the events of the morning and hardly blamed him. She was distraught too. No one expects to walk through an old forest and come across the dead body of a young woman.

Felicity thanked him, and Kevin closed the door. She tried to focus her thoughts on her dad. The dog whined at her feet, a woman she barely knew died in her forest, and Lance's suggestions for the plan left her so confused she didn't know where to begin thinking about it.

But right now the only thing that mattered was that her father had run off and no one knew where he'd gone, or why.

———

Felicity tapped in a reply to Jeremy's message, hit send, and dropped her cell phone on the seat beside her. He'd sent a text about the sighting of an old man hurrying along the shoulder of Heaven's Lake Road. The description did fit that of her dad, but Felicity couldn't imagine either how he would have gotten out there or why he'd have wanted to go there. If he wandered into the state forest thinking it was his own land, they might never find him. Or at least not soon enough to prevent a tragedy. She pushed the thought from her mind, started her pickup, and headed down Old Town Road to meet up with Jeremy.

When she'd first resigned herself to moving her father into the home, barely six months earlier, in the autumn, she'd struggled for weeks over how to talk to him about it. But in the end he'd surprised her with his willingness. He admitted he was confused and sometimes even startled by the noise that came out of the power tools, and sometimes he was angry with the folks who stopped and asked directions at the farm stand.

"I'm not myself," he told her once. "I guess I'm winding down." And then he rested his hand on his heart, as though checking on it.

Walter had liked the idea of Pasquanata because it was nearby and he knew other folks who'd gone there to live. She was relieved. She'd felt, then, that it was the hardest thing she'd ever have to do. But the aftermath surprised her. Her father liked it there, quickly made friends, and often had as much gossip for her as she had for him. They chatted easily unless he was tired, and then she made sure to leave early. He'd never given her any inkling that anything in the world he'd left behind troubled him.

Old Town Road was little used, except by the few people who owned property abutting it, and Felicity balanced the car along the center mound and the shoulder, avoiding ruts, downed branches, and mud. She peered into the woods on either side, kept the windows rolled down just in case her dad was in the area and called out. A doe stopped to take note of her before gracefully abandoning her forage for a less-trafficked area, but all else was still. Her truck bounded along at three miles an hour.

"I'm not dead yet," her dad had told someone at Pasquanata. The same thing he'd said to her.

The words flitted through her mind as she tried to recast them into something that made sense. He might be easily tired, confused about his moorings, but he hadn't yet taken to telling her things like "I won't be here much longer" or "You know I'm pretty sick, don't you?" She was used to hearing these things from some of the older folks she knew. But her dad had not yet made that transition. So what was he really saying, what had been misunderstood or misconstrued? She rearranged the words, but no other version made sense.

After an excruciating drive, she came to what she'd always called Nameless Road, and her father called That Road, and her mother called Where the Allens First Lived. She always thought of her mother, Charity, when she drove this road, a woman who'd died young, in her forties, not so far from Felicity's age now. At the intersection she spotted Jeremy's pickup, and Jeremy sitting on the lowered tailgate chatting with another man. Both stepped forward as she pulled up.

Felicity greeted Pat Holyoake. A master carpenter, he often showed up at Dingel Mantell's sawmill to place an order for special millwork. And now, apparently, he'd been working with Jeremy on one of his construction projects. She asked him about Nathan and how he was doing after the accident.

"He's never seen a serious accident like that," Pat said. "But he seems okay. Thanks for asking."

Felicity thanked him for volunteering to search for her dad.

He acknowledged it with a nod. Pat had wavy brown hair flowing loosely to his shoulders and framing his thin face, thus earning him the nickname Cattail. He was nearing fifty, older than Jeremy, and lived in another part of town. Felicity never ceased to marvel at the size of his hands; they seemed too large for his arms, as though he'd borrowed them from someone else. Dingel had once told her they were the result not of woodworking as a young boy, but of his years as a musician playing the cello.

"Someone near here spotted a man going down a dirt path into the woods and Pat remembered there was an old camp back in there," Jeremy said.

"Really just a one-room cabin," Pat said. "But I think your dad knew the guy who lived there near the end. One of those guys from an old family, kind of a character. He had no electricity but he had a well, and he had plenty of firewood, and he was happy out there."

"Who was it?" Felicity asked, confused. She didn't remember anyone living out there in the woods, but there was no reason why she should. They were skirting a state forest and private land.

"I don't remember the old guy's name right off, but it was a while ago. Anyway, I thought the cabin might be worth checking out," Pat said. "Since it's in the vicinity of where someone saw an old man walking, maybe your dad is there."

"I sure hope you're right," Felicity said. "It's getting late and I don't want to think of him lost in the woods all night." In truth, she feared she might never find him. The woods in that part of the state went on forever, and her dad could keep walking and disappear into history. She tried not to imagine him stumbling over downed trees, then sitting down too exhausted to continue. She didn't like thinking of him as old and fragile instead of as the strong and capable man he'd always been.

———

The dirt road had never been more than a well-worn dirt track with the occasional shovelful of gravel tossed into a mud puddle. Over the years the grass had grown up in patches, like tufts on a mangy dog. Jeremy estimated the cabin was less than two miles in, and he was close enough. In half an hour or so they could see it ahead through the trees, sitting on a low rise off to the left, with the lane petering out below. Farther in and higher up someone had built a blind, where hunters sat in wait for their quarry, usually a meandering deer. But the makeshift rungs nailed into the tree had rotted and the rest looked like no one had used it in years. Perhaps the same someone had also built the set of four broad, deep steps up to the cabin, which were now uneven from years of frost heaves and neglect. Shrubbery and debris might have buried them but for the effort someone had made to sweep them clear. Pat led the way. He pushed open the door and stepped aside.

The cabin was not at all what Felicity had been expecting. Straight ahead was a small wood-burning stove with a pipe leading into a concrete-block chimney. Each wall on the right and left held one plain sash window. Parts of the walls had battens of insulation pushed between the joists, but otherwise the cabin offered only the plank exterior against the weather. To the right was a small bed pushed against the wall and closer to the door stood a rattan chair with cushions and a blanket. To the left was a sink with an old-fashioned hand pump. An open cupboard held bowls and pots and other cooking equipment.

On the floor was a tattered braided rug. Everything was clean and the fabrics brought color into the drab space.

Felicity stood on the doorsill, taking in the cabin. She had expected an abandoned shack falling apart from neglect and perhaps pilfering. Instead, this was a cabin where someone had been living. She could smell it and see it. The cabin was clean, tidy, and extremely well cared for. But there was something more. She crossed the room and sat on the bed. It barely squeaked even though rows of steel coils held up the mattress.

"Do you smell something?" She sniffed and leaned over the bed. A thin piece of flowery cotton hung from the window and she brushed against it as she moved about, trying to get closer to the odor. "Partly it smells like an antiseptic and partly like something else, but I can't quite get it."

Jeremy shook his head as he poked among the bottles in a cupboard in the near corner. Finding nothing, he walked past the window to the far corner, where he turned over the top logs on the wood pile.

"I wouldn't trust that old stove," Pat said. He rested his hand on one side, then the other. He pulled open the door and knelt down, taking a piece of kindling and poking among the ashes. He put in his hand and rested it there. "Someone might have been here a day or so ago."

"I don't think Dad was here," Felicity said. "Something happened here, but Dad wasn't here. I'm sure of it. He has a distinctive soap fragrance and if he'd been here anytime today I'd smell it, even through that other smell." She glanced around the room but her eyes barely focused. Now that she believed her dad hadn't been here, she wanted to get on with the search. She was growing increasingly concerned as the afternoon advanced.

Jeremy walked along the periphery of the small room. "Pat, if he came down this path, where would he go from here?"

"Where would Mr. O'Brien go from here, assuming he knew where he was and wanted to be here?" Pat walked to the open door and looked out.

"That's a lot of ifs, isn't it?" Felicity studied Pat. "But yes. Where would he go?"

"If he went in a straight line, continuing from the lane where it peters out, straight ahead, he'd be going east southeast. As the crow flies, your farm is about four or five miles in that same direction. But that's as the crow flies. There's a lot of hilly terrain between here and your farmhouse."

"And he would know that," Felicity said. Both men turned to her, expectant. "He would know that because he bought a piece of land, no, two pieces, from someone out here. He once told me they were a gift to my grandmother, his future mother-in-law."

"Your grandmother?" Pat began to smile but stopped when he saw how absorbed Felicity was.

"When did he buy it?" Jeremy asked.

"Before he married my mother."

"That's kind of unusual, Lissie. Are you sure about that?" Jeremy waited.

"He said it was his way of convincing her he would be a good son-in-law."

"That's what he told you?" Pat asked.

Felicity glanced at the men and smiled. "It does sound odd, doesn't it? I always thought he was joking, you know, a special mother-in-law joke because my parents were so young when they met. But maybe it wasn't a joke. Maybe this piece of land is special to him and he's remembering how important it was in persuading my mother to marry him and he wants to make sure nothing has gone wrong with the property. Or something like that."

"Is he confused like that when you talk to him?" Pat began to look worried.

"No. At least, he hasn't been. The damage from his stroke is manageable mostly. His heart is weak, and that surgery didn't help. He may forget things and get confused but he's still here in the present, though he mixes up memories and then gets confused trying to sort them out. He's mostly okay when I visit but something seemed to set him off this morning. I never thought about what would happen if he ran away from Pasquanata." In truth, Felicity found the whole idea almost overwhelming—her father running off, an old cabin still being lived in, and bits and pieces of land lying forgotten. In years past, her dad could have spent weeks in a forest with few if any ill effects. He knew how to live off the land, finding berries and greens to eat, building a cabin and staying warm. But he wasn't that Walter O'Brien anymore, even if he thought he was.

"Well, we have a few hours of daylight before we have to worry," Jeremy said. "And you have to bring in the sheep before it's dark."

"Oh, the sheep." Felicity shut her eyes for a moment. "I can't forget about them. And I left the dog in the house with the cat. I hope they're all alive when I get back."

Jeremy patted her shoulder and led the way out.

"It really does smell funny in here, though." Felicity stood in the doorway, looking back. "What did you find in the cupboards?"

"Just the usual. Some cleaning stuff, lye and ammonia and bleach and antifreeze for the pipes, nothing special."

"Have you noticed any smoke that could be coming from up here?" Pat asked.

Felicity shook her head. "I'm not sure I would see anything at this distance, with the terrain as it is. The crow would have to fly over a small mountain, and that pretty much blocks what I can see. And I haven't been looking anyway."

"Let's keep going. We should spread out," Jeremy suggested. "We can stay within sight and sound of each other, and even without cell reception we should be able to let each other know if we find anything." The other two agreed. Each took up a position approximately forty feet apart and the trio set off into the woods.

Felicity almost wished she'd brought Shadow and let him track, but there was no guarantee the dog would pick up the scent of her dad and follow it. She came to a squirrel stumbling about near a tree, falling on its back, and then crawling to a rotting log. It seemed to be looking for something on the ground. Any other time she would have given in to her curiosity, but not today. She skirted both squirrel and log, glad the trees hadn't yet leafed out fully and she could see deeper among them. Every now and then she stopped to listen, but the area was settled in its silence.

They hadn't been gone long when Felicity heard a shout from Pat and headed in his direction. When she and Jeremy reached him, he pointed to a shoe.

"That's Dad's!" Felicity picked it up. She felt the warmth of relief flooding through her.

"It looks like he took a tumble and got his foot caught," Jeremy said. "But seems he's still on his feet." He suggested they call in Kevin's searchers, and did so.

"We can go ahead on our own in any case. I don't want to wait," Felicity said. Pat agreed to wait for the police, and Jeremy accompanied Felicity.

They hadn't gone far when they heard a groan and the sound of a sapling breaking. Felicity hurried forward, and through the trees she saw her dad's bright green sweater. She broke into a run, stumbling over downed branches, nearly collapsing into holes. And there he was, pulling on a sapling to keep himself erect.

"Oh, Dad!" She walked up to him with her arms outstretched. But she thought better of embracing him when she saw the expression on his face. Walter O'Brien was looking at her as though she were the most peculiar person he'd ever encountered.

He stumbled backward, landing on a boulder, which, fortunately, was high enough to serve as a rough seat. "No, no, you can't be here. No one can be here." He caught sight of Jeremy. "What's that man doing here?"

"Dad, that's Jeremy Colson. You know him. We've been looking for you."

"Why?"

"You left Pasquanata and everyone thought you were lost."

"I'm not lost. I know where I am. Why are you here?"

"Walter, we thought you might like a ride back to Pasquanata," Jeremy offered. "You picked a great day for a walk. The best time of year."

"I'm not dead. It's a secret, you know. I know what's going on."

"We know you're not dead, Dad. And we're very glad you're all right."

"Why wouldn't I be?" His face was flushed and his eyes skittered from one to the other, and then to the trees. "Why wouldn't I be? Old Zekey's gone. I'm not."

"You mean Ezekial Bodrun?" Jeremy asked. "That was his cabin we passed back there, wasn't it?"

"Smart guess," Felicity mouthed to him.

Walter looked harder into the forest, breathing heavily now and slumping on the rock. "I always keep my word. Old Zekey did too." He swung around to stare at Felicity. "Why are you here? You don't belong here."

Felicity managed to smile. "I found your sneaker. Can I help you put it back on?" She stretched out her hand with the sneaker. Walter bent over and sniffed the rigid, coiled black laces.

"Sure. If you want. Don't know why all the fuss." He lifted his foot with effort, and Felicity knelt down and slipped on the shoe, pushing hard against the stretched-out socks and his swollen ankles.

"I'm not sure he can make it all the way back to the road," she said as she pulled on the safety laces.

"The others will be here soon enough," Jeremy said. "You picked a nice spot, Walter." He leaned against the boulder and relaxed, looking around him. "It's very peaceful here. I could stay here all day."

"No, you couldn't. Neither of you." He cast a wary eye at Jeremy and then Felicity. She hoped he'd calm down once he was back in Pasquanata, in a familiar setting. She wanted to ask him why he'd run off, but instead she waited in silence for the police to arrive and help them carry her father out of his beloved woods. Jeremy conducted a fractured conversation with her dad while she studied the trees, the slope of the land, and the boulders and rough landscape, wondering what it was about this area that seemed to mean so much to him. Whatever he'd been looking for, she would have to figure it out on her own.

Six

On Thursday evening, Felicity collected the sheep from their grazing among the old apple trees and herded them back to the barn. Shadow followed along, showing no sign that a dog would ever have anything to do with sheep except to avoid them. She maneuvered them into the barn, which wasn't hard since they knew there'd be sweet grain waiting for them inside. Once locked in, they settled down for the night. Felicity was ready to set aside work and worries and enjoy an evening with a friend—dinner with Loretta Colson, Jeremy's mother.

She took one last walk around the barn. Like many others in the area, she was used to seeing narrow paths beaten into the earth around the corner of a house or barn or shed; coyotes ran in packs and liked to check out the neighborhood. Now that she had expensive sheep to care for, she watched for any changes in the landscape, just in case the coyote pack seemed larger or other animals seemed to be involved. She hadn't seen the bobcat whose den she and Lance had come upon, but she knew it was out there.

"Okay, Shadow." She opened the door to her pickup and the dog jumped in. If nothing else, he was becoming calmer and learning to trust. He was also catching on to the rules of the farm. She held out her palm with a treat.

A few minutes later she pulled onto the shoulder and parked in front of Loretta Colson's house. But she didn't get out of the truck. Instead she stared hard through the windshield. In front of the old Colson farm, where Jeremy lived just down the road from his mother's 1950s ranch, sat a black Jeep SUV. Felicity gripped the steering wheel as she watched for some sign of activity, but no one came out of the farmhouse.

After several minutes, she climbed out of her pickup. She clipped a leash on Shadow and let him jump down to the road. She would have stood in the middle of the pavement watching the Colson farmhouse if Shadow hadn't pulled and whined and tugged his way to Loretta's front door. Felicity didn't even notice it was open until Shadow dragged her inside.

"You can't see anything from here." Loretta slammed the door and headed through the archway into the dining room.

Still absorbed by the sight of the black Jeep, Felicity barely noticed herself taking off Shadow's leash and letting the dog run through the house where he'd stayed for a few days before moving to Felicity's farm. She turned at the sound of a soft whoosh.

"What's that?"

"Your first beer." Loretta sat on the far side of the dining table and pushed a brown bottle across to her. "Sit."

"Did I just see what I thought I saw?"

"I've got more in the fridge." Loretta lifted a bottle to her mouth and took a long pull. Then she drew out a pack of cigarettes from a shirt pocket and tipped one out, offering it to Felicity, who shook her head. The candy dish now turned into an ashtray already housed four filters and mounds of ash. Loretta lit her cigarette and blew a steady stream of smoke up to the glass-and-brass chandelier. She was built like a piece of electrical wire—long and thin and mostly supple. Her hair was the same color as the cigarette smoke swirling above her.

"That black SUV," Felicity said, sitting down with a thud. "That's Marilyn Kvorak's, isn't it?" Marilyn Kvorak was a local real estate agent.

Loretta pushed the beer closer to her guest. "Drink. It's been a bitch of a week."

"You're not talking about my dad running off or the dead woman on my land, are you?"

Loretta shook her head. "Want a boilermaker?" She turned around to the buffet behind her and picked up the bottle of whisky. "I had two this afternoon after Jeremy left."

"Am I going to be upset, really upset?"

"I hope not. I wish I were—dangerously upset—then I could die and be done with it."

"He's had an offer, hasn't he?"

"Worse."

"Worse?" Felicity turned to look through the picture window. The land was not yet shedding its straw look, and the buds that would soon give the trees a pink hue were still only dark spots. The earth was waking up, but gradually. "What could be worse?"

"The buyer is someone who wants to start an experimental farm to test things, like chemicals or hybrids or whatever." Loretta stared at the whisky in her left hand and the beer in her right, as though not sure which one to go for first.

"Oh. He never said a word to me." Felicity didn't want to add that she and Jeremy had always agreed that neither one would sell without first talking it over with the other. For their entire long relationship, she'd trained herself not to feel possessive—he was free and she was free. But now faced with the prospect of Jeremy taking this step without discussing it with her, she felt her heart speed up. She felt like she was suffocating. And she knew what Loretta would say if she admitted how bad she felt about this. Felicity pushed aside her beer and reached for the whisky. She found a small glass in the built-in china cupboard and poured herself a shot. "What about Daniel?"

"Jeremy bought out his brother's interest years ago," Loretta said. "You know that."

"I was hoping maybe Daniel could stop him in some way."

"I wish."

"Jeez, experimental." Felicity took a sip of the whisky, pursed her lips and wrinkled her nose at the burn in her mouth and throat, and then took another sip. "But I like Marilyn."

"So do I." Loretta lit another cigarette and swore at the candy dish.

"I feel sick." Felicity finished her whisky. "Oh! That's it! I feel sick."

"You said. Have another." Loretta pushed the whisky bottle closer.

"No, no, you don't understand." Felicity reached across the polished dining room table and slapped Loretta's wrist.

"Girl, I always liked you, but you are one bundle of strangeness."

"Listen to me, Loretta. This is important. Feeling sick—it reminds me of what I smelled when we were looking for Dad."

And then someone knocked on the door.

Marilyn Kvorak pulled out a chair at the dining table and sat down. "Mind if I take off my shoes?" She pulled off one high-heel shoe and then the other without waiting for an answer. "I love my job but my feet hurt sometimes."

"Wear sneakers." Loretta coughed out a cloud of smoke.

"I suppose in your job you have to always look like you're going to an office," Felicity said.

"Where's my son?" Loretta asked.

"He said he had to see to his cows. I know they don't give milk anymore so I figured he just wanted to get rid of me." Marilyn rubbed her toes and glanced at the bottles on the table. "Got any more?" Felicity directed her to the fridge in the kitchen, and Marilyn walked out to the other room barefoot. "Having a party this weekend?" she asked when she returned with a beer bottle and an opener.

"This is it." Loretta glared at her.

"You know, Loretta, my dad says he remembers you from high school," Marilyn began after taking a sip of her beer. "He said you were the sweetest girl in your class."

"He's lying."

Marilyn sighed and took another sip. "Yeah, I figured. He likes to always say something nice."

"Annoying, isn't it?" Loretta leaned back in her chair, looking morose and not a little drunk. "He's not coming over here, is he?"

"Who? My dad? Oh, you mean Jeremy. I don't think so. He was polite but he's not interested."

"He's not selling?" Felicity swung around in her chair. "I knew he wouldn't."

"That's not what you said a few minutes ago." Loretta reached for her beer.

Marilyn looked from one woman to the other. "It's too bad. It's an offer you wouldn't believe. I told the buyer that Jeremy wouldn't be interested but he kept upping the offer and I had to tell Jeremy, but he said no, for sure. No interest whatsoever."

"Damn!" Loretta grinned as she banged the beer bottle down onto the table. "This calls for another beer."

"Loretta, you're drunk." Felicity pulled the whisky bottle away from her.

"So?"

"You're next on the list," Marilyn said to Felicity. "I saw your pickup out front so I thought I'd warn you. This man is very determined. He wants a piece of land with forest and he's looked all over the state, he says, and this area is perfect. Perfect."

"You're seeing dollar signs, aren't you, Marilyn?" Loretta leaned forward, resting woozily on her arms.

"Come on, Loretta. There's nothing wrong with selling property for a good price."

"I'm not selling either, Marilyn." Felicity leaned back, relieved now that she knew Jeremy wasn't selling.

"You haven't heard the price yet." Marilyn lifted the beer and sipped. She lowered the bottle and named a figure. Felicity paled and Loretta swore.

"You can't be serious," Felicity said.

"I checked him out. He has the money." Marilyn shrugged. "You should really think about this. This is the kind of offer that comes only once in a lifetime and I can make it happen."

"Are you getting carried away here?"

"This is real money, Felicity," Marilyn said. "More than you'd see if you piled up every bill you earned for the rest of your life."

"Who is he? Some mad scientist who wants to experiment on our farmland?" Felicity screwed up her face in disgust.

"Where did you get that idea?" Marilyn glanced at Loretta.

"What?" Loretta slurred the word but the women heard her.

"Really, Loretta." Marilyn glared at her. "Not everyone who wants to buy land around here is the devil."

"How do you know?" Loretta glared back at her.

"He's a gentleman with money, and he wants a nice quiet place, away from the hubbub of tourism and unbridled growth." Marilyn's nostrils flared in suppressed anger.

"How about Saskatchewan?" Loretta's eyes began to droop.

"So who is this man?" Felicity asked.

"I'm not supposed to say. He's afraid he'll be deluged with strangers offering him their land when he knows exactly what he wants. He wants to make the choice of what to look at, so he doesn't want his name given out." Marilyn frowned. "But, since he's decided to make an offer to you, you do have a right to know. His name is Franklin M. Gentile." She pronounced it Gentilli.

"He's with the mob. I knew it." Loretta sat up, looking shocked.

"Loretta, don't be like that." Felicity scowled at her. "What does the M stand for?"

"Marshall," Marilyn said. "Loretta, it's spelled g-e-n-t-i-l-e."

"Why didn't you say so?"

Marilyn shut her eyes and took a deep breath. "Why is everything so hard with you?"

"I don't get it, Marilyn," Felicity said. "With that kind of money he could go anywhere. Why here?"

Marilyn began tapping out the reasons. "A quiet area, no big tourism push that draws lots of traffic—he dislikes traffic—nice rural area, genuine, nice people. No celebrities. It sounds ideal."

"Okay, that's the official reason. What's the real reason?" Felicity said.

"You got me." Marilyn shrugged. "But he's got the money and here is where he wants to be. He says it's perfect."

"For a mad scientist." Loretta articulated every syllable.

"Loretta, this is where he wants to be."

The three women considered this, each casting it in a different light.

"Well, you can tell him I'm not interested," Felicity said.

"Hey, not so fast." Loretta tried to sit up straight. Felicity knew exactly what was coming: a suggestion that took various forms but always had the same goal. "Listen to this. You sell your property and then you and Jeremy can work his farm. It's an idea," she added quickly when she saw the expression on Felicity's face.

"That's not a bad idea, Felicity. I mean, you and Jeremy ..." Marilyn rested her feet on the chair crosspiece. She still wore pantyhose and used clear nail polish to stop runs. She had done so that morning, Felicity guessed, from the clear shiny spot stuck to her leg just above her knee.

"Not you too, Marilyn!"

"Okay, okay. Just hear what Mr. Gentile has to say. Take a walk through your property with him and hear him out."

"Why? Think about this. He wants to buy bad farmland?" Felicity had progressed from frowning to scowling. "Don't you wonder about that?"

"He'll explain what he's interested in, so you'll see there's nothing to worry about," Marilyn said. "I've talked to him a number of times and he's just a regular guy who has enough money to do what he wants, and he wants to live a quiet life."

Loretta piped up. "A regular guy with enough money to do what he wants? They don't exist."

"Loretta, you're much too cynical," Marilyn told her.

Whatever Loretta was about to say was lost when Felicity raised her hand. "Doesn't it seem strange that he's offering so much money for what is, realistically, very poor farmland? I mean, there are lots of quiet areas in New England. Some of them very picturesque."

"She's right, Marilyn. There must be more to this. Is he some kind of advance man for a fracking company?"

Marilyn blanched. "Don't say anything like that. Don't use that word. We don't have that kind of land."

"So he's after something else." Loretta wasn't going to give up. "Something he's not telling us about."

"You're too suspicious, Loretta. I told him we care about our neighbors."

Loretta grumbled and reached for the beer.

"We do, Loretta," Marilyn said. "And besides, I checked and he's not tied to any oil drilling company."

"You checked?" Loretta studied her. "Maybe I've misjudged you, Marilyn. I know I'm hard on you. I know I am. But I don't want my boy selling that farm just for money."

"What else would he sell it for? Fame? The Nobel Prize in animal husbandry?"

"I think we've all had too much to drink, and I feel like I'm going to be sick, this time for real." Felicity leaned back and then bolted for the bathroom. When she returned a few minutes later, Marilyn was putting on her shoes and Loretta was resting her head on her arms. In another minute she'd be snoring.

"I'm gonna make some coffee," Felicity said.

"No thanks." Marilyn stood up. She looked at Loretta, head on her arms, eyes closed. "Sometimes I envy you. My sister moved out to California so she could go off the grid. She and her husband make less than eight thousand dollars a year, so they don't have to pay taxes.

They have solar panels, and they barter for everything they need. But she told me she goes weeks without talking to anyone but her husband." She winced as she tried to wriggle her toes in her shoes.

"And you'd go crazy living like that," Felicity said.

"I would. And so's my sister."

"And so would I. I live without money because I'm no good at making it. But I sure wouldn't mind having more of it."

"That buyer—"

"Save your breath. That's not the way for me." Felicity looked over at Loretta, now snoring softly. "We were going to have dinner, so I think I'll go out to the kitchen and see what's there. I'm starving and I was thinking about something I wanted to ask her."

"If you change your mind…" Marilyn patted her arm and headed for the front door. Felicity heard it slam just as she opened the refrigerator door and stared at two shelves of brown bottles.

———

"You're a good cook, did you know that? Don't roll your eyes at me, girl." Loretta reached for the ladle and filled her plate with another serving of vegetable and sausage casserole. She grabbed the salt shaker and gave it a good turn upside down a few times, and then slid it across the table to Felicity.

"It's a miracle you're still alive, Loretta."

"So my doctor tells me." She wiped her mouth with her napkin and continued chewing. "Where'd you get the wine?" She nodded to the bottle of cabernet sitting near Felicity.

"I walked down to Jeremy's and borrowed it. He declined to join us because he says he knows how you get when you've found the whisky bottle."

"What's that mean?" Loretta sat up straight and gave her head a little jerk.

"I don't know. I've never seen you drink whisky before. I guess you save it for really special occasions." Felicity took a sip of her wine and returned to her meal.

"Well, thanks for staying." Loretta looked like she was getting ready to burp but she caught Felicity's eye and modified her behavior. "Living alone does things to you."

"Hmm. If you say so."

"Look, honey, I'm sorry I did all that." She looked over the dishes and casserole as though searching for evidence of her earlier behavior. But Felicity had cleaned the table, prepared the supper, and waited for Loretta to sober up, which she'd done remarkably quickly.

"No problem."

"I fall apart when I think of Jeremy leaving." Loretta seemed to lose interest in her meal and pushed her plate away. "And the idea of him selling the land. It means so much to me, to him, to all of us."

"I think he knows that. Even Marilyn knows that."

"She was awful pushy tonight." Loretta scowled at her plate. "I don't remember her being that bad."

Felicity placed her fork on her plate and slid it along the edge, back and forth a few inches. "Loretta, I want to talk about something."

"Sure, go ahead." The older woman reached for her beer but thought better of it and pushed it away, along with her plate. "You sound serious."

"I am." Felicity leaned forward and tried to gather her thoughts. "You know we found a young woman on my property yesterday, and I don't know what she was doing there or how she came to die there."

"Sasha Glover."

"Yes, Sasha." Felicity went out to the kitchen and returned with the coffee pot. She poured herself a cup and one for Loretta. Loretta poured milk into hers and Felicity added milk and sugar to hers. "Dessert," she said with a smile, lifting her cup.

"Good thing too. I'm full, honey. So, go on about Sasha."

"The thing is, I'd just seen her the day before. She came by the farm to thank me for being there when Clarissa died." Felicity sipped her coffee. "I didn't tell her Clarissa was already dead when Jeremy and I reached the car. She talked about Clarissa and how close they were and how Clarissa was talking to her about how important it was to appreciate the land and all. Anyway, she said Clarissa had something to tell her but only after she talked to me. She made it sound important."

"Whaddya mean, important?"

"She didn't say. I got the feeling she was hoping I knew, or could guess, so I could tell her." Felicity turned to look out the window, now black with only the reflection of the women sitting across from each other at the table. "She talked about farming."

"So?" Loretta swiveled her coffee cup in the saucer.

"I got the feeling she was disappointed I couldn't tell her anything, but then I showed her a lady's slipper and that seemed to cheer her up. Like it helped her make peace with Clarissa's death."

"There's something else, isn't there?"

Felicity turned over her fork and moved around a slice of sausage, pushing it through the vegetables. "When we found her in the woods she was just sitting there. I felt something was wrong, but I couldn't put my finger on it. I stopped thinking about it because next thing I knew, Kevin showed up with news that Dad had run away from Pasquanata and no one knew where he was."

"Yeah, that would throw me off too."

"I never anticipated him doing that, Loretta."

"It happens, honey. It's part of the deal."

"I guess." She closed her eyes for a moment. "It just feels like so much of my life is coming apart. Maybe it's Marilyn with all this talk about selling land." She pushed her fork across the plate again, turning it over and using the tines to draw squiggly lines in the sauce. "I was completely thrown off balance when Kevin told me about it." She glanced up at Loretta, who watched her with a half-smile. "I don't know what's wrong with me tonight."

"I do," Loretta said, "But every time I say anything, you have at me."

"I don't do that, Loretta."

The other woman shrugged. "You and Jeremy ... " She shook her head.

"Right now, I'm just worried about Dad."

"Sure you are." Loretta leaned to one side and gazed around the dining room, as though looking for something else to do.

"Anyway, when we were looking for Dad we found an old cabin out there."

"Lots of old cabins around."

"Someone had been living in it, so we searched it. I smelled something but I couldn't guess what it was. But tonight it came to me. It was vomit. I'm sure of it. Someone was sick in that cabin. And I think I got the same smell from Sasha when I got close to her body."

"You think Sasha was in the cabin when someone was sick in there? Or you think Sasha was sick in there?"

Felicity shrugged. "I don't know. I don't know what she was doing on my property and I have no idea why she would have been in Zeke Bodrun's old cabin."

"That was Zeke Bodrun's cabin?"

"Do you know who he is?"

"Oh sure, one of the last Swamp Yankees, at least around here. Well, maybe not the last. You never know who's living out in the woods hoping no one notices them." Loretta leaned back and gazed up at the ceiling. "Jeez, I'd forgotten about him. And that cabin was still standing? It's been years since he died. He'd be way over a hundred by now." Loretta shook her head, her eyes dim with memories. "Old Zeke. Him and your dad used to be thick as thieves."

"I knew they were friends, but you make it sound like it was much more than that." Felicity rested her arms on the table. "He was my grandfather's age. Wow, Zeke and my dad? Are you serious?"

"Dead serious, girl. Your family and Zeke's weren't the type to be friends, but your granddad and Zeke seemed to have some kind of understanding. They used to help each other out, and they respected each other. Your dad and Zeke shared a love of pranks and secrets and hunting. But even back then Old Zeke was getting kind of strange."

"How do you mean?"

"He'd get in his pickup and drive away and no one knew where he went or if he was coming back. And once he said he might never come back if he found what he was looking for." Loretta snorted. "No one took him seriously. He was always playing mysterious, the older he got. He was normal for a while there."

"How do you define normal?"

"He had a family, a girl and a boy, both about my age now, or maybe a little older. The grandchildren are around. Clarissa was one, of course, and there's some others. He raised his kids like a regular family. I think he worked for some farm equipment company. Anyway, after the two kids were grown, he got a little strange."

"Not the kind of person I think of as a friend of Dad's."

"Well, they were pals for a while. I think your dad did him a good turn and then he did one for your dad. Something about a gift for your grandmother, your mother's mother."

"My grandmother? Faith?"

"Yeah." Loretta rested her forehead on her templed fingers, trying to recall the memory.

"What else do you remember?"

Loretta shook her head. "Not much. Sorry, honey. It was so long ago and I was just a girl. Well, a teenager and not interested in much outside myself. To me Zeke was an old guy even then."

"Maybe it'll come to you." Felicity didn't know if she was disappointed or not.

"All I remember is the whole thing was kind of odd, like if your dad didn't take care of it, whatever it was, Zeke got it back or something like that."

"Oh. That sounds like an animal, an award-winning cow or something." Felicity frowned.

"Oh, Lordy, no. Zeke wasn't one for animals unless he could shoot them."

"So not a farmer."

"Old Zeke wasn't so strange back then. It sort of grew on him. He found that cabin and moved in and forgot about his family and they went on without him. Kind of strange, but then he was kind of strange." Loretta stared into her coffee. "I'll miss Clarissa. She had an old-fashioned name because of him, she told me. He wanted to hear that name continue. He was like that. She was kind, too."

"Clarissa." Felicity whispered the name. She thought she would never forget it, or the woman's death.

"She was a really good pet foster mother. She saved Shadow." Loretta looked over at the dog sprawled in front of the window, where he'd slept peacefully through the drinking bouts and supper preparation and now the after-supper chat.

"He's not this serene at my place," Felicity said.

"I don't have a cat."

Seven

On Friday morning, as soon as she finished her chores, Felicity drove down into the center of West Woodbury. She spent a few minutes chatting with the town clerk as she handed over half of the real estate taxes due for the quarter. In addition to being short, they were late, as usual, but no one seemed to mind. Feeling depleted, she walked down the street to the Morning Glory Cafe for a morale boost. Bettes and her husband, Gill, had inherited the cafe from his mother. Just before he and Bettes could finalize their decision to open only for morning coffee and pastry so both could get other jobs, a group of artists had bought the Mill, the old industrial building where the cafe was located. Business picked up enormously. As Bettes remarked often, thank god artists can't cook. Felicity nodded to an acquaintance and slid onto a stool at the counter.

"You're looking down in the mouth," Bettes said as she poured a mug of coffee and slid it across the counter to her.

"Just paid my taxes." Felicity reached for the coffee and wrapped her hands around the hot mug.

"Say no more." Bettes selected a pastry from the plexiglass case and set it on a plate. "Think of it as a sympathy card."

Felicity laughed and thanked her. A young woman dressed in paint-spattered combat pants and a heavy blue jersey slid onto the seat beside her.

"I saw you coming down the sidewalk, and I just wanted to tell you how sorry we were about what happened at your place." When Felicity looked confused, the woman introduced herself as Nikki, an artist from the Mill, and explained, "About Sasha Glover."

"Thank you. Did you know her?" Felicity put down her pastry to listen.

"Yes. She wasn't an artist, but some of us ran into her at art events. She was a buyer for a shop in Pittsfield and we invited her to visit the Mill. We were hoping she'd take some of our stuff. Anyway, when we heard she'd died on your land, we wondered what happened. And then we heard about the bobcat."

"I don't think the bobcat had anything to do with her dying. There weren't any visible signs of injury anyway." Felicity paused. "I only met her once, when she came to the farm after her cousin's death. What was she like to work with?"

"Very professional. She looked carefully at things and asked a lot of questions. She knew what she wanted for the shop, but she was ready to look for something new." Nikki shrugged. "We all liked her and it seemed like a real opportunity, and now she's gone. I sound really self-involved, but most people don't appreciate handwork the way she did."

"They'll be getting another buyer, won't they?"

"Yeah, I guess. But it's easier to buy cheap stuff from China than order regularly from local artists where each piece is a little different." Nikki reached for a menu. "I just wanted to let you know we were thinking about Sasha. I liked her and I'm sorry she's gone."

"I liked her too."

"We used to see her in the cafe, with her boyfriend." Nikki's nose twitched just enough to give away her feelings. She tapped the edge of the laminated menu on the counter.

"Don't know anything about him."

"You're not missing anything. He was bossy. One time I saw them here, in the cafe. He was looking at a map and punching in GPS locations and she was bored, but he kept telling her to wait just a little longer." She pulled a face. "He wasn't very considerate of her."

"Do you remember when this was?"

Nikki looked at her as though she hadn't fully noticed her before. "You mean here, in the cafe?" She looked around at the empty booths. "Maybe a month ago. I'd just met her at the trade show in Pittsfield, so not so long ago. Something made me think they were looking for property to buy and he wasn't sure where things were."

"Did he say that?"

"Well, not exactly. She wanted to leave—it was getting late, almost ten o'clock, and he said we don't have forever to do this, so let's get this done."

Felicity repeated the words softly to herself.

"You look worried," Nikki said. "Is something wrong?"

"No, just sad for Sasha." She decided not to repeat what Sasha had said about land and heritage. "Do you remember his name?"

Nikki shook her head. "Kyle something. I'm sorry about Sasha. Like I said, we all really liked her. And her dying on your land has to make things unpleasant for you. I didn't mean to bring up anything that's a problem." Nikki didn't seem to know what to do with the menu now and slid it into a slot in the metal holder for napkins. "I think I'll come back later. It's too early for food for me."

———

After Nikki left, Felicity listened to Bettes chatting with Gill in the kitchen, watched a car drive by, and heard the faint sounds of a radio playing elsewhere, perhaps in one of the studios above. She selected one of the local newspapers left stacked in a corner by the door and began paging through it. Since finding Sasha dead in her woods, she had found her thoughts drifting back to the night she'd fired her shotgun into the apple orchard. She'd tried to put the experience out of her mind, as though she really had imagined an intruder trying to get into her farmhouse. But Sasha's death had ended her complacency.

And now this report, of Sasha and her boyfriend arguing in the cafe, perhaps not far from where she was sitting right now, sent chills up Felicity's spine. Sasha had come to Tall Tree Farm right after her cousin's death to learn something, something important that Clarissa had not been willing to tell her until after she'd spoken with Felicity, but she never got the chance. At this point, Felicity felt she couldn't just walk away. She rifled through the paper looking for Sasha's obituary but found only the paid announcement, which was as brief as anyone could make it.

"Bettes," Felicity began, dropping the newspaper on the counter, "did you ever hear of a secret about the woods around here?"

Bettes shook her head. "My dad took me out scavenging once. We were supposed to take a road trip out West but he got laid off. But he didn't want me to miss out, so we went out to the Berkshires and hiked around and found all sorts of Indian arrowheads and pieces of pottery."

"Wow! That's so cool." Felicity smiled, thinking how fortunate Bettes was. "I had no idea you could find things like that around here."

"You can't." Bettes picked up the newspaper, folded it neatly, and returned it to the stack. "My dad had salted the hiking trail so I wouldn't be disappointed. There's nothing hidden out there." She crossed her arms but went on smiling at the memory.

———

Felicity left her pickup parked in front of the cafe and headed for the town's main street. She walked along a row of storefronts, with the fabric shop on the east end and Trunks and Treasures at the other. Between them was the Flagg Insurance Company, where insurance and real estate agents rented desk space. Seton Flagg had given up sales in favor of building management, and then ran for local office. Since being elected to the Massachusetts General Court as a representative for the district that included West Woodbury, he had learned the art of letting the business run itself. He was sometimes there and sometimes not, but today he'd returned to the town for office hours.

Felicity and her parents had sought out Seton Flagg with a number of issues over the years, attended his fundraisers, which were mostly ten-dollar-a-person bean suppers, and knew his extended family. He was the first person Felicity thought of when she thought of government. She could hear his horsey laugh when she opened the front door.

"He's in the back," a woman at a desk said without pausing in her typing. She had her coat draped over her shoulders and fingerless gloves on her hands, a sure sign that Seton was meeting with a steady stream of constituents and the front door had been opening and closing all morning. Felicity stopped to share news about her dad before threading her way among the desks to the two-room office in the back.

"Hi, Felicity!" A young woman in a navy suit, white blouse, and low-heeled navy shoes greeted her. Alexis had joined the office soon after college and had a natural ease with people. "Representative Flagg is in a meeting, but he'll be out soon." Three men hunched together in a corner, speaking in soft voices, and two women sitting on a bench beneath a window shared an image on a cell phone. "Let me see what's up now." Alexis rose and pushed open the door that was already standing ajar. She murmured, and a moment later Seton burst into the room.

Felicity often found Seton Flagg a little overwhelming, with his over-the-top greeting, his effusive enthusiasms for all things West Woodbury, and his intense expression no matter what anyone was talking about. Tall, with unruly red hair and the light pink skin that went with it, he seemed to need a lot of oxygen, and Felicity often felt drained after spending time with him. It was a reminder of how quiet her life was. She sat down in front of his desk and relayed her conversations with Sasha Glover and with Marilyn Kvorak.

"Sasha Glover? Terrible." Seton shook his head. "Clarissa Jenkins? Sad, very sad. Nice woman." He frowned. "You think she knew something about your property and wanted you to know?"

"Sasha seemed to think Clarissa had something to tell me but wouldn't talk about it until she'd spoken with me first," Felicity explained. Now that she'd said it openly, she wondered if it really sounded as odd as it seemed. But she'd liked Sasha, and got the sense the young woman was trustworthy and reliable. Something had driven her to the farm, and Felicity wasn't going to abandon her and her memory until she knew what that was. When she thought about the offer from Marilyn's client, she was certain she was on the right track.

Seton's fleshy cheeks and nose folded in, and his red hair trembled. "Nope, I haven't heard any rumors about your land or that area." He lifted his hand. "But let's check." He swung around in his chair to face his computer, punched a few keys on his keyboard, and peered at the screen, looking it up and down as though the words were riding an escalator. "Nope again. Nothing about your property or even our county on my radar." He rested his elbow on the desk and continued to stare at the computer.

"I thought you might know if something was going on that might push investors to start buying up land," Felicity said.

"Out here? That would be something."

"Sasha didn't say that, but like I mentioned, Clarissa left her with a feeling that it had to do with land, and she talked a lot about that." Felicity paused. "And Marilyn's client's offer was very impressive."

Seton pursed his lips and studied her. "Made you wonder?"

Felicity nodded.

"Hmm. Would me too." He leaned to the other side in his chair and punched a few more keys, scanning the text and images.

"I figured if there was anything to know, you'd know it. The government's not up to anything?"

Seton jerked his head back. "It's always up to something, but I assure you, Miss Felicity O'Brien, it's not up to anything out here." He sighed and swiveled around in his chair. "I wish. We could use some more jobs out here, repair some of those bridges we risk our lives on every day. Sometimes I think no one even knows we're alive out here." He swung back in his chair. "But in answer to your question, no, whatever Clarissa Jenkins wanted to tell you, it doesn't look like it's anything tied to the state government. And that Gentile guy is no-wheres in my stuff."

Felicity stood up and thanked him for seeing her.

"But I'll keep an ear out," Seton said, standing up also. "And you let me know what you find out. It does sound like something but I can't say what." He walked with her to the door. "How's your dad?"

━━━━━

Felicity stepped out onto the sidewalk. The air was brisk, the cold end of winter that held a hint of the spring season to come. She'd let herself be deceived by the warmth of the sun and wore only a light Polartec jacket. She stopped to zip it up. Across the street she saw a man standing on the opposite sidewalk, and at first she was amused to think he was doing the same thing—zipping up a jacket after misjudging the warmth. But it wasn't a jacket zipper he was holding in his hands.

Lance Gauthier was shuffling through a number of scratch tickets, frowning and scowling. After doing this once or twice, he tidied them together and tore the bunch in half. He turned to the doorway behind him, where a small trash barrel was positioned. Barely noticing what he was doing, he tossed the torn pieces into the barrel and walked up the sidewalk, his fists balled at his sides. Most of the tickets made it into the barrel, but a few pieces of shiny paper floated to the ground. Lance didn't notice. He was already halfway up the street to his truck when the fluttering fragments came to rest on the cracked cement.

Felicity waited until Lance had driven through the intersection, then crossed the street to the cramped convenience store. She gathered up the fragments of the lottery tickets and shuffled them into a neat pile. Inside the trash barrel she saw the other pieces. It didn't take a genius to figure out that Lance Gauthier had just lost three hundred dollars on thirty ten-dollar scratch tickets. She dropped the papers into the trash can and headed back to her pickup. Could Lance's spending on lottery tickets be behind his eagerness to include extra land in the cutting plan? She understood the pressure of too many bills and too little cash. Holding thousands of dollars in assets didn't help when the bills came due. But she'd never felt so pressed for money that she'd considered exploiting anyone. If Lance was spending hundreds of dollars on lottery tickets in one go, then to her mind he'd lost his perspective, and that meant he was capable of anything. It also meant she'd have to keep a closer eye on him.

With that resolve in mind, Felicity turned her thoughts back to her meeting with Seton Flagg. Even though he'd reassured her, she wasn't satisfied. Seton was well known for his uncanny ability to suss out what was coming down the pike, but that could mean only that Clarissa's news was not yet on his horizon.

Felicity had one more idea for a way to set her mind at rest. She looked up at the sky. Noon. Warm. Lunchtime.

A single truck was parked in the sandy lot at the head of the trail leading into the woods. She parked alongside and climbed out of her pickup. She checked the hood of the other truck, felt the warmth of a cooling engine, and stepped onto the trail. She dodged a barrier with a *Do Not Enter* sign hanging from the bar and continued walking. She listened to the friendly sound of frozen ground crunching under her feet and inhaled the crisp, fresh fragrance of crushed grass. After a half hour she emerged into a clearing that ran through the countryside, the pathway for high-tension lines.

Three months ago, on a Sunday morning, she'd run into an old school friend, Handly Matthews, outside the Morning Glory Cafe. With his love of the outdoors, Handly had surprised everyone by going to law school. And then he surprised everyone again when he went to work for utility companies, identifying and clearing rights of way for utility companies all over the United States. Everyone was mad at the utility companies, he said, but no one was mad at him. He liked talking to people and he was a good listener.

Handly had surveyed in Montana and New Mexico and now was back in Massachusetts. But not for long, he said. He never knew for sure where he would go next until he went. He loved the uncertainty of his life and traipsing around new territory. As he'd told Felicity, he was especially good at finding spots where he could relax, maybe eat lunch, hike a bit, and then get back to work without losing any time. He'd told her about a new place he'd found for lunch, and she set out along the clearing to find him. After hiking for almost half a mile, she heard someone call out.

"Hey, you!" Handly swept his arm in a wide arc. Felicity waved back and hiked up the side of the open swath of land to the rocks where her friend sat with his thermos and sandwich. "Am I getting a visitor out here?"

"Looks like it." Felicity hopped up onto a nearby boulder and looked down into the valley. "Nice out here." Even with the sun full on her, the wind blowing up through the pathway chilled her.

"How'd you find me?" Handly rested the thermos on his thigh.

"You told me where you were checking things and eating lunch these days, and I figured out which trail you had to use to get in here." Felicity had to admit he'd picked a beautiful spot. Over the hill was a well-traveled road, but only occasionally did she hear cars. The trees, even in their bare winter state, muted most of the traffic noise. She wished she had more time to find places like this and enjoy them.

"You ignored all the 'do not enter' signs, didn't you?"

"I did. What did you expect?"

Handly laughed. He sounded so relaxed, and Felicity guessed his easy way of reacting to people helped win over skeptical landowners. For him, getting permission to cross private property to either build or service utilities was easy. "So are you here to flirt with me, or do you want something?" he asked.

"Do I flirt?"

"No, big fail there, Felicity. Big fail."

She laughed. "I do have an agenda."

"Go for it."

"Where do you go after here?"

He looked at her, waited, then blinked and shrugged. "That's your question? Okay, I'm going back out West, probably Montana again. I'm just about done here."

"Done because you don't like what the utility company offered, or done because there was nothing offered?" She pressed the palms of her hands onto the warm stone. It smelled so clean and fresh out here despite the heavy wires above her.

Once again, he looked at her as though her question was odd, unexpected. But he answered it anyway. "Nothing more out here for me. No work, if that's what you mean. This was a small job and I took it because the money was okay and I like to come back to New England once in a while, see family and get out in the countryside." He waited for her to comment. "Is that what you wanted to know?"

She nodded.

"Why?" Handly rested the thermos on the boulder and gave her all his attention.

"I was just wondering if a utility company was up to something and keeping it quiet. Since you're working on something out here, you might be the only one outside a board room to know about it."

She turned to look at him, letting him take it in. "You're pretty good at figuring out whatever the hidden agenda is."

He shook his head several times. "No one's even thinking about anything new out here. First, the money is out West, and the resistance to just about everything is here in the East." His face warmed with a broad smile. "You might think I'm in on all the secret stuff, but only if my supervisor is pissed at his boss."

"And is he pissed at his boss?" Felicity grinned.

"Wicked pissed."

"So? What can you tell me?"

"'If Mr. Effing Genius ever gets his head out of his ass you might get back East in the next millennium but don't count on it.'" He spoke in a whiny, nasal voice, with his lips pursed and his nose wriggling.

"You don't like your boss and he doesn't like his boss." Felicity laughed and Handly joined in.

"That obvious?" He sobered. "So, no, nothing going on here. What got you worrying about it? Someone trying to scare you into selling your place?"

Felicity brushed the grit from her hands and rubbed her palms down her thighs. Now that she'd gotten the answer she'd hoped for, she relaxed. In doing so, she realized just how stressed Marilyn Kvorak's news had made her. She was more than relieved. "Someone has been sniffing around the larger farms in West Woodbury offering big bucks. Much more money than the land is worth."

"And you thought that meant a stealth invasion by some big bad utility company." Handly smiled at her and held out half of his sandwich. She shook her head. He took a bite and went on talking after a minute. "Nope, they can't really do things like that, but they'd sure like to."

"You keeping them honest?"

He grinned, took another bite, and waved the sandwich at her in lieu of tipping his hat. "Something like that." He finished his lunch, then crushed the plastic bag and stuffed it into a soft-sided lunch box. "Rest easy, Felicity. It's not anyone I'm connected with. My guess is he's an independent contractor, maybe looking for a quiet piece of land that the real owner wants without anyone knowing he's out here."

"Hmm. A straw buyer." She considered that. "Would a straw buyer want to keep his name secret?"

"Sure. If the real buyer wants to avoid attention, he'd want his people to do the same." Handly dropped the lunch box like a football and gave it a kick, sending it flying to land right beside his bag of tools. "Don't worry too much about it. Whoever he is, it'll come out. It always does."

Eight

S aturday morning was visiting day at Tall Tree Farm, and Felicity looked forward to it. After her conversations with Seton Flagg and Handly Matthews, she'd begun to feel confident that she could handle whatever it was the mystery buyer was up to. Whoever it was didn't have the government as backup.

Felicity slid open the barn door and chivvied her small flock outside and over to the paddock. She spread out hay and filled the water troughs, then left them to graze while she finished her morning chores. The three fiber artists who owned the sheep arrived on schedule and, as expected, bleary-eyed at eleven o'clock in the morning. Felicity met them at the fence and listened to them admire Minnie, Lady Bountiful, and Jezebel, her three charges, each name chosen by the individual sheep's owner.

The artists seemed satisfied with leaning against a railing and admiring their stock, but Felicity was taking no chances. She led each animal over to the fence, undid its cloth coat, and urged the specific owner to check out the wool. She combed it out every Friday afternoon in anticipation of the Saturday visit but she wanted to make sure the artists were familiar with the coat. She didn't want any surprises after the first shearing, which was coming up soon.

Nola Townsend leaned over Minnie and cooed to her as she ran her strong hands through the thick coat. She grabbed tufts of wool, literally getting a feel for it. She rubbed the wool between her fingers and pressed them onto Minnie's back. Minnie munched on a carrot, a favorite treat that was sure to keep her rooted to the spot while Nola went through her inspection. On any other Saturday morning, Felicity would have spent more time trying to engage the artists in learning about their sheep. She was a firm believer in general interest leading to skill and skill leading to commitment. But today she had other issues on her mind, namely Nathan Holyoake and Sasha Glover.

She waved to the fiber artists as they drove down the driveway after their brief visit and hurried to her pickup. A few minutes later, she pulled into the parking lot of Kimball Hardware.

Felicity hadn't thought about Nathan Holyoake since speaking with his dad, Pat, and she hadn't been to the hardware store to ask the boy directly how he was doing. A distant cousin of the Kimball family that owned the hardware store, Nathan worked on Saturday mornings helping to mix paint and carry things out to the parking lot for customers. He was too young to work officially, but he always hung around until they found something for him to do. On the morning of Clarissa's accident Nathan had been on his way to school, and so dressed very differently from his Saturday morning attire of khaki pants and cotton shirt, but with no rips anywhere.

"I like that color," Felicity said, pointing to a square of pale yellow.

"I can make that for you, ma'am." Nathan Holyoake would soon look just like his dad, with the long face and the wavy brown hair. His Mohawk was tucked beneath his painter's cap. Felicity tried to ignore the "ma'am."

"How are you feeling after the accident? You were very helpful to the police."

"Yes, ma'am." Nathan grew serious. "She died. I thought she was going to hit me."

"Nathan, would you tell me again exactly what happened? I want to be sure I understand."

"I was riding up the hill and I saw this car coming and all of a sudden she turned like she was coming straight at me but then she went in the other direction, into the trees. I heard the crash. I could see the car."

"This is what you told Chief Algren, about her veering to avoid hitting an animal."

"Yup." He nodded in short sharp bursts and his hat slipped to the side.

"Which way did she turn?"

"She was on her side of the road and she crossed in front of me." Nathan's eyes widened and he pulled back, giving his chin a little jerk, perhaps recalling the feelings of that moment.

"So the animal went which way?"

Nathan looked blank. "I don't know. I guess it went the other way."

"A raccoon?"

He shook his head. "I don't remember."

"But you're sure you saw an animal cross in front of the car?"

Nathan frowned, his shoulders sagging. "I think so. Why else would she swerve like that?" His eyes hardened. "It wasn't me. I wasn't in the middle of the road."

"Oh, no, Nathan. I didn't think you were. I really didn't. I thought maybe a single coyote was out and about during the day and I wanted to know if that was the case. I have sheep, you know." Felicity was relieved to see him relax.

He smiled for the first time. "No, ma'am. It wasn't a coyote. I would have remembered that."

"I'm sure you would have." She thanked him for being so helpful and left. She had a lot to think about on her way to East Lanark. If she'd been riding up the hill and saw a strange car moving toward and then away from her, she too would have assumed the car was swerving to avoid hitting something. But she'd already seen it coming erratically down the road toward her driveway before veering off and continuing on its way. Nathan had filled in the gaps, just as Felicity would have. But she was pretty sure now there was no animal in the road.

———

The drive to East Lanark, where Sasha Glover lived, took less than an hour. Felicity turned onto the old Durston Road, crossed Heaven's Lake Road, and picked up speed on Lanark Road. She had no trouble finding the address and parked on a quiet side street.

From her research in a local online bulletin board, Felicity had learned that Sasha graduated from college with a degree in business. But she needed only to see the names of Sasha's parents to confirm some of what she'd already realized. Sasha was the daughter of Harold Williams Glover and Helena Bodrun Callahan, and the great grand-daughter of Ezekial Bodrun. She guessed he was mentioned as a courtesy for the old-timers who would remember him and his family.

The house where Sasha had lived was located almost exactly in the middle of a row of Queen Annes well cared for by their owners or tenants. Recently painted white, with a small front lawn, the house apparently offered modest but respectable apartments. The row of black mailboxes hanging beside the front door listed names as well as numbers; Sasha's name was on the mailbox for the second-floor unit. Since the young woman hadn't lived with her family, as Felicity learned when researching the address, she would have to settle for speaking with Sasha's neighbors for now.

She pushed the doorbell, hoping one of the other tenants would answer. She was not disappointed.

"Yes?" A woman held open the door and frowned at her.

Felicity introduced herself and explained her connection to Sasha.

The woman, probably in her late fifties, in black sweats and a purple jersey, swung the door open wide and shook her head with an apologetic smile. "I feel so bad about Sasha, and for her family."

Before the woman could say anything more, something crashed behind her and she hurried back inside, leaving Felicity standing in the doorway. She stepped into the hall and closed the outside door, then leaned into the apartment. "Can I help?"

The woman—M. Halloran, according to the mailbox for the first floor apartment—looked back and shook her head as she collected a cereal bowl and spoon from the floor while a child tried to right her chair. Felicity hurried in to help anyway, and the girl climbed back on the chair.

"My granddaughter. She'd scale Mount Everest if she thought there was cereal up there." M. Halloran seemed exhausted by the effort and Felicity wondered if she was the sole caretaker of the active little girl. "How about a cup of tea? I haven't talked to an adult in days."

Moments later the two women were settled on the sofa, where Maddie Halloran, as she introduced herself, could keep an eye on her granddaughter.

"Sasha's dad came around on Tuesday looking for her," Maddie said. Every few words she started to leap up, hand outstretched and calling "no" before her granddaughter stopped what she was doing and Maddie could settle back. Felicity thought the woman must have adrenaline pumping through her veins twenty-four hours a day.

"She was already missing then?"

"She didn't show up for work and her boss called Harold, her dad." Maddie stopped once again to yell at the little girl. "Her parents are divorced. She and her dad got along well, and they got together a lot."

"I didn't know." Except for the family name, Bodrun, Felicity hadn't found the parents' names familiar. "Did she have any siblings? Brother or sister?"

"She has an older brother but he doesn't live around here." Another lurch and the granddaughter rebelled. This time Maddie jumped up and grabbed the little girl. "Time for a nap. I'm exhausted." She tucked the child into bed in another room and returned, falling onto the sofa. Felicity held up her mug, afraid the jostling would slosh tea all over her.

"I met an artist who said Sasha was a buyer for an area business," Felicity said.

"Oh, yeah," Maddie said, turning to her. "She loved her job. Sometimes she showed me things she'd ordered. She'd buy a couple of pieces from artists and take them back to the shop, and even if the owner didn't want to order more, he'd still carry those pieces. She had his trust and it really pleased her."

Felicity asked about the name of the business, and Maddie produced a card for a store in Pittsfield. "They must do well in the tourist season." Felicity ran her fingers over the heavy paper stock and the embossed logo in the lower righthand corner. Anyone would be impressed with it.

"She was on salary, but she said she might get a commission also if some items did really well." Maddie settled deeper into the sofa. "She knew where she was going. She could be hard-nosed if she had to be. Tell me again how you knew her?"

Felicity took a sip of her tea and then put the mug on the table, pushing aside a pile of magazines to do so. "I only met her once. She came by to ask about my CSA garden, which I've just started. But she really wanted to talk about my property."

"Oh. I didn't know she was interested in farming."

Felicity decided it was time to take the plunge. "I didn't think so either, but they found her on my land, in the woods. Actually, I found her, and I'm not sure if her being there was an accident."

Maddie sat up and looked at her, then turned away, frowning. She pressed her lips together. She started to speak, then stopped.

"What?" Felicity leaned closer. "That means something to you. What?"

"I'm not sure."

"Whatever it is, I'd like to know."

Maddie glanced at her, then settled back. "I had a conversation with her about her boyfriend." She held the mug close to her chest. "Sasha didn't take it seriously. She was much too practical."

"What didn't she take seriously?"

"The idea of hidden treasure. You see what I mean? It sounds ridiculous."

"What kind of hidden treasure?"

"Sasha never said, because I don't think she believed in it."

"Can you recall exactly what she said?"

Maddie smacked her lips and continued to hold the mug. "It was only the one conversation. Sasha's boyfriend had this idea that one of her ancestors buried some kind of treasure in the woods and then lost control of the property, and if they could just get to all of it, they'd be as rich as Bill Gates."

"That might explain the map," Felicity said, growing thoughtful.

"I don't remember any map."

"Someone told me she saw Sasha and her boyfriend going over a map, but I never heard about buried treasure anywhere in this area."

"Kyle seemed to think it was a well-known family secret." Maddie gave Felicity a quizzical look.

Felicity considered the plausibility of this tale. "The whole idea is pretty far out there. I mean, hidden treasure in the forest? It's like kids playing pirates. Who would believe someone buried treasure out there?"

"Well, Sasha's boyfriend did." Maddie laughed.

Felicity looked across the room at the well-worn furniture, the dining table pushed against the wall, and the television sitting askew on an old bookcase. The apartment showed little wealth in its furnishings, and little evidence of an interest in housekeeping, but Maddie seemed a sensible sort, and so had Sasha. Neither one seemed like the type who would buy into a hare-brained scheme to make money.

"Does the name 'Bodrun' mean anything to you? The death announcement gave Bodrun as part of her mother's name."

Maddie shook her head, her interest clearly waning. "She might have been in that family line but she never mentioned it. I don't think she cared about that sort of thing."

"There's an old cabin on an abutting property. It isn't near where she died, exactly, but it isn't far from my farm's boundary, and you can walk straight down through the woods to where we found her. Her great grandfather owned it way back, and it looks like someone has been living in it recently."

Maddie sipped her tea. "You always hear stories around here about the old guys who went off hunting and never came back, or the one who sold the farm and put out the wife and kids and took off for someplace else. I never know if I should believe those or not. But maybe he was the one who buried the treasure?"

"Ezekial Bodrun?" This seemed too far-fetched to even consider.

———

Maddie had seemed to take a liking to Felicity, and now held out the key to Sasha's apartment. "A couple times Sasha locked herself out, so we exchanged keys." She looked at the key resting in her palm. "Her family will want to clean her place soon, but I don't think they'd mind if you went in. Do you know what you're looking for?"

Felicity knew the question would come and had prepared an answer. "I gave her a stack of my CSA pamphlets to hand out to places she visited." She paused. "They're expensive to print, and I thought if she hadn't given them out, I'd like to have them back."

Maddie didn't question this, and Felicity climbed the stairs to the second floor wondering what she'd find. She hoped to find a reason for Sasha being on her land, but then she hoped she wouldn't. What she really wanted was for the whole problem to go away—the person trespassing near her house late at night, the idea of buried treasure on her land, and the body of a young woman left to die in the woods. But life wasn't that easy.

The key slid in, the lock turning as though it were little more than a latch, and the door swung open. The three rooms were small; without walls they would have made a single room of average size in a new house. The furniture in the living room was modest: a futon with a blue plaid cover, a rattan chair with a cushion, and a small coffee table. A standing lamp in the corner illuminated a small table. In the bedroom a foam mattress sat on a platform. A third room seemed to be used as a work room or study, with three small tables lined up next to each other and covered with photos of jewelry and other hand-made items. Felicity picked up one brochure describing the work of artists at the Mill in West Woodbury. She rifled through the other materials but found nothing of interest.

In the bedroom closet, Felicity pushed aside hangers holding the kind of wardrobe she expected—a number of mix and match suit pieces, nice slacks, several pairs of shoes (apparently Sasha liked her shoes), and a row of purses (she liked these even more). On the dresser was a small jewelry box with little piles of bracelets and rings, reminding Felicity of the first time she saw Sasha, with her beringed fingers. She was about to give up and leave when she noticed a small stack of paper beneath a pillow on a rocking chair by the bedroom window. She pulled it out. It wasn't a stack of paper. It was a large map folded and refolded. She opened it up and spread it out on the bed.

The map covered Western Massachusetts and Southern Vermont and New Hampshire. Felicity didn't see anything special about it, but as she studied it more closely, she noticed several light pencil circles—one on part of a state forest, one near Zeke Bodrun's cabin, one near the boundary of her property, and another that covered the old highway and part of Old Town Road.

It was hard to tell if the penciled-in circles were doodles or intended to mark specific sites, but either way, Felicity wanted to remember them. She couldn't take the map with her, so she described the map and circles in a small notebook. She stuffed this back into her pocketbook, then refolded the map and returned it to the rocking chair.

In the living room, she studied a row of small, framed photographs sitting along the mantelpiece. These were the usual pictures of family gatherings, parties with friends, special trips. But behind one frame, near the end, leaned a photo of two people, Clarissa Jenkins and a man whose image was too blurry to be useful. It looked like a selfie badly done. But it also reminded her of the photograph Kevin Algren had found in Clarissa's car, the one he assumed depicted Clarissa and her fiancé. If this was the same man, he certainly didn't cooperate when the camera was around. Felicity slid the picture back behind the frame.

———

"You have kids?" Maddie leaned against the screen door, a cigarette in one hand, her elbow resting in the other. Felicity returned the key to Sasha's apartment and shook her head no. "I had my boy when I was still in high school but I managed to finish," Maddie said. "My parents and my boyfriend's parents made it a condition of helping us that we both do so. So we both did. But he took off and I stayed." She glanced back through the doorway. "And you're tied to a farm."

"Well, I inherited my family farm. I don't think of myself as tied to it, but in some ways I guess I am." Felicity understood how others saw her position, a still-young woman, not yet forty years old, bound to acres of land and an old house that always seemed close to collapsing, the money pit of the movies and the minefield of marriages.

"My son works his father-in-law's farm, and it's tough." Maddie finished her cigarette and dropped the butt onto the porch, grinding it out with the sole of her shoe. "He's in the hospital now for surgery. He hurt his back maybe a couple of years ago and he's been working through the pain, but he got addicted to those pills and finally his wife said, get help or get out."

"She sounds like a good one." Felicity smiled along with Maddie.

"Best thing that ever happened to him. So now he's in for surgery and then rehab."

"And you're picking up the slack." Both women glanced through the open doorway to the now-quiet apartment, where the grand-daughter was sleeping peacefully. "I saw a photograph up there of her mother's cousin, Clarissa Jenkins, and a man I didn't recognize. Was that her fiancé?"

"Coulda been." Maddie frowned. "I never met him, but Sasha said they'd just gotten engaged and were going to have a party to an-nounce it, but then she died. Sasha's dad might know who he is."

"It sounds like Clarissa was pretty close-mouthed about the rela-tionship." Felicity turned as a warm breeze swept up the porch steps.

"Sasha said the same thing." Maddie kicked the cigarette butt off the porch with the toe of her shoe. "Thought maybe Clarissa worried the family wouldn't approve."

"Are they like that? The disapproving type?"

"No, no. Sasha's dad is a real nice guy." Maddie stood up straight. "He'd stop to chat sometimes if he got here before she got home from work and he said a few weeks ago that he wanted Sasha to move closer to him."

"Where does he live?"

"The other side of Lanark."

"That's not very far," Felicity said.

"No, but he seemed kinda worried about her." Maddie crossed her arms. "He asked me once if I ever felt my son had turned into a stranger."

"Was he worried about anything specific?"

Maddie took a moment to watch a red car across the street pull into traffic. "He didn't say, but he wanted her to get ahead. She knew how to do it—work hard, keep your nose clean, learn as much as you can, and be the best one—she told me that when she was getting ready to ask for a raise. But I think she was beginning to be too hard-driving. Her dad was successful, yes, but easygoing, and Sasha was losing that easygoing style. I guess he was worried she was hanging around with the wrong people."

"Like Kyle?"

Maddie lowered her chin and looked hard at her. "Exactly like Kyle."

Nine

Felicity's phone rang just as she was about to pull onto the road. She was pondering the map she'd found in Sasha's apartment and almost didn't answer her cell.

"I'm heading over to your place," Jeremy said, "but I thought I'd check to make sure you were there."

Felicity explained she was on her way back from East Lanark.

"I don't want to know what you're doing, do I?"

"It's not that bad." Felicity explained she'd been intending to offer condolences to Sasha's family. "But I got sidetracked, sort of."

"Sort of, I'm sure."

"Her dad lives not far from here. It's getting late, but if you can check on the sheep for me, I can swing by his place on my way back."

"Sheep, huh?"

"You can handle three sheep, can't you?"

Twenty minutes later, Felicity pulled up in front of a small white farmhouse set back from one corner at River Bend Junction, which was little more than a few houses at a crossroads. She knocked on the door and stepped back, waiting. A man in his fifties, his eyes still bearing the shock that must have hit him when he first learned about his daughter's death, held open the door and stood facing her. She introduced herself, but when he made no response, she wondered if he'd heard her. She began to explain further but he interrupted her.

"Yes, I know who you are." Mr. Glover stared at her a moment longer. "Chief Algren came out to tell me. They found my girl on your land."

"I wanted to tell you how sorry I am." Felicity spoke slowly, touched by how hard he was struggling to hold himself together.

She was about to offer to return at a later time when he stepped back and invited her into the small, neat farmhouse. He led the way into a sitting room and turned in the middle of the floor to face her. "I was just sorting through some pictures. Would you like to see them?" Without waiting for an answer, he walked into the dining room, where a number of photographs in different sizes were laid out on the table. "For the viewing. I thought they'd be nice, see her how she was." He picked one up and handed it to her, and after she admired it and replaced it, he handed her another. They walked around the table, passing photographs back and forth of Sasha at various ages.

"This looks like Clarissa Jenkins," Felicity said, holding up one picture. Mr. Glover leaned closer.

"Yeah. That's her."

"I heard she'd just gotten engaged, before her car accident."

"Hmm. Yeah, I think Sasha mentioned that, but I never met him."

"Did Sasha?"

He tipped his head to one side to think, pulling down his mouth. "She never mentioned it. They used to see each other all the time. Clarissa's death hit her hard. They were close." He gave himself a shake, as if to remind himself to keep his feelings in hand. "That's her with her brother." He held out a recent photograph showing Sasha and a young man in a racing outfit standing next to his bicycle. "I can't imagine why she would be in your woods. She never cared about outdoorsy things. Not at all like her brother." He peered at her, an apologetic smile trying to form around his mouth.

"Does your son live around here?"

"He lives out west. He loves it out there. Sasha visited him and he took her hiking and camping. She said it was okay but nothing more. Her boyfriend, Kyle Morgan, likes to get outdoors, but he's more into scavenging. He goes out with a metal detector on the weekends and vacations and looks for old stuff in cellar holes, that sort of thing."

"Does he ever find much?"

Mr. Glover might have laughed if he hadn't been so overwhelmed with grief. He shuffled together a stack of photos and slid them into a box. "He's always chasing easy money. He goes out looking for stuff to turn over for a fast buck. There's nothing in it, but it keeps him occupied."

"Like buried treasure?"

His sharp glance told her she was right. "So you've heard about that?" He rearranged another stack. "I think I'll just use those." He nodded to a slew of perhaps ten photos lying along the edge of the table. Felicity agreed they were attractive and showed Sasha at happy times in her life. "Let's sit down." Mr. Glover waved his arm toward the living room, and Felicity crossed the narrow hall with him. He sat and threw himself back in his chair, gripping the arms. "Fool. Her boyfriend, I mean. She told me she was fed up with him."

"Did it have to do with the idea of buried treasure?"

Mr. Glover gave a harsh laugh. "She was disgusted with all that. He was sure he was onto some so-called buried treasure. I kept telling him this was nonsense, but he didn't listen to me." He bolted forward. "You find an old letter in the attic. One person picks it up and thinks, Wow! You could send a letter for two cents back in the fifties. And then another notices how thick the paper is. And another reads the letter and thinks how different people sounded back then. But there's always one who looks at the stamp and thinks, Hey, this might be worth something to a collector. That's Kyle. Always looking for how to cash in without doing any work. That wasn't Sasha. She dated him a long time back in high school, but you know how it is. She grew up and he didn't. She hadn't broken it off with him, but I know she got sick of him. Told me so. She was getting ready to tell him their relationship was over." His grief flooded in again, held at bay for barely a minute by his indignation.

"Did any of this treasure business have anything to do with Ezekial Bodrun?" Felicity didn't want to jump to any conclusions, but it was hard not to see this tale of Kyle's hunt for buried treasure along with the map she'd found in Sasha's apartment as a distortion of old family lore.

"Zeke Bodrun?" Mr. Glover stuck out his chin and moved it as though chewing. "He had that cabin and that bit of land. Had another piece. He was always about land."

"Did you know him?"

"Only when I was a kid," he said, shaking his head. "He was quite a character in his last years."

"What happened with his land?"

Mr. Glover shook his head. "He didn't pay his taxes regularly so maybe the town took it after he died."

That sounded too pat, but Felicity knew she could find out. "When we passed his cabin recently, it was in good repair," she said. "Looked like someone was living in it."

"There might be some cousins around who took it over."

"Do you know who his heir was?"

"My wife, ex-wife I should say, never mentioned a will or anything. Zeke outlived his wife, but he left a piece of land to his granddaughter Clarissa. Helena told me about it. He was very fond of Clarissa." Mr. Glover's voice softened, and he seemed soothed by the warm memories. "She used to take meals out to the cabin even though he said he didn't want anyone to bother him. She was just a kid. She liked taking in strays even then. He was an old man and she was a teenager. Took him an old dog that no one else wanted, and that was the beginning of it. After that she'd go out and check on the dog, make sure it had food and all, and then she started taking casseroles for him." He paused to remember.

"That's not what you'd expect to hear about Zeke Bodrun, from what I know of his reputation." Felicity brushed her hand along the soft velveteen fabric of the sofa.

"You can't go by gossip." Mr. Glover stood and walked over to the fireplace, straightening a silver frame on the mantel. "Few people really know anyone else, but Clarissa knew her granddad. He adored her, Helena said. Trusted her too."

"She's the one he left land to?" Felicity asked, and he nodded in reply.

"He was a cranky old guy, and secretive, as if he had anything to be secretive about. Helena and her mother knew one side of him, and Clarissa knew another. Guess that's why he gave her that piece of land. She said it was only good for a wood lot and since she didn't heat with wood she had no use for it. She gave it to Sasha a few years ago, as soon as my girl was of age, maybe eighteen or twenty. I don't recall exactly."

Felicity listened to this tale unfold with increasing uneasiness. "Zeke Bodrun gave his granddaughter a wood lot and she gave it to Sasha?"

"When Sasha told me and was actually excited about it, I was very happy. Surprised but happy. I was hoping it would get my daughter more interested in life out here."

"Maybe persuade her to stay around after her career got going?"

Mr. Glover looked at her over his shoulder. "Too obvious? Course, it doesn't matter now."

"Did you ever visit the wood lot with her?"

"I wish I had, but I never did."

"Where did she say it was? Do you recall?"

He smiled and shook his head, keeping one hand on the mantel to steady himself. "She tried to tell me but she couldn't be sure of the names of the old roads. I had to laugh. She kept saying, it's on this road. No, maybe that one. I only remember her telling me you could see Wisp Hill from there, and she had to find the entrance through an old stone wall off Old Town Road."

"Are you sure she said Wisp Hill?"

"You okay?" Mr. Glover asked. "You look kinda pale. Yes, that's what she said."

"I have an idea where this wood lot might be." Felicity paused to think. She had a very good idea where that wood lot had to be, and she knew exactly where Wisp Hill was—at the northernmost point of her property. If Sasha wanted to get to her wood lot without using the abutting road, she would have to walk through Felicity's property, and the best approach would be from the road leading to the old cabin.

"Now that Sasha's gone, who owns that land?" Felicity asked. "Did she leave a will?"

"A will? She wasn't even thirty years old. Who has a will at that age?" Mr. Glover rubbed his hand down his face, his two-day-old beard still dark brown like his hair. His brown eyes would probably shine if he weren't so sad. He returned to his chair, easing himself into it.

"If she has no will, does her property go to you?" Felicity didn't want to think about a piece of land floating around with no definitive owner, certainly not with strangers looking to buy land at outrageous prices and others searching for treasure. She knew Old Zeke's reputation, in her family stories at least, and his love for plots of land that looked to be useless. Some of them certainly were, but it seemed he'd considered the land he gave to Clarissa special.

"Me or her mother. Don't know which. And if something happens to us, then to her brother." He leaned sideways in his chair, stretching as if to relieve the pain.

"I think I've tired you out." Felicity rose. Again she offered her condolences.

"It's good that you came." Mr. Glover pushed himself out of the chair. "I'm glad to have a chance to talk about her. I didn't want to call Sasha's mother. We haven't talked much since the divorce." He took a moment to straighten up. "I've been alone and angry since I heard. But I needed to talk about her, get my bearings again. She had so much to offer the world. She was the light of my life." He walked Felicity to the door. "I'll let you know when the service is. Perhaps you'll come."

She assured him she would.

"We're combining the services—Clarissa and Sasha. It seems right. They were close."

And it will be easier on the family, Felicity thought. But still painful.

She turned the key in the ignition and listened to the engine rumble to life. It sounded like the way her brain felt—a jumble of noise firing and spitting energy. By the time she reached the old highway and turned toward West Woodbury, she was resigned to a morning spent under the pickup in her future. When she turned into her driveway, she wasn't surprised to see Jeremy's truck. But she was surprised to see Chief Kevin Algren's car right behind it. She drove around both and parked near the barn.

Entering through the kitchen, Felicity could hear the men chatting in the living room, but not what they were talking about. She walked into the front room. The chief was nearly hidden in her dad's over-sized green recliner, his hands splayed on the upholstered arms. Jeremy stretched out on the sofa. A fire burned in the fireplace. It wasn't enough to heat the room but offered a pleasant warmth to those seated nearby.

"You guys look comfortable," she said, quickly adding, "Don't get up."

Kevin ignored her, as she guessed he would, and followed her back into the kitchen. "I was beginning to wonder when you'd get home. Got a minute?"

"Of course." Felicity picked up the cat's water bowl and filled it from the tap and then added kibble to the cat's dish. Miss Anthropy watched from her chair under the window but didn't get up. Shadow, after greeting her energetically, returned to watching the cat from the far corner of the room. "You must have learned something."

"I've learned I need a more formal statement about Sasha Glover's death, so you need to come in, maybe tomorrow morning or afternoon. Can you do that?"

"Sure. Tomorrow's Sunday."

"You're right. Okay, Monday."

"Something's happened. I can tell."

"You can always tell." He pulled out a chair at the kitchen table and sat down. "Don't look at me like that. I'm just tired is all."

"So why did you come by tonight?"

"To tell you to come in and make a statement."

"You could have done that over the phone."

The chief stretched his arm across the table and slouched deeper in his chair. Felicity pulled out a chair and sat opposite him, thinking about the uneven color around his chin and cheeks and forehead. At the moment he had a white forehead and bright red cheeks and chin.

"Okay. In very simple terms, Sasha Glover died of acute intoxication of ethylene glycol," Kevin began. "That's the chemical used in antifreeze, the kind you worry about your pets getting into."

"Antifreeze?"

He nodded. "She had vomit residue in her mouth, and plenty of antifreeze in her system."

Felicity swore softly. "So that rules out suicide."

"No speculating, Felicity."

"Is a detective from the state police taking over? What does this mean for you?"

"Detective Rendell would be the one. And he'll let me know if he wants me to do anything, and how and when." Kevin's color changed, his cheeks reddening even more. "He's running the show."

"Did he say anything else?"

The chief shifted in his chair. It creaked. That and a log breaking in half in the fireplace were the only sounds in the house. "They're checking out some other chemicals in her blood samples."

"So, more than antifreeze killed her?"

"We don't know yet. It's too soon to tell, but I got friends over there and they let me know what they're finding. They're not done yet. It's all preliminary."

"You look sick, Kevin."

"I feel sick. Sasha was barely twenty-four." He spoke softly now, the way he always did when he spoke about a life ended. "It seems she was drugged and given plenty of antifreeze, enough to kill her. It tastes real sweet, and she wouldn't have noticed it in something sugary like a soft drink."

"So she might not have noticed right away?"

Kevin nodded. "Maybe she ran off and vomited, but it was too late. That's all speculation." He shut his eyes. "It looks like she was out there for at least a day, alone."

Dying alone, Felicity added to herself. "That makes sense. She came to the farm on Tuesday morning, and we found her Wednesday afternoon. And I heard she didn't show up for work on Tuesday. The whole thing is pretty awful." She paused. "Does anyone have any idea why she was on my property?"

"Do you?"

"Well, sort of, but it doesn't make any sense."

"Try me." Kevin's tone told her he meant business. "You went to see Mr. Glover, Sasha's father."

"Jeremy told you that?"

"I would have learned about it anyway."

Felicity wondered why Kevin seemed unable to get comfortable. He shifted in his chair and slid his black shoes across the floor.

"Where I found her was not far from Wisp Hill, which she used as a landmark to tell her dad where her property was. She had a wood lot that Clarissa gave her, and if it's where I think it is, Sasha could reach it by walking from that old cabin through my land. She could get there without going in by the old road." Felicity paused, expecting Kevin to ask a question, but he remained still, watchful. "If you're right about the drugs and the antifreeze, then Sasha must have been poisoned not long after her visit to my farm."

"Mr. Glover called the police on Tuesday when his daughter didn't show up for work, but it was too early to file a missing person's report."

"You're very unsettled today, Kevin. There's something even more, isn't there?"

Kevin leaned back. "Rendell is letting me take care of telling the father this."

"Nice of him."

"Don't go getting on the wrong side of him, Felicity. He's a state police detective and what he says goes."

"Sasha's dad is heartbroken. He's still in shock. I'm sorry you're the one who has to tell him. What about her mother?"

"We'll go out there too." Kevin let his attention drift around the room.

Shadow had inched his way closer to Felicity and she reached down and began to pet him. He sprawled on the floor, content. "If it hadn't been for this guy, we might not have found her."

"Detective Rendell is in charge of this, Felicity, but if you know anything or find out anything, you can tell me. I know you're not as easy with everyone, so you tell me and I'll tell Rendell." Kevin stood up. "I sure want to know who did this to Sasha. Antifreeze poisoning isn't pleasant. It's cruel." He grabbed his belt and gave it a tug.

"Are you losing weight?"

"Don't be ridiculous." He looked around for his hat and headed back to the front room to get it. "You cooking?" he said to Jeremy.

"Seems so." Jeremy stood and the two men shook hands.

"Don't let her get any wild ideas." Kevin waved his hand above his head as he went out the front door, not bothering to turn around and look at either one of them.

Felicity waited for the chief to get into his car and back out before turning to Jeremy. "He's not well."

"He knows it."

"He told you something?"

"He asked about the farm, the extra work, and then about my dad. What he was looking for were the warning signs of a heart attack." Jeremy paused to give her a gentle kiss. "I get that kind of thing once in a while. People wondering what happened. Dad was healthy and then he dropped dead in the barn one day. It's kind of scary."

Felicity liked to think they were too young to worry about such things. But also, she didn't want to think about anything happening to Jeremy.

"What else did Kevin say?" She followed him out to the kitchen, where Jeremy opened the refrigerator and pulled out a package wrapped in butcher paper.

"He said Natalie's on his case to get a checkup."

"Is he going to?"

Jeremy dropped the package on the counter and turned around to lean against it, his hands cupping the edge. "I think he's hoping someone will just take him to the ER and get it all done for him." He wrapped his arms around her as she stepped into his embrace. She looked up at him, thinking about how neatly they fit together.

"You're guessing."

"But a good guess."

"Another log?" Jeremy tipped his head toward Felicity but made no effort to get off the couch and put one on the fire. Felicity glanced at the dying embers but couldn't bring herself to get up either. "It's getting late. This place is too comfortable."

Felicity rested her hand on his arm and rubbed gently. "You have cows and can't stay, and I have sheep and can't leave." He turned and smiled.

"That's about the size of it." He watched the fire spit its way to dying. "It'll be smoking soon." He went over to the fireplace and stirred the ashes. When he was confident they would die safely, he pulled a heavy screen onto the hearth and hooked it in place. Shadow sat up and watched.

"I'm going over to see Dad tomorrow."

"How's he doing?"

"He's been agitated since he took off, but he gets a little calmer every day." Felicity had her bare feet stretched out to the coffee table and wiggled her toes beneath the light woolen throw that covered her legs.

"Have you gotten anything more out of him?"

"Not much." She watched Jeremy sit in a chair and pull on his socks and boots. "Mostly some incoherent jabber about Ezekial Bodrun and promises. None of it makes any sense."

Jeremy tied his boots and sat back. "You're not going to stay out of this, are you?"

Felicity pulled off the blanket and sat up, crosslegged. "You sound like Kevin." She folded the blanket and draped it over the back of the couch while Jeremy moved to sit beside her. He reached for her hand.

"I don't want you to get into something dangerous."

"I'm not stupid, Jeremy."

"You're not, but some of the others around here are."

Felicity nuzzled his neck. "If you'd heard the way Sasha's father talked about her, Jeremy, you'd want to find out what happened too. She wasn't someone who would just be wandering around in the woods, mine or anyone else's."

"Promise me you won't do anything without telling me." He waited for a reply. "I don't want to worry all the time."

"Do you worry about me, Jeremy?"

He turned to her, a bemused smile on his face. "Of course I do."

"I don't want you to worry," she said. But what she really wanted to say was that just hearing him tell her this made her feel so much safer. "Or Loretta."

"Yeah." Jeremy turned away. "I may have to have a talk with her before she kills herself."

"She's lonely. And a little scared. And Marilyn Kvorak showing up with a prospective buyer didn't help. Anything more on that front?"

"He's definitely not with any of the big gas or oil companies."

"You were thinking of a new pipeline running across the state?"

He nodded. "But any pipeline stuff is off the table. Besides, if they wanted to cross my land—or yours—they'd just take what they needed by eminent domain after a lot of fighting."

Felicity filled him in on her conversation with Handly Matthews.

"He's a good man. But I'll keep checking, if only to keep Loretta from harassing Marilyn for information."

"Your mother's scared about the future, Jeremy. She's not where she expected to be at this age."

"Where did she expect to be?"

Felicity ran her hand along his arm. "She probably thought she'd be a social butterfly with a passel of grandchildren."

They'd had this conversation before, about how his mother hared off in different directions—binge drinking, taking in stray dogs, running a political campaign for a friend—all as a way to make sense out of her life. She had four grandchildren but only one lived nearby. But the real question that festered was why had Jeremy fallen for Taylor's mother and a marriage that lasted barely three years before she up and left. Loretta never gave up hope that things would progress between her son and Felicity, but Felicity and Jeremy had grown so comfortable in their long-term relationship that neither one seemed to think about what more they could have. The idea crossed Felicity's mind occasionally, but then something else would come up to claim her attention and she set the question aside.

"She was never that kind of mother."

"She knows that. So what? If we didn't have dreams a little different from reality we'd never reach out for more of life. So what if she was unrealistic?"

"My younger brother has three children. They count, don't they?"

"But they don't live near her and they're so different. I think she feels lost."

"Well, Taylor's coming home next weekend, for a long weekend. That should make her happy. Daniel's coming too, with the family. My daughter tells me she wants to talk." Jeremy pulled a face.

"Does Taylor know about the offer to buy your farm?"

"No. I don't know what her visit is all about, but it should be interesting."

"She didn't give you a hint?"

"Not a clue." Jeremy stood up. "I thought launching a daughter followed a certain strategy, but I guess I was wrong."

"What strategy?" Felicity followed him to the door.

"Give her lots of love and tell her she can do whatever she wants in life. And give her lots of role models. Like you."

"Now that's a pretty good line!" Felicity leaned into his embrace. "I love it when you lie to me."

Ten

On Monday morning, just after nine o'clock, Felicity crossed the street from the parking lot to Town Hall. She glanced at a window on the first floor and stopped in the middle of the street at the sight of a tall man leaning over the table where the tax assessment printout was displayed. She was late with the other half of her property taxes, and she prayed a lien hadn't already been recorded. She veered toward the steps and headed into the building.

The man she'd seen in the window bolted out of the assessor's office and into the hallway, knocking back a clerk. Her arms full of folders, the clerk didn't have a free hand to grab her glasses as they slid down her nose and off her face, dangling on their beaded chain. She fell back toward Felicity, who jumped forward and held her arms out to catch her. The man apparently didn't notice, continuing to walk toward the stairwell leading down to the police department and storage.

"Thanks," the clerk said. She clutched the files closer to her chest. "Not my day, I guess. I'm just glad I didn't drop these."

Felicity bit her tongue as she watched the man disappear down the stairs. "Clod. Him." She nodded toward the now-empty stairs. "I'm here for the bad news," she added.

The clerk laughed. "Taxes? We haven't got to the liens yet, if that's what you're worried about." She smiled. "Besides, Felicity, we know you're good for it." She winked and headed on into the office. Felicity followed her, and then went over to the table where she'd first seen the stranger in the window. The printout, organized by name, was open to a page that included her property.

Startled by the idea that the man she saw could be Franklin Gentile, the buyer working with Marilyn, Felicity jumped back, ready to run down the stairs after him. But before she could do so she spotted him walking down the sidewalk to the intersection, where he turned left and walked out of sight.

"Damn."

"You complaining about me?" Chief Kevin Algren walked up behind her.

Felicity spun around and shook her head. "Hi, Kevin. I thought I saw someone I've been trying to meet. Sort of."

"Sort of meet? If you're here to make your statement, go on down. I'll be there in a minute."

Felicity walked down to the police department. "Kevin's on his way," she told Padma. "Do you know who that man was who just came through here?"

Padma looked up from the small paper sack she'd been inspecting and shook her head. "I don't have a clue even though I'm right here in

117

the heart of town government." She gazed around at her empire of cast-off desks from the 1930s, stacks of old army green metal files, a row of lampshades looking for lamps, and folding metal chairs stacked in a corner. "He didn't even stop to say hello. You here to see the chief?"

Felicity nodded as they heard Kevin's footsteps on the stairs. "How's he feeling about all this?"

"Guess! He's miserable. I feel for the guy, I really do. He loves West Woodbury, but now that he's at the end of his career he says the things happening these days make him feel like he's a stranger here. He feels like he stayed too long at the party. He says—" Padma stopped to consider this. "Do people really feel that way?" She dropped the paper sack into an open drawer. "Good morning, sir." She chirped the greeting before Chief Kevin Algren had even made it all the way into the room.

———

The chief closed his office door behind Felicity and motioned her to a chair. "Don't tell me I look sick, Felicity. I just spent an hour with the town accountant who's trying to sell me on some kind of nature medicine." Felicity shut her mouth. She knew better than to tell Kevin exactly what she thought of the way he looked.

"I'm going to ask Padma to come in and type up what you have to say, but before I do, is there anything you want to tell me first?"

Felicity shook her head, then stopped. "Oh, there is one thing."

"I knew it." He closed his eyes and sighed. "Go on."

"It's not that bad, Kevin. Anyway, when we were looking for my dad, Pat remembered there was an old cabin back in the woods where we were searching. We looked in the cabin, just in case Dad might have been going there. Zeke owned that place. He died quite a while back, but that cabin is being taken care of. I thought someone had

118

been there recently and I was sure I could smell something, but I couldn't figure out what it was until much later. Anyway, after we started searching through the woods, I passed a dying squirrel."

"A dying squirrel?"

"You said the medical examiner found vomit in Sasha's mouth," Felicity said. "But there was no vomit on her clothing or her body when we found her."

"So?"

"So I think I smelled vomit in the cabin and I think she ran away and vomited in the woods and then whoever was with her, followed her and cleaned her up and left her in the woods, setting her up to look as though she just sat down to die."

"What's the squirrel got to do with it?"

"I think the squirrel ate the vomit. The poison was in the vomit."

"The squirrel ate the vomit?"

"Don't look at me like I have ten heads, Kevin."

"Okay, only five heads."

"I saw this squirrel stumbling around but I was too focused on finding my dad to pay attention. But it was weird."

"A squirrel." He pushed himself away from his desk. "Let me get Padma in here. Maybe you'll start sounding normal if someone else is listening to you."

"You have to check the cabin. Pat checked the firebox and he thought someone had been there in maybe the last two days, from the way the ashes felt." She swung around in the chair as he walked to the door and pulled it open. He called for Padma.

"So, I'm looking for a dead squirrel in how many acres? Six hundred? A thousand? Two thousand?" Kevin pointed Padma to the computer.

"Are you going to check out the cabin?"

"Old Zeke Bodrun's place?" Kevin sat down again. "Will it make you happy?"

Felicity grimaced.

"And I'll bring in any dead squirrels I find, too." He told Padma to type up the statement on Sasha Glover. "Ready, Miss O'Brien?"

———

Felicity managed to make it to the Pasquanata Community Home before lunch. Since her father's foray into the larger world, she'd fretted and worried and worked herself into as much of a state as he had been in the day he bolted. She found him in the lounge watching the birds outside the window.

"Pussy willows," he said when she sat down.

She checked his wardrobe on every visit and was pleased to see how well cared for he was—his clothes were always clean, the items of clothing made sense, and each item seemed to still fit. Today he wore his favorite khaki slacks and a light yellow shirt, well ironed, and a gray cardigan. She didn't know but guessed the nurses would have removed his cold-weather jackets from the closet, to discourage any ideas of stepping outside again. But she knew that was akin to magical thinking—if he wanted to go out he would, regardless of the weather and the availability of suitable clothing.

She leaned over him to the window to look at the pussy willows. "We have some behind the barn. I'll cut some and bring them in. A harbinger of spring, for sure."

He listened to her with a vacant look, an expression of thinking about something else while waiting until something she had to say caught his interest. "You're Lissie, come for your regular visit."

"Yes, Dad, I'm Lissie."

"I went looking for you." He reached across and grabbed her hand. "You need a sign at the end of the driveway."

"A sign for Tall Tree Farm?" Felicity's heart sank. She'd been thinking about repainting the sign during the summer. It was beginning to look a little ragged. As long as she could remember, they'd always had a sign at the end of the driveway. Perhaps there had been a time when there was no sign. Perhaps that was where he was now. This morning, she couldn't bring herself to correct him. Let him have his reality, if it made him happy.

He nodded. "Three words."

"I'll be sure to do that."

"It's special. It's what we called it when we were hanging out together." He lowered his voice to a whisper and looked around.

"You and Mom called it Tall Tree Farm when you were young?"

He wasn't listening to her. He'd drifted off on another memory. "Perfect name. But couldn't use it, couldn't use it. But it's okay now. No one will know and if they do, they can't do anything about it. Tall Tree Farm is forever."

She kissed his gnarled, stiff hand and then his cheek. At first she didn't know what he was talking about, and it didn't matter. But then, the foray into the past and the naming of the farm began to make sense.

"Don't forget, Lissie. It's forever."

"I won't forget."

"And no one can do anything about it."

She shook her head, still smiling, waiting to hear what he would say next.

"Old Zeke is gone now." He grew sad. "A true friend."

"You were great pals, I heard." Felicity was beginning to think she understood the heart of this friendship, but she could still be wrong. She wanted to be sure.

He eyeballed her, alert and suspicious.

"Loretta, Jeremy's mother, told me you and Zeke were great pals when you were young, before you married Mom." She hoped this mention of Zeke would lead her dad into a reminiscence that would shed more light on what was behind his seemingly inconsistent feelings about the Bodruns.

"Loretta." He relaxed and smiled at her once again. "Good-looking woman in her day. She had a little boy. Jeremy. And another one. Daniel."

"They're grown up, Dad. You know them."

He nodded thoughtfully. "Good farmers too. I always liked them, Jeremy especially."

"I'm glad, Dad. I do too."

That seemed to ground him in the present, and a warm smile spread over his features. His history with Zeke Bodrun would have to wait for another visit.

Eleven

On Tuesday, Felicity focused on repairing their farm stand. She drew a tape measure along a plank, marked it, remeasured, and set the tape aside. She gripped the plank with one hand and held the circular saw with the other, setting it along the line. She guided the saw through the wood and let the shorter piece fall away.

For the rest of the afternoon she cut and nailed, until the table with compartments and a roof that passed for her vegetable stand began to look sturdier than it had in years. She calculated how much produce she could display, and how many baskets she'd need around the base, to take in a certain income. And she had to make a certain income. That had become clear after her chat with the Pasquanata Community Home manager about her father's wandering off. It was obvious the income from the CSA garden wouldn't be enough, so she had to get serious about bringing in cash.

By late afternoon Felicity felt she had a strong enough structure to survive any unexpected late winter storms. She pulled out her father's trailer and leaned the stand against it until she could pull it down, letting it rest on what was little more than a wooden frame on wheels. She pulled it out to the end of the driveway and set up the stand on the cement base that had been poured years ago. Shadow explored the street in either direction, but returned within a few minutes. By then Felicity had shifted the stand into place and locked one side post onto the base.

As she stepped back to admire her handiwork, a small black hatchback pulled up in front and parked.

"Hey, Josie." Felicity leaned in the open side window and greeted the driver. Josie Halloway had delicate features and curly light brown hair, but her hands were often smeared with oil. She helped out her husband with his garage once in a while, mostly with the bookkeeping, but she wasn't above changing tires or oil or batteries or anything else that needed doing. Flat Road Automotive was a family affair if Bruce needed help. Not yet fifty, Josie was already a grandmother.

"You're early." Josie looked past her at the repaired vegetable stand. "Are you going to have an April crop?"

"I overwintered a lot of greens, so unless we go into a deep freeze I'm thinking I'll open up the garden and see what's there." Felicity leaned against the car door. "It's been such a mild winter and there's no reason to wait."

"I'm glad your dad is all right. I heard he ran off for a while."

"Well, we found him." Felicity glanced at the stand. "I hope it looks more inviting when it's packed with veggies. Looks a little pathetic right now."

Josie laughed. "They always do. There's nothing sadder than all those empty stands along Route 2 just waiting for warm weather and new crops. Are you going to Sasha Glover's service?"

"Is it set?"

"Tomorrow. Both Sasha and Clarissa." Josie's good cheer faded and she opened her mouth to say something, but she waited until an approaching car passed. She and the other driver acknowledged each other with a slight wave of the hand before she leaned closer to Felicity. "Two funerals in one family in one day." Josie turned to look at the farm stand again. "I hope you have something more upbeat on your agenda. Do you?"

"Not quite. I'm on my way to see your husband. My truck stalled the other day and I don't know why. Before I do anything I want to check with him."

"Well, he's there. But he's kinda grumpy today."

Felicity promised to keep that in mind. Josie went on her way, and Felicity put away her tools. Less than an hour later, she was pulling into Flat Road Automotive. She parked in front of the last bay and shut off the engine.

Bruce Halloway's automotive repair shop and garage sat next to a gas station, and it was hard to tell that the two were separate businesses. The gas station did no automotive business, by agreement, and Bruce never pumped gas. He leased some of his space to Hogie Dubois, who rented out and maintained a small fleet of cheap cars. Bruce also had the town's towing contract, and after an accident he could be found sitting in his tow truck parked behind the police cars. He had arrived on the scene of Clarissa's crash and towed away the wreckage after Jeremy and Felicity left. Today she found Bruce where she expected to, under a car.

"No one's supposed to come into the garage," Bruce said when Felicity reached the back of the bay where he was working. "Is that a dog?"

"It's me, Felicity. This is Shadow." The dog continued to sniff Bruce's shoes and pants legs and then moved to the doorway leading into a small office. Felicity tugged on the leash and led Shadow out to the yard and around the side of the building to shrubbery and trees. This seemed to please him and he snuffled and poked and scratched for several minutes, leaving Felicity to let her thoughts wander along too.

"How's your truck running?"

She turned to see Bruce behind her. Despite the chill he wore only a T-shirt over oil-stained navy work pants and heavy boots. He looked tired, and she wondered if he ever took a regular weekend off. He loved his work, and it meant that he often said yes to a customer when he should have said no and gone home to get some rest.

"That's why I'm here. I stalled going about twenty. Fortunately, no one else was on the road, but I want to check it out."

"How old is your car?"

"It's a 2002 Toyota Tacoma."

"Yeah, they do that." He pulled a rag out of his pocket and walked back into the garage.

"Maybe this isn't a good time. You look kinda beat."

"There is no good time." He tossed the oiled rag onto a cluttered workbench.

"Is that Clarissa Jenkins's car?" Felicity walked deep into the end bay, where a badly damaged sedan sat high up on a lift. She didn't have to crouch more than an inch to look at the undercarriage.

"You shouldn't go over there." Bruce sounded like he was telling her the time of day, not like he was giving her the warning required by his insurance company.

"Are you working on it?" Felicity stepped back and took another turn around the raised body.

"Not yet. The cops released it, and I just put it up there. I haven't done anything yet. I thought I'd buy it for salvage and repair it. My dumbest idea yet." He pushed his hands into his pockets.

"You don't think someone would buy it even after you repair it?"

"People buy wrecks all the time," Bruce said. "The buyer would have to insure it as a wreck, but it could still be a good car. It just means the buyer wouldn't get the same replacement payout if something happened to it, and the insurance premium would be a little higher. But that's not the reason it was dumb. You know cars pretty good. Take a look." He began to collect tools, leaving Felicity to inspect the vehicle on her own. She crouched under, then backed up and moved to the side.

"That's the brake caliper." She reached out to the front right wheel and pointed to a part.

"Yeah. Don't touch anything. You can look, but that's all."

She glanced at him, then moved down to a line, and then to a valve. "Bruce, what's going on? The bleeder valve is open. Are you working on it?"

"Nope." He crouched beside her under the car. "The bleeder valve on every caliper is open and the fluid reservoir is almost empty." He shut his eyes for a moment. "And the only fluid in it is water, plain old tap water." He opened his eyes and looked at her.

Felicity stared at him, and then ran her hand in the air alongside the caliper and the lines. She hurried to the other wheels. He didn't try to stop her or tell her she was wasting her time. "Would the water do anything?"

Bruce shook his head. "Water isn't going to stand up to that kind of heat."

"I wondered about the car when we came on the crash site. There were no skid marks on the road. It didn't look like she tried to brake." She stepped out from under the car. "What about the steering?"

Bruce picked up a screwdriver and tossed it onto the workbench. "Yeah, that too. Not the fluid—something else." He took a deep breath. "Now, there's no telling when this damage was done. Jeez, Felicity." His voice fell to a whisper. "Clarissa picked her car up from us on Monday morning. It'd been sitting here all weekend. Just out in the lot. The way I leave them. Just waiting for her to come and get it."

"We all leave our cars out there, Bruce."

Bruce opened his mouth to say something but turned at the sound of a car driving up to the gas pump. "I've never had anything like this happen. I called Chief Algren as soon as I realized what it all meant. He should be here any minute."

"No one else has looked at the car?"

Bruce shook his head.

"When would Clarissa have known something was wrong?" Felicity asked. "Could she have pulled over on Flat Road right away?"

Bruce shrugged and rested his hands on his hips. "Her car's an automatic, and those things drive themselves. You don't have to step on the gas to get them going."

"So she'd need her brakes right away?"

Again he shook his head. "Not for sure. She goes out here, down Flat Road, and turns onto High Street. The hill isn't steep, and at that hour, before seven o'clock or so, the lights are still blinking red or yellow, yellow on High Street. So if no one's coming she can go right through, and then she's climbing. She doesn't need a brake till she gets up to the ridge. There's a little turn, so maybe by now she feels something in the steering. But when she reaches the intersection and has to turn left, she has to know something is wrong. By then she knows she has no brakes and the steering is off."

Felicity listened, and when he finished they looked at each other.

"So she would have known just when she was coming toward my place."

"Yeah. She might have guessed earlier if she tried to brake at the curve, but for sure by the intersection. The road is banked there so that alone would have carried her through the intersection onto your road. The banking would have put the car into a turn and then it probably would have swerved back and forth with the layout of the road."

A car pulled off the paved road and onto the graveled apron for the garage. Both turned to watch the chief park and climb out of his car.

Bruce turned back to her. "I kept telling myself the damage to the steering system could have been done in the crash. The way things pop off if they're loosened isn't going to show after you've crashed into a tree. And they had an eyewitness telling them she swerved to avoid hitting an animal. But after seeing all that—" He waved at the underside of the car. A moment later he turned to nod to the police chief as he walked into the bay.

"Hello, Felicity." Kevin stared at her.

"You're not going to let me stay, are you?"

———

A few hours later, just before eight o'clock that evening, Felicity knocked on the door to the Algren home. Natalie Algren made and sold preserves and small handworked items, mostly small felt toys and animals. For the last several years she had sold her goods on Felicity's farm stand in exchange for time managing it.

"We just finished supper." Natalie led Felicity into the kitchen, smiling warmly and her green eyes sparkling. Natalie's short black hair shimmered like pure silk in the overhead light. She moved softly, easily, and though she wasn't a petite woman, she seemed to have the grace of someone light.

To Felicity's mind, Natalie Algren was the most remarkably and genuinely cheerful person anyone could ever meet. She seemed to move in a separate world, smiling at the oddities of human beings around her. Even when she'd had so much trouble with her ankles the previous summer, she'd remained cheerful and upbeat. Her mood never seemed false, and Felicity thought Kevin a fortunate man.

The two women settled at the kitchen table and went over the schedule for the farm stand. Natalie spread out on the table some of the things she was planning on stocking. The women compared estimates from previous years with final sales figures. They concluded their pricing and scheduling for the upcoming year in less than an hour.

"Kevin's fixing up the little stand I used last year," Natalie said, and headed out to get her husband. A moment later Kevin followed her into the kitchen, wiping his hands on a rag and then flicking it onto his sawdust coated jeans. "You're making a mess, Kev." He looked down at his legs, as though not sure what to do about them or the sawdust. Natalie appeared behind him with a hand vacuum cleaner and proceeded to tidy him up.

Kevin lowered himself into a chair and rested his arms on the table. "Any more of that?" He nodded to the coffee pot sitting on a warmer, and his tone was at once intimate and respectful. His wife placed a mug in front of him. "Felicity was at Flat Road Automotive this afternoon," he told his wife. He lifted the mug and took a sip. "It's police business, Felicity. I'm not going to tell you anything."

"Okay, I won't ask. I rebuilt my farm stand this afternoon," Felicity said.

"You got it set up too," Kevin said. "I saw it on my way home."

Natalie and Felicity glanced at each other. Her farm was certainly not on his way home.

"What were you doing out my way?" Felicity asked.

"Police business," Kevin said.

"Oh, tell her, Kevin. She has a right to know," Natalie said.

"What my wife means is that I have some public information, yes, because it was in the town notes. Some of it, anyway." Kevin tipped his head toward his wife, softening his words. He closed his eyes a moment, and when he opened them he looked straight at Felicity. "I was checking out a report of a 911 call from Clarissa Jenkins a couple of weeks back. It seems she made the call from her home, but when the Lanark officer drove up, a man was driving away and she didn't want to press charges."

"Was Clarissa hurt?"

Kevin tightened his shoulders and shook his head. "The report said one side of her face was red, as though someone had slapped her hard, but she insisted it was all fine."

"Did she give the man's name?" Natalie asked.

"She refused to press charges or say anything more." Kevin shifted in his seat as if about to stand up.

"That poor woman," Felicity said. "Maybe that's what she was going to tell Sasha. That her boyfriend is violent and she broke it off because of that."

"Maybe." Kevin's face was blank, giving away nothing of his feelings. "We'll never know unless she told someone."

Felicity glanced at Natalie and wondered if they were thinking the same thing. "And then she had that car crash."

"We can't jump to conclusions, Felicity."

"I know, I know, Kevin, but something very strange is happening around my farm. I thought it began with Sasha Glover. But after what I saw at Bruce's garage today and after what you just told me, I have to wonder if it begins even before the car accident. Perhaps even before the prowler at my place."

"Did you put up motion detectors?"

Felicity nodded. "Sasha's dad, Mr. Glover, told me something that seems worrisome. At first I dismissed it, but it's something to think about. Kyle, Sasha's boyfriend, got the idea there's some kind of buried treasure in this area. I never heard anything like that before, but that's what Mr. Glover said. Maybe Kyle was pressuring Clarissa about it."

"How's your dad?"

Felicity stared at Kevin, startled by his change of subject, but relented. "Better. Less agitated. He's still talking about something secret and I shouldn't tell anyone. Of course, since I don't know what it is, I can't, so that's just fine." She'd decided not to share more of her suspicions until she was sure she would sound less foolish, or at least less like Old Zeke.

"It's the way things are now," Kevin said.

"I didn't mean to be flippant. Whenever I think about him I get agitated too. Since he disappeared from Pasquanata, the home has had to hire additional help to watch him. At least that's what they're telling me. And I have to pay for this extra service—a mental health care giver, a special service for people in his condition, now that Dad has shown he can't be left alone."

"You have to pay?" Natalie asked. She'd come to stand behind Kevin, her hands resting on his shoulders.

Felicity nodded. "That's what they've told me. I have to come up with several thousand dollars a year."

"That can't be right, can it, Kevin?" Natalie leaned over her husband.

"I'm at my wit's end, Kevin. I'll get some cash from the farm stand and timbering. But short of selling land, I don't know where I'm going to get a few thousand extra every year for the rest of his life." Felicity looked at the tissues sitting on a bookcase against the wall and wished for once she could break into tears and have the relief of feeling all that worry and fear and anxiety flowing away. Instead she took a deep breath and swore softly under her breath. "Every time I see Dad he makes me promise not to sell anything and then the manager wants to know when they can expect a payment."

"You've given them something already?"

"Not yet, but I said I would soon. I had to. I was afraid they'd put him out and then what would I do?"

"Can they do that?" Natalie asked.

"Don't know," Kevin said. "But I can give you some numbers to call so you can find out."

———

Kevin walked Felicity to her car soon after she told them about the Pasquanata Community Home.

"Are you going to Clarissa Jenkins's and Sasha Glover's funeral tomorrow?" she asked.

"I don't think so." He raised his hand to stop her from saying anything more. "Felicity, don't ask me any more questions. I know you want to find out what I think, but this is police business, state police business."

"But you do know something."

Kevin glanced back at the house. "I felt so good just a moment ago."

Felicity smiled and opened the truck door. "And you will again, as soon as I leave."

Kevin lowered his head and looked at the ground before stepping closer to her. "I don't know if anyone is chasing hidden treasure—as absurd as it sounds. But I want you to be careful. Clarissa's car sat outside Bruce's garage long enough for someone to tamper with it. You take your pickup there. Natalie takes our car there."

"You sound so serious."

"Felicity, you live on a huge piece of land, alone, with a few animals. You're very vulnerable."

"My family has been on that land for almost three hundred years," Felicity said, a smile of incomprehension growing.

"Things aren't the same, Felicity. Just listen to your name and your mother's and grandmother's. All those words of virtue—Charity, Faith."

"And before them Hope and Devotion." Felicity's smile softened. "I know life is changing, Kevin. How could I not know? But I can take care of myself."

Again he raised his hand. "I know you have a rifle and a shotgun. But those arms won't do you any good against someone who sneaks around. Clarissa probably had no idea what was happening to her as she drove to your place."

"I'll bet near the end she did."

"Whoever is doing this could be someone you know, someone I know. We have no idea who is behind this, if it's one person or two, or even if the deaths are connected."

"It's Clarissa Jenkins's brakes, isn't it?"

"You never stop, do you?" He tugged at his waistband again.

"Dad was muttering about something secret, that I shouldn't tell anyone." She rested her hand on the open door. "It's possible there's some secret from years ago, something to do with land and Old Zeke. He and Zeke were close way back when. And lots of people know that."

"You know what I want you to do?"

"Run the farm and stay out of it."

"That's exactly it, Felicity." He spoke softly, as if he didn't want any of the neighbors to hear. The neighborhood was one of the few with homes facing sidewalks, well-tended lawns and shrubbery in front of a poured concrete foundation, and streetlights. Natalie had begun to turn off the lamps in the first-floor rooms, except for those that shone through the living room window. It was nearing ten o'clock, a time when almost everyone had settled in for the night.

"I don't know if this has anything to do with your dad when he was young or when he ran with Zeke Bodrun. Your dad was considered very shrewd for a young man, coming up with a way to get past a skeptical future mother-in-law, and we thought Old Zeke Bodrun had something to do with it. I heard your granddad traded him some cast-off lumber to repair his house some years ago in exchange for cutting firewood. We all heard things like that. And then Zeke moved into that cabin. But I never heard of real money or anything of value changing hands. That's just fantasy. You can look if you want, but I don't think there's anything there."

Felicity slid into the front seat. "Maybe I will. I have a few ideas. But I just wish I knew exactly what I was looking for." Kevin slammed the truck door and leaned on the frame.

"Oh, Felicity, we all wish we knew what we were looking for. Then we'd know when we found it." He patted the door and stepped away. "But you? You're sure to find trouble."

Twelve

The following afternoon Felicity parked near St. Peter's Catholic Church in a suburb of Lanark. She saw only two or three available spaces, but it was hard to tell if the cars parked along the street belonged to mourners or those going about their usual business. The few parking meters covered with blue plastic caps announcing *Funeral* didn't give any indication of the number of mourners inside. Felicity climbed the steps of the old Victorian church and stopped at the top to get her bearings.

The vast nave was empty and she thought at first she'd come to the wrong place, but as her eyes adjusted to the dim interior a man dressed in black, an official usher from the funeral home, approached her and pointed to a small chapel off to the left. She turned to the aisle and followed it to a chapel softly lit. The eight rows of pews were nearly filled. She slid into the last one, nodding to the older woman near the middle.

In the center of the second pew, a familiar head of yellow and green hair turned around and smiled at her. Padma sat beside her father, Dingel Mantell, and Felicity guessed he must have known the family. She recognized some of the other mourners, including Josie Halloway, who turned and caught her eye but didn't smile. Beside her sat Nola Townsend and another artist from the Mill in West Woodbury.

Many of the mourners were youngish women in their twenties, some with cell phones in their laps, judging by their concentration and posture. Others looked like friends of Sasha's parents, middle-aged men and women who would be doubly pained at the loss of one so young, perhaps one close in age to their own children. One funeral for two generations of the same family, Felicity thought. What could be sadder?

She let her mind drift until she caught sight of Lance Gauthier, sitting at the end of the second pew. He occasionally glanced to his right, to the front row, still empty, but not behind him. He nodded to one or two people but generally kept his eyes focused on the altar. She was mildly surprised to see him there, since he'd given no indication that he knew Sasha. It was good of him to come, Felicity felt.

"Hello!" The whispered greeting came from Maddie, Sasha's first-floor neighbor. She climbed over Felicity and settled in the pew. Apparently Catholic, she lowered the kneeler, moved forward, and prayed. After a minute or so, she sat back. "I'm so glad people have come. Her dad came to the house and he was so broken up I thought I'd have to call an ambulance for him."

"How's her mom?" Felicity felt remiss for not having visited Sasha's mother yet, but after her visit with Harold Glover, she wasn't sure she could face another grieving parent.

"She's devastated." Maddie studied the other mourners. "I heard she cried for two days nonstop, and then she got up and said she wanted to talk to the police. I don't know what happened but she looks pretty resigned now. You never know how people will react."

"I haven't seen her yet. I haven't been brave enough."

Maddie patted her knee. "Don't be so hard on yourself." She continued to scan the back of the mourners' heads and Felicity wondered if she was looking for someone in particular. "See that guy at this end of the second pew? That's Kyle. Ms. Callahan told the funeral home he wouldn't be allowed to sit with the family."

Felicity glanced at Kyle, and then at Lance at the other end of the pew. Kyle slouched, his head down and his rangy torso folded over, making his short spiky hair look like a weapon about to spear the person in front of him. She couldn't be certain if Lance had acknowledged Kyle earlier, but now she wondered if they knew each other, and if Lance had indeed known Sasha. But if he had, wouldn't he have said something?

"Do you know most of the people here?" Felicity asked.

Maddie gave her a short rundown on those whom she knew. Felicity pointed out Padma and Dingel, Josie Halloway, and a few others. "I'm surprised Bruce isn't here," she said half to herself.

"Why?" Maddie asked.

"Oh, no reason. Just they're usually together." That was pretty lame, Felicity thought, but Maddie seemed satisfied and turned to look at the other mourners.

"Who's that guy?" Maddie was looking at the end of the second pew.

"That's Lance Gauthier. He's a logger. He was with me when I found her." Felicity lowered her voice when a woman in front turned around and hissed at her to be quiet. "It's good of him to come," she added in barely a whisper.

"He looks really uncomfortable." Maddie studied the back of Lance's head for a while and gave a quiet harrumph. Before she could share her opinion, however, a door near the altar opened and the family, small as it was, filed in and took seats in the first pew.

———

Felicity followed Maddie through the reception line in the church hall, offering condolences to Clarissa Jenkins's and Sasha Glover's cousins and more distant relatives. She steeled herself for greeting Sasha's father and was relieved to find he had taken his feelings in hand and seemed almost calm. To his right was a small woman seated in a wheelchair. Felicity had noticed her entering with the family and assumed this had to be another aunt or distant cousin, but Mr. Glover introduced the elderly woman as his mother-in-law, Zenia Callahan.

Felicity offered her condolences, and the old woman offered her a thin delicate hand with a surprisingly strong grip. It reminded her of Jeremy's grandfather, who in the end couldn't speak or walk or even eat but could break tools in half when he was frustrated. The elderly woman accepted her condolences and then her attention faded.

To her right stood Sasha's mother, a woman who had hidden her grief behind a veil of formality. Felicity introduced herself and saw the flicker of recognition in the other woman's eyes.

"I remember hearing your name," Helena Bodrun Callahan said. She was well into her fifties, with thin lines crinkling around her eyes and mouth. She had the poise of a professional dancer, and wore her dark, wavy hair long and pulled back in a small knot at the nape of her neck. "Perhaps we could talk sometime."

Felicity spent the next half hour milling around the buffet table, where a number of church volunteers kept the platters full and the chatter light. She was used to this kind of funeral service, but Maddie grew restless almost at once.

"I don't like thinking about mortality," she said. "I'm not ready."

"You don't have to be," Felicity said.

"My sister-in-law came over the other day and all she wanted to talk about was her upcoming surgery. I hate that kind of conversation, the way people talk about their ailments and everything." She held a plate of sandwiches and brownies close to her chest as she looked furtively around her. "I think I'll go sit down."

Felicity was about to join her when Helena Callahan appeared at her side. A volunteer handed her a paper plate of selected food items, and the bereaved mother led Felicity to two chairs set apart from the others. She sat down and looked across the room at a group of young men lounging in the doorway and chatting.

"My daughter went to school with most of them." Helena stared at each one, and then looked over the other guests. "I told her when she was still in high school that most of these friends wouldn't last. She'd leave them behind as she grew." She looked down at her lap. "It was part advice and part my own ambition for her."

Felicity studied the younger guests. Yes, she could see how the advice would be true, based on what she'd learned about Sasha Glover. She did have ambition, as her mother wanted, but she seemed to have something more, a sense of the larger world and its possibility that she carried within her. "I've been hearing how good she was at her job, Ms. Callahan, and how much she loved it."

"She grew and they didn't." The woman turned to Felicity. "Please, call me Helena." Felicity nodded. "What was she doing on your land?"

"I have no idea. That's what I was hoping you could tell me." Felicity wondered how much the police had told the parents; if Kevin had indeed informed the mother of how Sasha had died.

"I was so surprised when her father told me she was found in the woods. She wasn't the outdoorsy type at all. She didn't even like gardening." Helena looked across the room at her ex-husband. "Sasha made a special point of staying close to her father. She was good at managing relationships, maintaining them. I wondered if she was waiting to see if her boyfriend, Kyle, was going to come along as she'd hoped, to mature the way he should, but she said no, she was done with him."

"She told you that?"

Helena nodded. "We talked a few days earlier, and she said she'd come by and we'd have a good chat. That usually meant she had something specific to tell me." She offered a wry smile. "She wasn't one for drama. If she had an announcement, she said so, made it, and went on with whatever she was doing." She settled back in her chair. "I was looking forward to it. I hadn't seen much of her lately and I thought it would be fun to catch up with her, hear whatever it was she'd decided. I always worried she'd tell me she'd taken a job in Albany or New York, but I got used to that because I knew it would happen and I wanted her to succeed and be happy."

The last words caught in her throat and she pulled away. "I was so proud of her." She brushed non-existent crumbs from her lap. "I'm a freelance booking agent for dance programs in the New England area, and I've been branching out into New York and the Midwest, so I was doing some traveling." She leaned back in her chair, and the metal chair legs squeaked. "I missed visiting with her. I loved listening to how she was getting on and what she'd just learned. She had that enthusiasm of the beginner you just know is going to make it."

Felicity murmured something.

"I have to stop talking like this. I'm not helping myself or anyone else." Helena Callahan paused to sit up straight and look across the room. "My mother is devastated, but she's grown philosophical, I guess."

Felicity followed her line of sight straight to the old woman in the wheelchair. Someone had positioned her at a table, where she was surrounded by a younger generation. "Sasha's grandmother… so she would be Ezekial Bodrun's daughter?"

"That's right." Helena nodded, apparently unaware of the change in Felicity's tone, from casual conversation to sudden interest. Instead, she took a moment to compose herself. "Sasha used to visit my mom after she went into the nursing home, when she was still a teenager. Not so long ago," she added wistfully. "My mother will feel the loss."

"Did she talk to your mom about her current life?"

Helena frowned. "I doubt it. Sasha was nothing if not diplomatic."

"I don't understand." It was Felicity's turn to frown.

"She would never talk to her grandmother about boy trouble, or man trouble now. She saved that for me." Helena gave a soft laugh.

"Did your daughter know how you felt about Kyle?"

"A little. Well, yes, I guess she did. After she told me she was probably going to break up with him, I didn't try to hide my feelings as much."

"Did she give you any idea of what she was thinking when she made the decision to break up with him?" Maybe this was the time, Felicity thought, or maybe it wasn't, but Helena Callahan had opened the door and she was glad to walk through. Helena must have known what she was thinking, because she shifted in her chair and peered at her.

"You mean, did she have a specific reason for ending it with Kyle?" She glanced across the room to where the man in question was slouching against a wall, next to a short woman whose green and yellow hair could only be Padma's. "Is that Padma Mantell?"

"I think so."

"Hmm. Well, as to your question, no, not that I know. I asked if something had happened and she said not really. She was just ready to move on. But I wondered. She seemed uncomfortable talking about it." Helena looked down at the plate sitting in her lap, the small sandwiches untouched. She noticed a side table and slid the plate onto it. She straightened her skirt and pressed her knees together, sitting with her calves and feet perfectly aligned. "Her cousin, more like an aunt, might have had something to do with it."

"Do you mean Clarissa Jenkins?" Felicity asked. "When your daughter talked about Clarissa it sounded like they were very fond of each other."

"Yes, they were. Clarissa and I were cousins. When Sasha and I and everyone else in the family learned about Clarissa's accident, we were devastated. And then my daughter. Now, we're numb." She glanced at her mother still surrounded by younger cousins and friends.

"I have the dog Clarissa was fostering." Felicity feared Helena would start crying.

"Oh, that cute little black dog? She was very good with him. When I first saw him I thought he should be put down, for his own sake, but she was really good at bringing him back. So you have the dog?"

"I do, and he's coming along. Loretta Colson got him from Clarissa and passed him on to me." Felicity was relieved to be able to say something positive in all this misery. She recalled Sasha's one and only visit to the farm. "Was Sasha interested in dog fostering?"

"Oh, no. Clarissa and Sasha were great friends, but my daughter didn't have time for a pet." Helena smiled. "Those two were very different. Clarissa was one for causes, and even though I didn't always agree with her I thought she was a good influence on my daughter.

She had such a sense of excitement about the world. She thought anything was possible if you put your mind to it."

"Even socializing an old hermit?" Felicity said. Helena glanced at her. "You mean Ezekial?"

Felicity nodded. "I heard Clarissa took care of Ezekial near the end. I suppose that fits with the fostering of stray dogs."

"Well, to the extent that anyone could take care of that old coot. He was my granddad too, and I loved him when I was a child because he was so different. My mother was sure she'd have to take him in at the end and dreaded having him around because he was so contrary, but in the end he died happy, in his cabin in the woods."

"Is it true Clarissa used to bring him meals and he grew quite fond of her and in the end he gave her a piece of land?"

Helena laughed. "Well, yes and no. He transferred a piece of property to her, but I told her then I didn't think it was worth much."

"Did he think it was worth something?"

"He told Clarissa it was more valuable than gold. It had something special." She shook her head.

"Do you think he meant that literally?" This sounded like it could be the beginning of Kyle's obsession with buried treasure.

Helena shrugged. "Who knows? He was always buying up useless property, wood lots with no access, marshy areas with vernal pools, and pieces that were all ledge, coyote hotels I called them. If he had trouble paying the property taxes on them, the town might take it and sell it for taxes, so who knows what he owned when he died. My mother wasn't happy about that, but I guess she sorted it out."

"So do you know what Clarissa did with the land?"

"Oh, yes. She gave it to Sasha. When Sasha told me Clarissa was giving her the piece of land our granddad had given her, I gave Sasha the same talk. Don't believe any of the nonsense. There's no surprise wealth there. This isn't a television show with an oil field hidden among the rotten trees. I don't know if she believed me or what she did about it."

She told Kyle, Felicity thought, and he became obsessed with finding whatever that treasure was. That's when she knew the relationship was going nowhere. "What happens with the land now?"

"I get it, I suppose. To add it to all the other useless land I have and can't sell." Helena didn't look pleased. "Sasha accompanied me when I went to update my will and she had one done at the same time. She said she should, now that she was a landowner." Helena brushed a wisp of hair from her eyes. "That was so typically Sasha—she'd do what she was supposed to even if it seemed silly. She had property, so she got a will."

"Was Kyle in the will?"

"Oh, no."

"Do you think Kyle knew?"

"Oh, yes, he knew. She told him she was doing this."

"Was he angry?"

Helena stifled a laugh. "Probably. He didn't like people disagreeing with him."

Across the room, the almost ex-boyfriend leaned against the door jamb; his worn hiking boots testified to his love of the outdoors. His jeans were neatly pressed and his jacket tidy if old, perhaps second-hand. But his white shirt and sweater looked new. As she watched him, he listened intently to one of Padma's stories. After a moment Felicity realized Helena was staring at her.

"I wish she'd left him sooner." Helena glanced over at Kyle.

"I've never met him and I've wondered what he was like. From what I've heard about your daughter, he seems such an unlikely partner for her."

"She could have had someone with a real future," Helena said, her sadness rolling through each word.

Thirteen

Felicity crossed the church parking lot, still thinking about Sasha Glover's prescient decision to draw
up a will after she took possession of the lot from
Clarissa Jenkins. Helena Callahan had promised to
let Felicity know if she decided to take any action,
such as selling the land or leasing it for timbering.
Felicity hinted she might be willing to purchase it.

Her thoughts drifted to her last image of Kyle,
and then to the way he and Lance had book-ended
the church pew. From that she jumped at once to her
new image of Lance as someone who played a lot of
scratch tickets. Was he someone who would gamble
on a piece of land rumored to hide a treasure? It
sounded absurd, but then seeing him the other day
with all those losing tickets seemed absurd. Felicity
wondered what she would do if she suddenly found

herself in competition with Lance for the same property. She was mulling this over when Josie Halloway fell into step beside her.

When they reached her car, Josie unbuttoned her dark brown jacket, slipped it off, and folded it so the pink lining became the outside. She dropped it onto the back seat. "My funeral outfit. It depresses me." She pulled out a light cotton golf jacket and slipped that on.

"No Bruce," Felicity said.

"Would you believe me if I told you Kevin asked him not to talk to anyone? So he decided it would be better to stay home."

"Yes, I believe it. He didn't want me around when he found me there at the garage looking over Clarissa's sedan. Kevin's afraid that if word gets out something was wrong with the car before it crashed, the rumors will get out of hand."

Josie winced. "I have a big mouth, I know. But I do know when to keep it shut."

Felicity slipped off her own jacket, draped it over her crossed arms, and leaned against Josie's car. She wore black flats with almost no heel, a habit she'd picked up years ago when she missed a train in Albany because she couldn't run fast enough in heels. She didn't mind missing the train, but she did mind not being able to run. The heels went into the Salvation Army donation box.

Josie fished in her pockets and pulled out a roll of Life Savers. She offered them to Felicity, who took a red one. She popped it into her mouth.

"I wonder if they tested Clarissa for alcohol," Josie said. Felicity squinted at her. "I mean, would they assume she was drunk because she was driving so erratically?"

"I think they would test her for lots of things including alcohol." Felicity rolled the Life Saver around her tongue. "Kevin said he didn't notice anything when the EMTs were moving her out of the car."

Josie folded up the Life Saver package and slid it back into her pocket. "Sometimes I hope they find she was sober and then I hope they find that she wasn't." She frowned when she caught Felicity's eye. "If she was drunk, then maybe what Bruce found means nothing. But then I'd hate to think Clarissa went so far downhill that she was getting drunk at seven in the morning. So maybe it's better that something happened to her car, but then I can't stand the thought of someone tampering with her car. And then I'm even more terrified to think that someone was skulking around our garage tampering with cars." She clenched her fists inside the jacket pockets.

"You're going around in circles, Josie. But I know what you mean. We all leave our cars in Bruce's lot. And the keys inside them."

"I don't want to think how easy it was for someone to tamper with the car in the lot."

"I just can't see Clarissa Jenkins or Sasha Glover in the middle of anything that would get them killed." Felicity stood away from the car. She brushed down the back of her pants automatically, and then brushed off her hands. "Sasha came by the day after the accident to talk about Clarissa, how she felt the land was special and things like that."

"Hmm. Strange."

"Maybe. There's a man offering a lot of money for farmland around here."

"Really? Why?"

Felicity laughed. "Exactly. Those of us who live here don't think the land's worth anything."

"Have you met him?"

Felicity shook her head. "But Sasha's boyfriend thinks there's something valuable on her land."

"Do you think Kyle and this buyer are after the same thing?"

Felicity shrugged. The thought had crossed her mind, as well as the fear that Mr. Franklin Gentile had enough money to buy some local help, although that wasn't what Josie had asked her. "What would it be, Josie? It's not like we have minerals to exploit or a history of buried wealth or something to attract treasure hunters." But Kyle and the buyer are definitely chasing after something, she thought.

The evening could not come soon enough for Felicity. She led the sheep to the barn for the night, fed the animals inside and out, made supper, and built a small fire. When she settled in her chair in the living room, Miss Anthropy jumped into her lap and Shadow circled the rug in front of the fire. Felicity needed this time to shed her feelings of sorrow over Sasha's death and the sadness lingering from the funeral. But then came the doubts about the two deaths.

"You're going to help me work this out, Miss Anthropy." The cat purred and rubbed her nose along Felicity's chin, and Felicity took that as a sign of agreement.

In front of her, on the floor, lay a large map covering almost the entire town. To this had been added several hand-drawn property lines and odd scraps of historical information written in small cramped letters. Felicity leaned on her arm and peered down at the tidy or not-so-tidy blocks of land. She wondered now that she'd never paid that much attention to the map. Her sense of space and location stemmed from following her parents around the property, and she had absorbed their sense of place.

As she looked at the individual blocks, she noted how the farm had been pieced together over the years, a wood lot this year and a wood lot a decade ago, and another wood lot decades before that. Little pieces here and there, more during years when times were good, and then decades of nothing. Several pieces had been added during the Great Depression, which made sense because people were desperate for cash. And then in the late 1950s a small piece of land that seemed too poor to care about, but it linked to another, larger piece that Felicity's father had timbered every few years. A productive piece and a scrub lot together. Both came onto the farm while Felicity's grandparents were still alive, before her parents married.

Her father had told her stories about each piece, turning the patchwork quilt of low-value farm and woodland into a mythic space. She leaned back in her chair and Miss Anthropy, annoyed at being disturbed, sat up and squinted at her. She blinked once and settled down again to continue her nap. Felicity scratched the cat's head and behind her ears. And then she remembered the notes she'd taken in Sasha's apartment. Sasha, or perhaps someone else, had marked four spots on the map Felicity had found in the bedroom.

Felicity scanned her notes and then located the four spots on her own map. One sat along an old fire road. She had no notes for this piece. A second piece stood far to the north of her property and, again, she had no notes on it. A third piece seemed to fit the location of Zeke Bodrun's cabin, and the fourth piece fit the description of the location of the plot Zeke had given to Clarissa.

She got a magnifying glass from the desk and held it over the notes on various plots, moving past the four marked on Sasha's map to plots she was familiar with. She paused at one plot to read the crabbed handwriting, which she recognized as her dad's. The note read simply, *Huston to Z. Bodrun, 5.5.51*. The date seemed significant. Zeke had purchased that plot before her parents were adults, but perhaps around the time when Zeke and her granddad had been friends. This piece abutted another piece her grandfather had purchased a few years later. She put away the magnifying glass.

Over the years she had walked with her dad through the woods, on the little trails he built, some of them linking deer paths. When he bought a lot that Felicity's mother thought was worthless, and she rolled her eyes to let him know just how worthless, he only smiled and said, "It's a buffer zone. Always good to have a buffer zone. Never know what might be out there." Charity would shake her head and go back to whatever she'd been doing. Walter would wink at his daughter.

"There's always timber, Lissie. Even if it looks useless, there's always timber."

This was mostly true. Their part of the state had never had a glorious history that left behind a residue for later searchers to uncover and resurrect. There were no elegant mansions, no grand hotels, no historic sites, no eccentric recluses hiding out. No rock piles suggesting early Nordic visitors or Indian settlements. It was poor farmland that had attracted those who couldn't travel farther or who thought they could make something out of nothing. They were mostly wrong. The heyday had ended in closed mills and a notch on the rust belt.

Her dad had been right, but not many people outside the area could have known that.

"People are so greedy and so deluded," Felicity said to the cat. Miss Anthropy opened one eye, purred, and went quietly back to sleep. Only then did she notice that Shadow was watching her, sprawled on the floor with both eyes focused on her, unblinking and still.

━━━━

Later that evening Felicity followed Shadow down the driveway, letting him snuffle his way along at his own pace. The dog had grown calmer, Felicity was getting used to the animal, and Miss Anthropy seemed to have accepted him.

At the mailbox, she pulled out a manila envelope and opened it. She peered in and read Lance's name at the top of a sheet of paper. Guessing this was the revised cutting plan, she pulled it out. She was right. She'd meant to speak to Lance at the funeral, but he'd left soon after the service and she hadn't seen him at the funeral meats. It was good of him to come, Felicity had thought, even though he'd seemed unwilling to linger. And then she'd put him out of her mind.

Under the ambient light, she scanned the description of work to be done. She thought she recognized the change in location but she hoped she was wrong. Curious and impatient, she dragged Shadow back to the house long before he was ready.

After clearing the dining table of piles of miscellaneous clutter and papers, for the second time that evening she spread out the map. With Lance's cutting plan in one hand, she leaned over the ridged and crumpled paper to get a clear sense of where he planned to work. Despite his earlier assurances, he wanted to come in from the northeast and cut a path through to a plot that had never been timbered, near where the bobcat had taken up residence. She recalled her dad's comments about various plots, including this one.

The three of them had gone out one spring to bring in blowndown trees for firewood, and her dad had pointed into the forest. "I tell people it's of no use and you will too," he told her. "Wood's no good, land's no good." She was perhaps ten years old at the time, and she'd looked up at him and nodded, solemn with her new responsibility though she wasn't sure what it was. She didn't see anything special about the trees, and she hadn't been able to decipher the smile on her mother's face. The jagged-toothed saw rested on her mother's shoulder. "She'll remember, Charity. When the time comes, our little girl will remember. She may not understand now, but she will later, when we get there, and then she'll remember."

That was what she'd been trying to recall when they'd come across the bobcat den.

Felicity looked closer at the map. It was a small lot, marked as scrubby with no special trees, and it sat in the middle of the property. It wasn't always the center of the farm, but over the years her parents and grandparents had bought up bits of land, so now the old plot was almost dead center. The plot itself had been forgotten until Lance told her she had to include it in the cutting plan now or in the near future. Which meant he'd been studying her farm more closely than she had.

Identifying the lot Ezekial Bodrun had given Clarissa, and she'd given to Sasha, had been easy. That one was located on Old Town Road, and was just another part of the woods left to grow as they would. She had passed it most of her life without even thinking about it. It wasn't her property, so she had paid no attention to it.

Lance had tacked the small plot in the center of her property onto the cutting plan. Perhaps he hoped she wouldn't notice, but this meant she'd have to revise once again. And she'd watch his reaction while she told him this. He was up to something—she was sure of that. But she didn't know if he was after the same secret as Kyle. And then she'd walk over to Sasha's plot and check on the boundaries, and then walk up to that plot that was so special to her dad. Since her father had managed most of the forestry planning until a few years ago, she was discovering there was more work than she'd anticipated. It was one thing to know all the trees and another to manage the paperwork.

Fourteen

An early morning shower the next day, Thursday, weighed down the stalks of the daffodils outside Felicity's front door and lining one side of the barn. The raindrops hung like crystals on the yellow-and-white trumpets, and the color alone put a lift in her step. The shower left the air smelling clean but moldy beneath the canopy along Old Town Road.

She moved gingerly among the small puddles dotting the nearly abandoned road, avoiding the obvious mud traps as she made her way past a falling stone wall on one side and a slanting shoulder on the other. She checked the GPS on her cell and concluded that in another hundred feet or so she would reach the corner of Sasha Glover's property. She didn't need the GPS coordinates, but she decided to learn to use the app in case some day she did need them. And now it was a game.

The problem with old plot lines on maps was they had no corresponding markers on real land, at least not until developers arrived. She wanted to make sure she found the correct piece of property to explore. Also, she didn't know how long this would take, but she wanted to give herself all the time she might need. She wore a backpack and carried a picnic lunch.

The official entrance to the lot was a break in the century-old stone wall, its form changing as the ground around it rose or fell, trees dropped limbs, and snow and ice shifted the rocks. But the more obvious sign was a barely discernible row of ATV tracks going in and out on a narrow path. Felicity followed these into the lot, which looked like any other wood lot in the area. Some pine and arborvitae, a few old hardwoods that would be worth something in the future, and a lot of windblown trees rotting in marshy ground. But as she walked deeper in, she noticed something else, something she would never notice while walking or driving past.

It was an old cellar hole, about forty feet from the entrance. She circled it. It wasn't an unusual sight. And like many of the remnants of abandoned homes from past centuries, the corner of a foundation, set into a once-low hill, still declared itself although the ground had changed, settling and filling in over the decades. But there, in the cellar hole, someone had dug several holes, going deep and piling up the dirt in neat piles. Felicity grabbed a stick, knelt down, and peered into the holes, poking through the loosened soil. She saw nothing that would have told her that the site was valuable.

She was used to seeing men and women, old and young, with metal detectors, searching for anything of interest in old cellar holes or wherever people might have lived and left behind an artifact or two.

They might find an old horseshoe, perhaps a scrap of an iron cooking pot, but she'd never heard of anyone finding anything truly valuable.

Ahead of her were several more holes. These had been dug earlier, perhaps in the fall, and the displaced dirt showed signs of having sunk into low mounds over the winter months, disappearing beneath fallen leaves and branches. The walls had begun to collapse, but the holes were still fully in evidence. Deeper into the woods were more piles of dirt fanning out in every direction, as though giant gophers had been digging tunnels and their entrances all over the New England landscape. Felicity checked the coordinates for the lot and began walking.

For the next hour and a half, she crisscrossed the wood lot, approximately fifteen acres, counting holes and piles, but only the one cellar remnant. Each hole was about the same depth, and none was noticeably larger than another. Some of the holes had obviously been dug months ago, before the ground froze, the piles of dirt sinking lower and the walls of the holes beginning to fail. Some piles were more recent, evidently dug when the ground thawed in the warm winter. None seemed to be the last, successful one, and Felicity wasn't even certain the digging had ended. Every minute she expected to hear someone calling out hey, what are you doing here? But she heard only her own footsteps crunching on the crusty earth.

Throughout her exploration she looked for signs of earlier timbering, but if any had been done, it hadn't been in recent years. Perhaps not even during her lifetime. When this had been Ezekial Bodrun's land, he'd done nothing with it except perhaps enjoy the solitude or pull out a windfall tree for firewood. But this piece was a good distance from his cabin, so Felicity looked for signs that he might have camped on the lot in earlier years. She found nothing except the usual evidence of recent picnickers who didn't take their trash with them.

After a while she crossed onto her own property and followed the slope up to the first of the two plots Old Zeke had sold to her dad, land that had never been timbered and now welcomed a bobcat. The lack of timbering seemed to be a theme in Zeke's life, though not in her father's. Felicity walked along the edge, into the center, and settled on a boulder. She tried to see what her dad or Zeke had seen, what had made them so interested in this piece. Fifty years ago, approximately when the transaction took place, it would have looked almost the same. But truthfully, it wasn't much of a piece of land. It all looked plain enough. Some good trees, but nothing spectacular. She headed back to Sasha's plot, wondering what she was missing.

Pulling out a canvas bag, Felicity began picking up old beer cans, plastic water bottles, scraps of plastic, and other detritus of the modern era. She carried the bag hooked onto her belt loop. She found most of the trash within a few feet of the stone wall and the dirt road, but occasionally she found something at the other end of the lot, along the northeastern boundary where the holes were most recent.

After two hours, Felicity knew she'd done enough. She sat on the stone wall, slipped off her backpack, and pulled out a sandwich. The road hadn't been used for general traffic in years, and she'd only used it once recently. This area had the kind of peace that most people never experience.

She began to eat her lunch. Beyond the trees to her west she could hear cars passing on the old road. Not far from here, Clarissa Jenkins had died in a crash. Felicity lowered her sandwich and looked behind her. She'd laughed when she'd first heard the story about buried treasure, thinking it the kind of story first graders heard in school that sent them running home and out into the back yard to dig up their parents' gardens. But someone had believed it strongly enough to spend hours and hours digging into a patch of useless ground. The warm winter had meant an early thaw and someone had returned to take advantage of that, moving from spot to spot despite repeated disappointment. Felicity turned again to the sound of traffic filtering through the trees.

Clarissa was dead. Sasha was dead. Could they have been murdered for this? Could someone have taken their lives for a myth about a piece of worthless land? All she could think about were the dozens of holes and little mounds scattered through the wood lot. All this couldn't be worth the lives of two vibrant, decent women. She felt her heart sink at the thought.

———

Felicity emerged from Old Town Road onto the paved highway. Ahead of her, parked along the shoulder, sat a black Jeep SUV and inside was Marilyn Kvorak. When Felicity approached within thirty feet, the real estate agent climbed out and walked a few feet to meet her. In her high heels, Marilyn wasn't about to walk much farther down the road, and Felicity didn't expect her to.

"It looks like you've been out hiking," Marilyn said.

"Sort of."

"Sort of isn't an answer, but I'll take it. Can I drive you back to your house?" Felicity climbed into the passenger seat and Marilyn drove them the short distance to the front door. "Got a minute?"

"I figured you didn't come out here to help random hitchhikers." Felicity got out and headed for the house. She went around to the side, slid off her boots, and opened the unlocked kitchen door. Marilyn followed her.

"You know everyone locks doors now."

"So I've heard." Felicity dropped her backpack onto a chair and bent to greet Shadow. When that was done, she went to Miss Anthropy curled on her chair and let her know she was still the number one animal in the house. The cat purred. She went to the stove and filled a pot with water, which she set to boil. "So what's up?"

"Not a lot." Marilyn found two mugs in the cupboard and put them on the kitchen table. "I think tea in the afternoon is just right. Not so much caffeine that I can't sleep but enough to get me through the rest of the day."

"And night. I heard you're showing houses at night now." Felicity stretched out her feet and wiggled her toes. Her socks had holes in the big toe and she could feel one developing in the heel. Darning wasn't her favorite activity and she wondered how long the socks would last before she'd have to get serious about mending. Or buying a new pair. Was she the only person left who still darned socks? "That's got to be hard on the sellers."

"Sellers want to sell, and I want them to sell for a good price, so we accommodate." Marilyn poured boiling water over tea bags in mugs. "Tea bags okay?"

Felicity thought it was a little late to ask, and since Marilyn seemed to be the hostess here, she said it was fine. "You still haven't told me why you're here."

"I need your help." Marilyn replaced the pot on the stove and sat down. "For some reason I always think you'll have brown sugar in the sugar bowl or a jar of honey on the tea tray. You being so earthy and all." She dipped a spoon into the sugar bowl and scooped out a heaping teaspoon of refined white and poured it into her tea.

"Earthy?"

"You know, healthy food and all that."

"There's honey in the cupboard and brown sugar in there too if you want. But you seem to be okay." Felicity watched a second teaspoon pour into the mug. "But the chemical makeup is the same. Sugar is sugar."

"You're so down to earth."

"Hence, earthy." Felicity added a little sugar and then a dollop of milk. "So, you must have something difficult to ask me because you're not usually so uncomfortable with the small talk." She stirred her tea.

"I just want your help."

"You said that."

"Do you think I'm missing something in life?"

Felicity stirred her tea and stared at her. "You came here to ask me that?"

"Well, sort of."

"You live in a garden apartment. I thought you loved it there."

"I do. But everyone I know wants a yard with a garden and all that stuff." Marilyn sipped her tea but Felicity could see her watching her out of the corner of her eye.

"Okay, Marilyn. This isn't like you." Felicity swung around and leaned on the table, facing her.

"I hate myself sometimes. I get so smarmy."

"Yup."

"Okay, okay. I'm here because my client insists I make an offer even if you reject it right off the bat." Marilyn raised her hand and shut her eyes. "Just hear me out."

"I've already said no."

"I know you have and I told him you weren't interested, but he said to make the offer. Spell out all the terms. If you don't like it, he won't bother you anymore. Okay?" Marilyn pushed her tea away and

Felicity guessed the second heaping teaspoon of sugar had been the result of nerves. "He seems to think you'll be interested."

"I wonder why," Felicity said, more to herself than Marilyn. "What does he look like?"

"What difference does that make?" The real estate agent looked genuinely confused. "He's not from around here."

"Okay. Make your pitch."

And Marilyn did.

"Do you know anything about him?" Felicity asked at the end of the speech. "I mean, how did he find out about us?"

"How does anyone find out anything?"

"Word of mouth, newspapers, television."

Marilyn picked up her mug to take another sip, noticed it was empty now, and put it down with a frown. "What's you point?"

"Does this Mr. Gentile know anyone else here, other than you, I mean?"

"Don't know. Never asked." Marilyn shrugged.

"I asked you what he looks like. Is he tall, thin, clean-shaven?"

Marilyn studied her mug, looked around the kitchen, and then at Felicity. "You have a point to all these questions?"

"Maybe. So, what about him?"

"I vetted him, Felicity. That's what you need to know. Don't you trust me?"

———

Even though it was late afternoon by the time Marilyn drove away, Felicity headed out to her vegetable garden to begin removing the pine boughs that had been protecting the plants throughout the winter. The weather had been so mild during the cold months that she could almost promise everyone an early crop from overwintered veg-etables, but she'd restrained herself to avoid costly and embarrassing setbacks. She desperately wanted the CSA garden to be a success, and she went to work with Marilyn's words ringing in her ears.

The reasoning the enthusiastic buyer had given for wanting a chance at her property had seemed, well, reasonable. Tall Tree Farm offered solitude, or isolation depending on your point of view. There was no one nearby to complain about the smell from the sheep. The farm wasn't surrounded by newcomers eager for the pleasures of country life and the conveniences of the more sophisticated urban world. Farmers in this area were less likely to find strangers enjoying their land, taking photographs, walking the dog, or finding a nice spot for a picnic. Nor would they find suburbanites dragging away what they thought of as free firewood or free stones for their garden wall.

Felicity gathered up another load of pine boughs and carried them to a large pile. She flung them onto it and looked around. Her farm, she had to admit, was not manicured. No one would ever get the sense that this was a place for visitors, with nicely situated animal pens, polished saddles waiting for riders (even if there were no horses), an unexpected sprout of daffodils or other flowers in season. There were no paths lead-ing into protected and picturesque groves, with a bench hewn from a log or a rusty seat pried loose from an old harvester.

The price being offered was so high that it had taken her breath away. Yes, the man's reason for the offer made sense, and yes, she ap-preciated not being cheated, and yes, Jeremy had turned down the offer Gentile made on his place, as she knew he would. But Marilyn had urged her to at least think about it, and Felicity promised she would. And she meant it. She would think hard on why this man who insisted on remaining a stranger wanted to pay at least three times what her property was worth. And how was it that Gentile seemed to know so much about the timbering practices in this area? Whoever he was, he seemed to know something she didn't, and she was going to figure it out.

Felicity was never more aware of the limitations of a working farm than when someone like Marilyn Kvorak pressed her to consider the alternative. And the alternative always seemed to highlight her weaknesses—an old farmhouse in constant need of repair (like any other old house), an old barn that looked ready to collapse (like every other old barn), a yard that looked like an auto shop had just moved out (tools nearby made work easier), and a series of paddocks that were picturesque only in photographs of rural poverty (painting a fence was a waste of money and time). But looks were deceiving. She knew that. And so did Marilyn.

She pulled off more pine boughs, added them to the pile, and walked through the now-visible rows of overwintered vegetables. Beneath the straw, lumpy and gray, was the promise of a good start and an easier year. It was still too early to uncover everything, but Felicity was impatient. She knelt down. She lifted a clump of straw and peered underneath. Yes, there was the promise. For the first time in her life, she loved kale.

Felicity replaced the straw and went down the beds, checking every few feet. Yes, she loved kale and she loved radishes and she loved parsnips. She didn't really, but that hardly mattered, not this year. She was practically giddy with relief. She could feel her prospects improving. She could feel it down to her sweaty socks and callused heels. And not because of the offer for her land.

Fifteen

The next day, Felicity all but whistled her way through her morning chores, moving the sheep, mucking out the barn, filling grain bins, moving some of the straw covering, and mending another hole in the back wall of the barn. It wouldn't do for a scrawny coyote to slither inside and eat her profits.

By noon she was happy to step into a hot shower and think about her first harvest, which was really only days away. By the end of April she could be making her first deliveries, gaining not only grateful customers but a reputation for an early start. The O'Briens had traditionally had an early harvest because her dad always overwintered a few vegetables, but most people had stopped bothering with this practice. So here she was, outstanding, when in fact she was really rather ordinary. Felicity heard herself singing badly off key.

She was still cheerful and almost ebullient as she pulled into the Berkshire Nursing Home over an hour away from West Woodbury. The building was two stories set on the edge of a small town, with tall windows on both floors facing the mountains. It was easy to see why families chose the place. Unlike the Pasquanata home, which was built in a meadow on a quiet road, the Berkshire home offered gorgeous views. Felicity wondered if the services could ever equal the view of the mountains through the seasons.

Zenia Bodrun Callahan had a room on the first floor, at the end of a long corridor. Because Zenia could still walk, Helena had insisted her mother be given a room with access to the outdoors. "She likes getting out and smelling the fresh air and the dirt. She loves the smell of dirt," Helena had told Felicity at the funeral.

Felicity found the elderly woman in a chair by the window, a book lying open on her lap, one hand curled on the pages. But she hadn't fallen asleep. She was staring out the window, caught in whatever reverie the late-winter sun had evoked. Felicity rapped lightly on the door. Zenia turned a curious face toward the sound.

"I remember you." The woman let both hands rest on the book now, her fingers splayed over the pages. Felicity positioned a chair for herself. "It was good of you to come to the service. And now I get a visit too." Zenia smiled as though it were the most ordinary thing in the world for Felicity to drive over an hour to see her.

Felicity offered her condolences again.

"You don't have to explain yourself. I know Sasha died in your woods." The old woman grew sad for a moment. Her eyes were still a clean bright blue, and her white hair fell softly to a short ponytail caught with a black ribbon. Felicity could easily see what Helena would look like when she reached this age. "I'm not so vain as to think strangers want to visit me. What did you come for?"

"I hope you don't mind."

"I'm always glad to talk about my family."

Felicity nodded. "Sasha was given a piece of land by your niece, Clarissa Jenkins. Do you know about this?"

"As I recall, that plot was accessible from a road, not like some of the pieces my father purchased." She turned to look out the window, where the sun pricked light from old leaves.

"Yes, I've heard about some of those from your daughter." Felicity paused, waiting for Zenia to turn back. "I've also been told that your dad and my dad, Walter O'Brien, were good friends years ago."

Zenia laughed, a sound like spring rain. "Thick as thieves, and sometimes I thought that metaphor was truer than not." She closed her eyes and inhaled. "Oh, they could go on." She opened her eyes and studied Felicity. "What is it you want to know? About something they did together?"

"I know they had some land transaction that was important to my dad, but I don't know the details. Were they going into timbering together, something like that?" Felicity sensed Zenia was still sharp and curious, and anything withheld would be by choice rather than disability.

Zenia turned to the window again and grew pensive. "There was a piece of land your dad wanted, and my dad was glad to give it to him. They helped each other out, little things mostly, but that land seemed to be important to your dad. I don't know why. It wasn't worth anything. When my dad sold it, he told my mother they weren't losing anything." She paused. "We were poor, to be truthful. All we had was our land and most of it wasn't worth much."

"Your dad never said why he wanted to give it to my dad?"

Zenia shook her head. "I was young then and parents didn't tell their children everything in those days." She returned to smiling. "By the time I might have appreciated why it mattered to my dad he was off on something else. He took to traveling." Zenia smiled as though imparting a great secret. "If someone had told me he was going to leave his beloved woodlands and travel around the country, I wouldn't have believed them. Or him."

"But he did just that?"

"He had a list of places he wanted to see and off he went. We never knew when he was coming back or if he was coming back."

"Where did he want to go?"

"Oh, around and about, you know. A few places up in New Hampshire, and then up in Maine. My mother went with him a few times. She'd never been out of state, except maybe across the border into Vermont or New Hampshire. Maine seemed far away, and she had a good time, but she said trees are trees wherever you find them."

Felicity softly repeated this to herself. "Did she say anything else?"

Zenia shook her head. "Every time she came home she said the same thing. Trees are trees wherever you find them."

"How long did this go on?"

"A few years. But he was always back for hunting season. I remember when I was a girl he used to get a deer early in the season and bring it home, dress it, and we'd invite everyone over and sit around the table and eat almost the whole thing. Some winters we lived on deer meat. Plenty others did the same thing. One year we went to four houses for their first kill. Dad would never miss that."

Felicity began to feel disappointed. She'd hoped the discovery of Zeke's traveling would tell her what she wanted to know. "It sounds like he went to ordinary places."

"I don't know about that. But once he went down to Maryland. And he went another place, not so far south. Near New York. It made me think of cows."

"New Jersey?"

"Yes, that's it. And then he started going west. He went to Indiana, of all places."

Felicity listened to the sounds of nurses and aides passing along the hallway, pushing medication carts, answering buzzers, greeting visitors and patients. The sounds remained distant, dissonant with the tales coming from Zenia.

"It made him happy, all that traveling. He came back from each trip feeling more and more chipper." She smiled at the recollection, then began smoothing out the still-crisp pages of her book. "He was downright cheerful. Grumpy before, and now he was cheerful." She laughed. "That was a change."

"He never told you what he was doing the traveling for?"

"No, he never said a word. He just said he knew what he was doing."

"When did he start to become a hermit?"

"Hmm, maybe when he was in his seventies or older. After most of the traveling my mother died." The color seeped out of her face. "She anchored him, and when she was gone, he began to drift, you might say."

Zenia was growing tired. She tried to hide it but her lips quivered and she took short quick breaths. She had been generous with her memories, but the effort had been physical, as well, and it was beginning to show. Felicity thanked her and prepared to leave.

"I'm glad to get to know a little about him," she said.

"Did it help?"

"I think so."

"You look like you have one more question, dear. Go ahead and ask it."

"It's an odd question and I feel foolish even considering it."

"Go ahead. I won't mind."

"Did your father ever talk about hidden treasure?"

Zenia pushed her head forward, as though suddenly hard of hearing. She frowned at Felicity and then leaned back in her chair. Her fingers wrapped around the book covers, holding on tight. "That is a strange question."

"Yes, it is. I'm sorry to waste your time with it."

Zenia turned to the window again for a moment. "That reminds me. I heard my parents talking one day, near when my mother died. I heard them through the open screen door. I can hear my mother saying, even now, the treasure we leave them is our love. It's enough."

Felicity nodded. It was the kind of thing her parents would say.

"I don't know what he was doing near the end, but he felt his life had been worthwhile. I think of that. I want to feel that way, and I guess I do. But he really did. He felt he'd done something important. He loved this part of the country. He saved all those useless bits of woods and swampland." She paused. "We choose what matters to us, I guess."

———

Felicity had gone to the Berkshire Nursing Home in the hope of learning something useful from Zenia Bodrun Callahan and came away with confirmation of most of her suspicions. She could easily imagine Zeke in his final years, a man satisfied and perhaps even a little smug that he had pulled off something that mattered to him. She turned onto the old highway and was soon traveling well above the speed limit.

Her father had talked often of Old Zeke, as he called him, and even though Felicity had never met him, she'd begun to feel she knew him. And now, after learning about Zeke's travels, she started to feel she liked him as much as her own father had. She loved the idea of the old man traveling the country to satisfy a whim, of his achieving something that made him happy and not feeling the need to tell the world and garner the praise of strangers.

She could easily imagine Zeke Bodrun traipsing through the New England woods, his wife hiking along behind him, and this at a time when hikers met few others on the trails. The explosion in outdoor tourism didn't take off until the 1960s, and those who hiked and camped in the 1950s could drive into any national or state park and expect to find a camping spot or RV slot for the night. The highway system was still new enough to not be crowded, and the national park system had not yet attracted so many visitors that parking lots filled up before mid-morning. Zeke and his wife would have had their pick of sites wherever they went.

And he chose such peculiar places for a backwoods New Englander. Zenia's list of states her father visited was not complete, she'd insisted, but she'd wondered aloud at the end of their conversation if he might have been doing some genealogical research on his own, perhaps visiting grave sites of his earliest ancestors in North America. It was the kind of thought that made sense to Zenia as a child of the twentieth century. After all, people once traveled miles and across counties to track down old documents before anyone thought of the internet and online files. Perhaps Zeke had been an early scout on the heritage trail.

That seemed the most plausible idea to Zenia, but Felicity felt something else had motivated the trips. Her walk through Sasha's plot earlier had left her with a sense that she was seeing but not understanding.

And now, after talking with Zenia, her understanding was beginning to shift, still fuzzy but growing sharper.

Felicity saw the flashing blue lights in the rearview mirror before she heard the siren. She glanced down at the speedometer and immediately put on her blinker and pulled over to the side of the road. She didn't know how much speeding tickets were these days, but she had a feeling she was about to find out.

She lowered the window and handed over her license and registration as requested. The state trooper walked back to his car. At least she didn't have any other tickets or legal problems. She closed her eyes and prayed. When she opened them again, the trooper was standing next to the door. There was little other traffic on the road.

"It's customary to hit the valleys when you drive, not just the tops of the trees." He handed back her license and registration through the window.

"I was actually thinking about trees," she said, glancing at a paper in his hands, by the window.

"Never thought trees could be so exciting. Any trees in particular?"

"Maine, New Jersey, Maryland."

"Hmm. I visited the Pine Barrens in New Jersey once. Some of the oldest untouched pine forests in North America, and all of it on some kind of sand." He handed the piece of paper to her. "I'm giving you a warning. I just want you to get home alive."

So do I, she thought, especially now that things are beginning to make sense.

———

Shadows lengthened as Felicity drove into the mini mall and parked in front of the hardware store. She disliked running to the store for every little thing. But sometimes even she ran out of three-penny nails or garbage bags. She walked through the aisles, picking up the few items she needed. She met Jeremy at the cash register going over an order slip.

She dropped her purchases on the counter next to him. "Is Taylor here yet?" The clerk totaled up her order and she paid with a credit card. "Isn't this the weekend she's coming home?"

"It is. And you're expected. We're having a few people over Sunday afternoon, so I'm counting on you being there."

"As long as it doesn't go on too long."

"I know, sheep."

Felicity reached for the paper sack and receipt, and the two walked out together. "I have a question for you, Jeremy. What would you do if you were Zeke Bodrun and you found yourself in New Jersey?"

Jeremy stopped by her pickup and waited while she tossed her purchases through the open window onto the passenger seat. "Are you serious?"

"Yup. What would you do?"

He looked across the parking lot and the few cars passing along on the old highway, rested his hands in his pockets, and pulled a face. "If I were Zeke, from what I hear about him, I'd get in my car, turn around, and drive home."

"Yeah, that's what I thought." Felicity shrugged and opened the pickup door.

"How did you come up with that question?"

"I met his daughter, Zenia Callahan, again today, and we had a long talk. She told me her father took to traveling in his later years and one of the places he went was New Jersey."

"Hmm. There's nothing wrong with New Jersey, but it's so built up. I wouldn't have thought Zeke would visit a place like that. Where did he go? What part?"

"Don't know. His daughter said he didn't talk about his trips, but they made him happy."

"Then he found something in New Jersey to like," Jeremy said, and that seemed enough for him.

But it wasn't enough for Felicity. As she drove home, she wondered about Zeke's almost extreme change of character. He went from a man who loved to be in the woods and loved his hometown and the surrounding forests to a man bitten hard by the travel bug, so much so that he wandered up and down the east coast and then out west. And Felicity could only think of one reason to account for it.

The idea preoccupied her until she was driving down her driveway to the barn. From there she could see the three sheep clustered at the paddock gate, their little snouts rising at the sound of her engine. They looked so stolid and unmoved that she began to feel self-conscious under their unflinching gaze. She unlocked the gate and began to chivy them toward the barn but she needn't have bothered. The trio remained bunched together as they trotted, to the extent sheep ever trot, to their nighttime accommodations. Once in the barn each one gave her a look of such reproach that she pulled out a few carrots to mollify them.

Sixteen

On Saturday morning the fiber artists made their weekly visit to the sheep, leaning on the railing to ooh and aah and critique the burgeoning wool coats inside the paddock. Felicity had to admit, the sheep looked pretty good, and she felt like rewarding them with a treat. What did you give sheep for a treat? Carrots, yes, but what else? She'd have to ask someone, since the question had never occurred to her before.

Nola Townsend climbed over the railing, gripped the thick wool and gave it several twists and turns. Minnie, her sheep, ignored her. "I've had more pre-orders this spring than I've had for the last two years total." She stood up and walked between the sheep back to the fencing, where she paused to stare at them.

"That's good, isn't it?" Felicity couldn't tell by Nola's expression if she was pleased by this or not. It sounded like a good thing, but she didn't know anything about selling handmade knitted goods. Or wall hangings. She'd gone into Nola's studio late one afternoon, just to take a look at the kind of things she made. She found the usual sweaters and caps, but she also came to a halt in front of a tightly woven, multicolored block approximately two feet by four feet hanging on the wall. She loved the abstract design, the varied tension of weaving, and casually picked up the dangling price tag. She stood there with her mouth hanging open, gaping at the four-figure price. Fortunately, the artist wasn't there to see this. She left, wondering if she was charging enough to care for the sheep.

"It's both good and bad," Nola said. "It means I have to schedule my time better to meet all the deadlines, and it also means I may have to buy more wool, which means more sheep or more wool at auction." She climbed over the fence. The other two artists had wandered off to examine the garden, which was more and more revealed to the sun.

"This is lambing season, so you could start going around to farms and picking out what you want. When they're weaned, you'll get a call and we can go pick up the new one, or new ones. Do you think you'll want more than one?" Felicity asked.

"I'm not sure." Nola rested her folded arms on the top rail. "Part of my sales pitch is that I talk about buying the wool and carding and spinning it myself. Now I'm going to talk about raising my own sheep." She glanced at Felicity and tried to suppress a smile. "I'm massaging the truth here, but you know what I mean. I'm selling items made from wool that I've cared for from first growth to final product."

Felicity couldn't help smiling at Nola's canny ways. For the months she'd cared for the sheep, she'd thought mostly about keeping them safe and healthy, their wool protected from the ordinary scruff of living mostly outside. She hadn't really thought about the condition of the animal's wool as long as it was suitable for spinning. Seeing the wool from Nola's perspective was almost disorienting. Nola wasn't thinking in terms of little baby's caps; she was thinking in terms of art and aesthetic appreciation.

"I can look into some lambing farms and see what they have. Another Merino?"

"Not sure yet," Nola said. "I was thinking about maybe llamas or alpacas."

Felicity knew nothing about llamas and alpacas, but she couldn't let that stop her now. "Llamas? Alpacas?"

"But I decided to stick with sheep. I like working with the wool, and right now is probably not a good time to experiment with something new." She turned to smile at Felicity. "But maybe someday. I like trying new things."

"Just let me know," Felicity said, wondering what llamas and alpacas were like to work with. She'd have to find some to meet. "I have plenty of room."

"Let's talk more about the lambs in a couple of weeks." Nola glanced behind her at her fellow artists. "They're not as excited about this opportunity as I am. I'm the only one looking at expanding. My pre-orders have been so good that I would be a fool not to."

Felicity had to agree with that. When opportunity fell into her lap, she wasn't going to send it away.

———

By late morning Felicity made it to the Pasquanata Community Home for a visit with her dad. She had a lot of questions today, and she hoped he would remember at least a few things. Ever since he'd run away, he'd had periods of great agitation and then great calm, as though he'd settled something in his own mind. But if he couldn't remember that he'd settled something, he grew agitated again, and then she and the staff had to calm him, offering reassurances for they knew not what. She hoped he wasn't on the verge of another stroke or heart attack.

Felicity walked Shadow down a hallway, to give the other guests an opportunity to visit with him for a few minutes before going to find her dad. Shadow was now a practiced nursing home visitor, and everyone was glad to see him. After half an hour, she found her dad in a sitting room watching out the window. He seemed pleased to see her, and expectant too.

"Did you bring me something?" he asked as soon as she sat down.

"I brought your favorite sandwich from the Morning Glory Cafe." She opened the package, but he only looked at it. Sometimes his taste buds seemed to shut down, and other times he savored an unexpected treat. "I also brought pussy willows. I have long stalks now sitting in a vase in the kitchen." And I'm just waiting for them to turn and start dropping sprigs all over the table and floor, she didn't say. "I left some at the front desk here. Is that what you were thinking?"

"Good. Spring is important."

"We all feel better when the season warms up. Everything smells good." She resettled herself in her chair, ready to begin, knowing that the conversation could easily go awry. "I met Zenia Callahan."

"Zenia?" He frowned. "Peculiar name."

"Yes, isn't it." Already this wasn't going well.

"I knew a Zenia." He looked about him, as though he'd mislaid her nearby.

"When was that?"

"Oh, ages ago. Zeke's little girl, though not so little. He always called her his little girl. He had a son too. Can't remember what happened to him. A war maybe." He tried to think through that one and began to mumble about World War II, which he'd been too young for.

"That's the Zenia I met. She's quite old now."

"Zenia Bodrun?" He peered at her, then looked her up and down, perhaps silently criticizing her wardrobe or wondering who she was.

"She was telling me about her dad in his last few years." Felicity waited, took a sip of her water, hoping against hope her father would find something in her words to trigger a reminiscence.

"He loved that cabin." Her dad smacked his lips, and that seemed to bring to mind the sandwich sitting on an unfolded paper wrapper on the small table in front of him. The paper was creased like a series of snow-capped mountains, and he gently patted the tallest peak. Then he picked up his sandwich and began eating.

"She told me about how Zeke liked to go traveling in his later years." Felicity waited, ever hopeful. Her dad put the sandwich down and stared at her. He wiped his fingers on a paper napkin and then tugged at his shirtsleeves. He studied the length of each one, and she could imagine him standing in front of a lawyer stalling before he had to answer a question. The thought startled her. Where had that come from? He rested his curled fingers in his lap and lifted his chin, looking at her over his nose. She had the oddest sensation that he wasn't sure he wanted to know her anymore. He looked suspicious. He glanced around the room and pushed the sandwich away.

"Nothing wrong with taking a look at the rest of the world."

Felicity nodded and picked up her sandwich. Whatever tale she had hoped for had evaporated under the intense heat of her father's suspicion. She gave it up and began to talk as if to herself. "I was just hoping you'd be able to tell me why some people are so curious about our land. One guy is looking for hidden treasure, and he's digging up his wood lot like a gopher. And another guy says he wants to buy the whole thing and live like a recluse, all alone deep in the woods. And Lance is determined to go where I keep telling him not to. And frankly, I'm feeling besieged without knowing why."

Her dad's face softened. "I trust you, Lissie. I've given you everything I had to give. I taught you everything I had to teach. I trust you." He reached out and patted her hand, then reached down and gave the same pat to Shadow. "He's growing into himself, isn't he?"

After leaving Pasquanata, Felicity drove to Flat Road Automotive. It wasn't on her way home, but she was curious to know what had happened with Clarissa Jenkins's car. She found Bruce at the back of the garage. When he saw her, he walked to the front of the empty bay.

"My truck's fine at the moment," she told him when he asked her what the trouble was. "I got a speeding warning yesterday."

"That's not a bad thing," he said, turning to look at the blue pickup over his shoulder. "It's better if you get out on the highway and open it up once in a while. Vehicles start to fall apart if you let them sit in the driveway or only drive them around town at low speeds."

"I'll keep that in mind the next time I'm stopped. I'll tell the trooper it's my mechanic's fault."

"Okay, no work necessary. So what's up?"

"I noticed that you don't have Clarissa Jenkins's car here anymore." She looked around her.

Bruce shook his head and led the way into the office. As often as Felicity had brought in her pickup for work, she'd never wanted to stay long enough to sit on what passed for a couch or any of the wooden chairs. They were simply too dirty for her. She wondered if anyone sat there while they waited, or if everyone did what she did—

told Bruce to return the vehicle to her house or call her over at the cafe when he was ready.

"You don't look very happy, Bruce."

"I wonder why." He shrugged and dropped the rag he'd been carrying onto the counter, which he stepped behind. He hit a key on the computer, checked a couple of messages, and then turned to her, muttering mostly to himself. "Kevin said they could take it, so they did." He fell into the chair. "I am so frigging—" He glanced at her and skipped the end of the sentence.

"I hope you're not out a lot of money."

"Money and time. Mostly time." He looked around the small space. "Maybe I should have kept my mouth shut."

"You couldn't have done that."

"I dunno. I never expected this."

"Did Kevin say anything?"

"I suppose he'll tell you." Bruce leaned back and looked up at her. "Want a Coke?" She shook her head as he reached down to a small cooler below the counter and pulled out a well-known red can. He popped the lid and poured some down his throat.

"I don't think I'm going to like what you're going to tell me."

He lowered his eyes as if ashamed of what he had to say. "Anyone could have walked in and done whatever they wanted to the car. I have no security, as Kevin pointed out to me with every other breath he took."

Felicity winced.

"Kevin thinks they can estimate when the lines were opened and maybe even where—out there." He tipped his head toward the parking area. "He's pretty sure it'll show it happened right here, early in the morning."

"You mean, just before she picked up her car?"

"Yeah. So he wants to know who was here. And do I have a camera on the premises?"

"Do you?"

"Are you kidding?"

"How about the gas station, or Hogie?"

"Hogie? Are you effing kidding me? I'm sorry, Felicity. But this is a bitch. Forget Hogie and his junk cars. Hogie has maybe two decent cars to rent and I never know if they're here or not. Sometimes it looks like he leaves his wife's car and sometimes it's another car I've never seen before, and sometimes he has a regular company rental car, like Hertz or Avis or Enterprise. I don't know where he gets his cars. I mean, I know he buys them in New Hampshire at the auto sales, but really, I never know if a strange car is his or someone else's."

"Kevin really got to you."

"He said I could be liable, not offering reasonable care for someone else's property," Bruce said, lowering his voice. "And the family could sue."

"Oh no." Felicity took an involuntary step back.

Seventeen

Felicity hung up the dishtowel and wiped down the kitchen table with a sponge. It had been a long but mostly satisfying day. Chief Kevin Algren's advice on how she could respond to her financial problems with Pasquanata Community Home had elicited what she could only call an improved attitude on the part of the manager when they'd talked after her visit with her dad earlier in the day. It was remarkable what a strategic call to a state agency could accomplish.

Even so, the Pasquanata manager's monetary request had shown Felicity just how vulnerable she was. If she was vulnerable to people like the nursing home manager, a slick land buyer could be dangerous. It was time to arm herself with information if not cash. She sat down at the kitchen table and opened her laptop. By her right hand a mug of steaming green tea promised to soothe her jangled nerves, depending on what she found. And if that didn't work, Miss Anthropy was ready with a quiet purr and a warm body. The cat jumped onto her lap and settled down.

She knew the name of the man who had proposed buying first Jeremy Colson's farm and then Tall Tree Farm. But that was all she knew, and since it wasn't a particularly distinctive name, she guessed she might end up finding a few hundred people called Franklin M. Gentile. But at least she might be able to whittle the list down and then pry more information out of Marilyn. She typed in the name, hit return, and waited.

To her surprise, instead of seeing a list of hundreds of people with both or one of the names, she faced a list of perhaps five or six people. She typed in the full name again—first middle last—in quotes, and this time the search engine listed three results. So, Franklin M. Gentile wasn't as common a name as she'd thought. She went down the list, clicking on links for all three.

The first Franklin M. Gentile lived in Portland, Oregon, and sold insurance linked to extreme sports. She thought he looked the part—muscular, shaved head, robust features, and a mountain bike mounted on a dusty Jeep. His life seemed to revolve around the high desert country. The quiet life Mr. Gentile said he wanted, however, would have been anathema to this Mr. Gentile. She checked him off as unlikely.

The second Franklin M. Gentile was fourteen years old, lived with his parents in a suburb of Baton Rouge, Louisiana, and wanted to be a designer of video games. He'd already produced a few for his friends, and Felicity declined to follow a link to appreciate his prowess on the screen. She checked him off as unlikely to be Marilyn Kvorak's client.

The third and last Franklin M. Gentile was a retired science teacher from Bangor, Maine, without wife and child as far as Felicity could see. She squinted at his photograph, which smiled back at her. The picture was fuzzy, but to the extent she could make out a face, he in fact looked like a science teacher: serious but approachable, someone the kids could trust and talk to about their problems. And it was difficult to tell for sure if he was the man she'd seen—fleetingly—in Town Hall.

Mr. Gentile had several awards to his credit and had continued to teach until his very last day, declining early retirement, buyouts, or anything else that might pull him out of the classroom. He was now tutoring students for college exams and AP courses. His only other interest was fresh water and ocean kayaking, for which he wore a helmet. Felicity couldn't help smiling at the image of him in his headgear. He was definitely a dork.

It was possible this was the same man she'd seen from a distance in Town Hall, his appearance altered by the light or camera or something else. But even so, where would Mr. Gentile of Bangor, Maine, get all that money to buy out Jeremy or herself? She buried her fingers in the warm fur of Miss Anthropy.

———

Felicity pushed aside the mug of tea, now growing tepid, and spread out her map of the area. She studied the boundaries of her farm, north to south, west to east. If she were a stranger, coming in from outside, what would make her stop and look at this part of the state?

The offer made through Marilyn had been in the seven figures. At first Felicity had found it offensive, as though the only thing necessary to make anyone part with land held for generations was money. Certainly there were those who would be glad to sell a farm that barely paid its way. Seven figures, even high six figures, could change a person's life.

It could mean the difference between a family living in poverty or near it to a family moving into the middle class and paying for college educations for the next three generations to make sure the family stayed in it. Felicity stood up, dumping Miss Anthropy from her lap, and leaned over the table, studying her land, Jeremy's land, and a few other properties in the area.

She ran her finger over the plot lines, imagining the landscape at each section, recalling the experiences of walking through this part or another, the rocky landscape, the fallen trees, the places that would yield good timber, and the animal tracks. She was kind of glad to have found a bobcat on her land, though she hoped she'd never meet it face to face. Though reportedly shy, bobcats, like any wild animal, could surprise humans with their unpredictable behavior.

Miss Anthropy mewed, and Felicity looked down at her standing by the chair. Yes, she thought, I insulted you. She folded up the map and sat down, letting the cat jump onto her lap again. Shadow inched closer, his snout resting between his paws, his eyes fastened to the cat. The cat ignored him.

The old hand-wound clock struck nine, the spring grinding so loudly that Felicity wondered if it would last another day, let alone another week or year. She'd have to fix it when she had time. But right now she wanted one more look at the only likely candidate for her Franklin M. Gentile. She typed in his name and waited, then began searching through links to learn more about the science teacher. There wasn't much.

She found a photograph of him setting off on a group ocean-kayaking trip along the Maine coast, and another of him leading a group of students for an annual walk to clean up litter. She increased the size of the photographs but all she got was more of the helmets. He seemed to like helmets. After a little more digging, she found a single photo of him without one, as a graduate student looking studious and, yes, dorky. Still, he sounded like a reasonable fellow, and if a clean environment was important to him, she could understand why he might want to live in an out-of-the-way place. She understood that. And yet...

It wasn't unheard of for a quiet, unmarried man or woman to work diligently at a job and squirrel away money, investing it wisely and building up a large portfolio. Felicity could imagine Mr. Gentile doing that, recognizing the bonanza that lay hidden in start-up biotechnology companies or perhaps in the stories his students told him after they graduated and returned home to visit family and friends. Perhaps an especially bright student had founded one of the great research labs making fantastic discoveries and piles of money. And perhaps Mr. Gentile had been an early investor. Perhaps.

Felicity leaned back in her chair and watched the blinking cursor. And perhaps, she thought, Mr. Gentile is just trying to reel us in before ... before what? Before his partner carries out his side of the scam? Before he slips in and steals what Kyle has found at long last? Before he pulls a legal fast one, cheating her out of her property? Those seven figure offers were just too good to be true.

———

Some time after midnight, Felicity awoke to the sound of an animal whining. She thought about this for a while, as the awareness grew in her consciousness. She could see through her one uncovered eye that daylight had not yet arrived, nor had the moon risen enough to filter light through the trees and into her bedroom. She rolled over onto her back and listened. She sat up and looked around. No Shadow. God, had she left the dog outside?

Felicity threw off the covers and ran down the stairs in a jersey, pajama pants, and bare feet. At the bottom she saw the dog, circling around the living room, going from window to window but not jumping up to look out.

She walked from window to window on the first floor. The new motion detector lights at the back of the house hadn't gone on, but those on the barn had. Resigned as well as nervous, Felicity slipped on her boots and hung a flashlight around her neck. She opened the cabinet and lifted out the shotgun. Whatever it was, she might as well scare it or him off before all the animals grew too agitated to go back to sleep. She flicked on the outside lights and again saw the motion detector on the barn blink on and then off. She opened the door and stepped onto the low front porch. The breeze was negligible.

Ever since she'd driven off the intruder almost two weeks ago, her nights had been quiet, with no sign of any unwanted guests. Felicity had begun to think she'd made her point, to man or beast, and her farm would be left alone. But she'd been wrong. Kevin had warned her, and she'd ignored him beyond putting up more motion detectors. She hated to admit now that he'd been right.

In the chill, she could hear a little mewling coming from the barn and headed for it. She didn't have to go far before she sensed she was not alone. Just as she stepped to the far corner of the barn, the motion detector came on, and she caught the swish of an animal moving into the shrubbery. Coyotes would have made less noise, and she would probably have caught more eyes in the woods shining back at her. It sounded like the bobcat had come calling, not for sheep but for barn mice.

Felicity lowered her weapon and moved closer. But there was nothing to see or smell. She wasn't even sure which direction to aim in. It might be a false alarm. Perhaps. But after her near encounter before, she wasn't going to make any assumptions. She circled the barn and house but saw no sign that anyone had returned to finish the job they'd started almost two weeks ago. The sheep grew calm, and Felicity, after a moment's hesitation, went back into the house. She returned the shotgun to the cabinet and locked it, but didn't unload the weapon.

Eighteen

Of all the things Felicity enjoyed, thinking up recipes was not one of them. Whenever she went to a community event, she tortured herself over what to bring. If the hosts had asked her to bring tools and help fix something or paint a room, she'd be there early and stay late. But instead, she was expected to bring a dish to share, and this sent her into a blue funk.

She had a standard dish to take to potluck dinners, usually a simple salad or dessert, but after a while even she grew tired of her offerings and tried to think up something new. Today was one of those days when her brain couldn't get beyond potato salad or garden salad or gingerbread or sugar cookies. In an act of desperation she pulled out a cookbook, opened it, and poked her finger onto the page. The recipe beneath her index finger was pasta, cheese, and tomato pie. She hadn't tried that before, but she was desperate for something new. She would make it for Jeremy and Taylor's party this afternoon, a leisurely Sunday gathering.

If she were being scrupulously honest with herself, Felicity would admit there was more riding on the afternoon than a simple get-together with family and friends. Taylor had arrived on Friday for the long weekend with her dad and grandmother, usually a normal event. Of course, Jeremy had said that his daughter wanted to talk, and only later learned she was bringing a few friends with her to meet everyone. And that was not a normal event.

Felicity put a pot on the stove to boil and began pulling out the ingredients she needed. Shadow sat under the kitchen table watching, ever alert for the prowling Miss Anthropy, and Miss Anthropy sat on her chair beneath the window, ever alert to misbehavior by the other residents.

Jeremy had been open with her about his plans for the farm, or the lack of them. As soon as Taylor was twenty-one, which was not very far away, he planned to put her name on the deed and offer to turn over the farm to her. She was already his heir in his will, but once her name was included in the deed, she would have a say in the disposition of every aspect of the property. Unspoken between Felicity and Jeremy during this quiet conversation late at night, curled under the sheets in Felicity's bedroom, was the understanding that Jeremy was doing this without having any idea about his daughter's intentions.

Taylor knew her dad planned to do this. They had talked about it. Jeremy had laid out the options as clearly as he possibly could: sell the farm, rent the land out to other farmers, divide and sell some and keep some, keep it all and do nothing with it, develop it all. There were, if not endless, certainly a fair number of possibilities. Land was, after all, useful. And no one was making any more of it, except perhaps the Dutch.

Felicity turned on the oven and greased a pan. After reading the recipe through a few times, she concluded it was a variation on lasagna, and she knew how to make that. Maybe the afternoon would go well after all.

———

Cars lined the road in front of the Colson farm. Half a dozen men occupied the porch off the kitchen, their jackets open to the unseasonably warm weather. Felicity recognized Daniel, Jeremy's younger brother, and stopped to say hello before making her way into the kitchen and depositing her contribution on the dining table.

"You been busy." Loretta came up beside her and inhaled the aroma of the still warm dish. "Something new. Looks good."

"Quite a crowd. I thought it was mostly family today," Felicity said.

"So did I, but Taylor must have called her friends and invited them and their families, so here we all are." Loretta turned around to gaze at the guests clustered in the living room, and beyond in the kitchen. "I haven't seen Dan's kids in ages, months even."

"How's Taylor?" Felicity skirted the issue of Daniel and his family, a sore point with Loretta.

"Better than ever." Loretta grinned. She wore an old gored burgundy corduroy skirt, a white silk blouse, and a black sweater. She was more dressed up than Felicity had seen her in some time, with the exception of weddings and funerals, of course.

"You look pleased."

"Honey, I am so tickled."

"Tickled?" Felicity squinted at her. "That means something's up."

"I'll leave it to Jeremy to tell you."

Myriad possibilities ran through Felicity's imagination, and she resolved to stem the flow before she made herself sick with anxiety. Loretta went off to get a drink—non-alcoholic, she volunteered—and Felicity went looking for Taylor, to say hello. She found her in the room Jeremy always called the office, a room filled with papers, computers, books, and a couple of comfortable chairs. Taylor perched on the arm of one until she saw Felicity, and then jumped up and fairly skipped to the doorway to give her a hug. After introducing Felicity to her college friends, she led the way to a corner of the front hall, where they found seats on the stairs.

"This is quite the party." Felicity took note of the familiar faces passing through the hall and in and out of the other rooms.

"I guess I got carried away." Taylor waved to Natalie Algren. Felicity nodded. "I called a friend and then another and pretty soon I'd called almost everyone I know, in West Woodbury and beyond."

"And your dad was so glad you were coming home he didn't mind at all."

"Yeah. So he called Uncle Dan. It's so cool to see everyone here." Taylor accepted a glass of Coke from a friend carrying around a tray. Felicity took a glass of spiced apple cider.

"You picked a good time to show your out-of-town friends the area. It's been so mild that you can get out and walk around, get the lay of the land, without climbing through snow and ice." Felicity sipped her cider. After a moment, she realized Taylor wasn't speaking. She just sat there holding her glass and running her finger through the condensation. When she noticed Felicity looking at her, she smiled.

"Yeah."

"Yeah," Felicity repeated. "I'd love to ask what's going on, but I guess I should wait until you and your dad decide to tell the rest of us."

"Yeah."

Yeah, thought Felicity. If this was the extent of Taylor's conversational abilities, developing a relationship with her as an adult was going to be difficult. And she'd been such an adorable and chatty little girl. Felicity held a kaleidoscope of images of Taylor as a child, in her red boots covered in glitter on her way to the annual fair, in her overalls when she snuck out of the window to sleep on the porch roof, in the favorite blue-and-white dress she wore to the parties Felicity took her to the year she turned ten. For some reason known only to Taylor, turning ten was momentous, and Felicity had found herself driving the girl back and forth across the county for music lessons, riding lessons, overnights with friends, and other events.

"I was going to come in May, for Dad's birthday, but I just wanted to come now. We have a long weekend at school—something to do with the founder—so here I am." Taylor lifted her shoulders as a substitute for doing a little jig and continued to smile and nod to the other guests. "This party was going to be just the family and you. I mean, you're family."

Felicity felt the heat rising up her neck to her cheeks. She hoped the girl didn't notice. She wondered why she felt embarrassed to hear Taylor acknowledge her relationship with her dad.

"Yeah." Taylor basked in the warmth of greetings from those passing by, and in a moment that could only be considered a throwback to her childhood, she said, "Gran brought chocolate cake and raspberries."

"There's probably still some left."

"I can't wait to tell everyone." With that cryptic remark, Taylor leaped to her feet and ran off to get something to eat.

———

Before Felicity could follow her, Jeremy sat down on the step beside her.

"She's beyond happy," he said.

"It shows."

He took a pull of his beer and the two of them watched guests pass by, picking up snatches of conversation.

"She sounds like she's here to make an announcement," Felicity said. "I was so curious, I was afraid I'd try to wheedle it out of her, but I managed to control myself." They sat close together, their upper arms touching, and she felt the familiar comfortable warmth of his body. She smiled as he pressed his leg against hers. "You're feeling bold today."

"I live here." He turned back to the guests. "And pretty soon Taylor will too."

"Oh. Is that the announcement? She's leaving college?"

"No, nothing like that. She has one more year and I'd be more than disappointed if she quit now." His smile was given readily, but after each person passed by he grew serious. When he spoke again, he looked down at the uncarpeted stair and spoke softly. "The friends she brought home with her..."

"The ones she wanted you to meet? I met a few of them."

"She brought three special ones." He looked around, perhaps checking to see who was within earshot. "I've heard her talk about them. They seemed to be pretty steady friends. Two are from Ohio, and one is from Maine. But they all have one thing in common."

"Should I guess?"

"They all say they know something about farms. One of the kids from Ohio grew up on a farm with corn and some dairy cows. One guy visited his cousins on a farm every summer. The guy from Maine has relatives with a chicken farm. His family is still there. He says they do okay."

"Do the others' farms do okay?"

Jeremy pursed his lips. He wasn't frowning exactly, Felicity thought, but he was taking time to phrase things in a way that seemed best. It was the one visible sign of discomfort. "One family sold out to a developer."

"Not so unusual."

"And as my mother repeatedly reminds me, I'm basically a developer."

"Your mother is always hoping for a purist in the family, all farming and no construction, but she'd be miserable if you ever started acting like that." Felicity finished her cider and slid the glass to the corner of the riser and the wall. "She likes to admire purists strictly in theory."

"You may be right."

Felicity glanced at him. It wasn't like Jeremy to suddenly withdraw into an easy comment. She squeezed his hand. He smiled and let his gaze linger.

"She and her three friends want to farm here." He looked at the front door, now ajar, as people went in and out. "They're talking about building a herd to ten, maybe, to get started, and going into the cheese business." He gave her a long look.

She waited for him to continue, but she knew what he was thinking: they think they know what they're getting into, but truthfully they have no idea. Even Felicity, working alongside her parents year in and year out, didn't understand what the burden was until she'd taken it on alone a year ago when it became clear her father's heart condition wouldn't allow him to continue running anything, and then it had hit her even harder after she placed him at Pasquanata, capitulating to the reality of his decline. Four young people taking on the burden of making a farm pay were getting into more than they could possibly understand.

"My brother told her she was crazy." Jeremy might have been smiling but he hunched over as he spoke, and this seemed more telling than his words. She would have expected him to be happy and reservedly optimistic, but instead he seemed tense. "I've gone over some of it with her—the investment in milking equipment, licensing, inspections, building a market for product."

"And? Any doubts glimmering behind the enthusiasm?"

"She and her friends produced a business plan they'd worked up at school."

"Really? And how was it?" Felicity swiveled to face him. A business plan for a new artisanal dairy business? Taylor was way ahead of them, farther than Felicity had imagined even in an unguarded moment.

Jeremy nodded several times before glancing at her out of the corner of his eye. "It's doable. And they're not asking me for all the capital." His hands clenched and unclenched as he spoke.

"This is a lot more than I expected, Jer." She could hear the undertone, feel the pull of the totally unexpected, a riptide dragging away his future. Instead of hearing the news of a daughter getting started on someone else's farm, he was facing the prospect of handing over his own but in a way he'd never considered. "It's a surprise, that's for sure. I wouldn't have expected so much so soon."

"Me neither."

"Well, it's still early days, isn't it?" Felicity nodded to another friend passing through the hall. "When it comes time for her to really take over, you'll have a better idea of what kind of farmer she'll make." She hadn't expected to face this watershed so soon, but she held back from saying that.

"I owe you an apology, Lissie." Jeremy looked hard at her. "I told her—in a moment of insanity, maybe—that she could go right ahead with her plans."

"Oh." Felicity looked down so he wouldn't see the shock in her eyes. There was no point in reminding him they'd discussed the transition at length and agreed that it would be best to ease Taylor into full responsibility gradually. That idea seemed to have faded away. She looked out at the other guests, trying to hide her feelings.

"I guess I was trying to jump start the rest of my life," he said. "I should have told you."

"No reason. We're not—"

"Married?" He put his arm around her shoulder. "Still, I should have told you. We talked about it over and over again, and we agreed how we'd do this, and then I went right ahead without telling you. I'm sorry. I shouldn't have jumped without letting you know."

Felicity leaned into him before pulling back. Some days their relationship was so easy, but sometimes they both remembered that they weren't married to each other and they could take nothing for granted. "Thanks. Well, it's done. And now you have a future farmer in your life."

"It feels like it's more than that," he said. "For the first time in my life I can see myself living without Colson Farm." He opened his clasped hands and looked at his palms, as though reading something there. "I could go anywhere, do anything."

There was nothing she could say to that. She listened as he explored the idea, nodding to people passing in front of them as he tried out the feeling of being untethered for the first time in his life—his daughter grown, his mother taken care of, his farm in other people's hands. "Taylor will make a good farmer, I know that."

"She's a sensible girl," Felicity said.

"I think so."

"This is sort of changing the subject," Felicity said, trying to absorb the idea of Jeremy living anywhere but in West Woodbury, "but does she know about that offer you got from Marilyn's client?"

"No, and she's not going to."

"So you don't think it's legitimate."

"Let's say I have my doubts, and I don't want to see my daughter tied up with something that could lead to trouble."

Felicity nodded. "So let me tell you about a dork I discovered on the internet."

———

By five o'clock Felicity was glad to drive home to her farmhouse, and equally glad to see only four cars scattered along the drive. Earlier in the week, to her surprise and delight, Nola Townsend had asked if she could bring a number of artists out to the farm for a day of plein air painting. After Nola had explained what that was, Felicity said yes with alacrity. They agreed on a fee per artist and shook hands.

The arrival of the artists that morning had brought more activity and shouting and calling back and forth than Felicity had ever heard on her land. She'd watched the group, from teenagers to senior citizens, gathering up their equipment and heading off in different directions. So when she returned in the late afternoon, she expected to see a few of them planted in the pasture, or among the apple trees, or near the sheep. Instead she saw half a dozen artists leaning on their cars, going over the experiences of the day. She climbed out of the pickup and looked for Nola.

Shadow bolted across the small lawn, spun in the air, and jumped up a few times before calming himself. Felicity took this as a greeting.

"It looks like you had a successful day," she said to Nola. The artists looked tired and sweaty but seemed intent on admiring each other's work before giving up and heading home. They'd arranged a number of canvases on the ground, or leaning against the side of the barn, so they could discuss them.

"Most of them have left already, but reluctantly." Nola glanced over her shoulder. "It was a very successful day." With a discretion Felicity had to admire, Nola pulled out an envelope and handed it to her. Felicity could feel the soft mound of paper money inside and folded the envelope to put in her jacket pocket.

"I'm glad it worked out." And she really was. After all, how often did anyone find surplus cash in her bank account? And all because strangers liked to paint trees and wanted their own wool. This was a strange world.

"It really worked out." Nola gave her a questioning look.

"And?"

"They'd like to come back, soon."

"Really?" If Felicity had been slouching, she wasn't now. "How soon?"

"Next weekend? They'd like to do Saturday if possible."

Felicity and Nola walked over to the cars where the artists were gathering up their canvases and equipment. The women, and they were all women, wore floppy hats or straw hats or other head coverings as though they expected to be outside in full sun. Such headgear wouldn't be necessary for another couple of months, in Felicity's view, but the women had wisely worn heavy shoes or hiking boots.

She strolled past the paintings, curious as well as trying to be diplomatic. She had no idea what she was looking at for the most part, but she didn't care. They were all wonderful in her view.

"You were very kind to let us take over your farm for the day," one woman said. Felicity told her she was very welcome, though she would hardly have agreed to really let them take over the farm. "I found a great spot on the other side of the enclosure."

"So the painting of the sheep is yours?"

The woman nodded. "Nola tells me that she owns one of them."

Felicity and the woman discussed sheep for a while. Another artist carried her canvases to her car but stopped to listen to them. She balanced a small canvas on her knee and held it toward Felicity.

"I found the greatest spot, with those red buds on the trees and just a little water in a swampy area. But I couldn't figure out what those little mounds were. What are they?"

"Mounds?" Felicity stepped closer and looked at the painting. Fortunately it was done in a realistic style, but it still made no sense. She lifted the canvas and moved into a different area, with more light. "I think I know where you were." She described the spot. "You took that path from behind the barn?"

"I walked farther than I meant to, but it was so peaceful and I wanted to get a scene that gave me a specific feeling. And I wanted some kind of variety. Something with less gray."

"Gray is about it this time of year," Felicity said. Still, those mounds troubled her. They were in the wrong location.

"It looks like some animal digging, like a giant squirrel looking for coconut sized nuts."

"Yes, it does." She handed back the canvas and hoped the artist wouldn't ask anything more. The question was troubling, and the possible answers even worse.

Nineteen

Just after eight o'clock the next morning, Felicity took the trail the artist had indicated and followed it through the still-bare trees along the boundary of her farm. The new buds gave the forest a pink glow, and there was a warmth to the early morning. She knew it wouldn't last, however. A late-winter snowstorm was predicted for later in the week. Whatever fell might not last, but it would dampen the warming ground and her efforts for an early harvest. The woods would once again take on a winter stillness.

Felicity stuck to the description of the path given by the artist, forgoing shortcuts to ensure she saw exactly what the other woman saw. She had to be certain before she took any action. She hadn't told Kevin Algren about the mounds she'd discovered on Sasha's wood lot, since those weren't on her property.

And Sasha Glover had had a right to do whatever she wanted on her own land, even if it was a foolish search for nothing. But she was gone now, and Felicity couldn't imagine Helena out digging. It sounded like Kyle had decided to continue his quest even after Sasha's death. And if the artist was accurate in her description, Kyle had extended his search onto Tall Tree Farm.

The red blazings on selected trees had not yet faded to a pale dirty orange, and Felicity walked on the outside of her boundary to keep her bearings. When she came around a rocky outcropping where deer had scuffed through the leaves, she saw what she'd hoped she wouldn't. There, well within the blazed trees that marked her property from the few acres Zeke Bodrun had given to Clarissa and Clarissa had given to Sasha, were the telltale signs of Kyle's search for hidden treasure. And even worse, these mounds were recent.

Felicity walked in from the boundary and counted seven holes. As she moved among them she could discern no logical reason for Kyle's choice of location to dig. She saw nothing that would attract him, and no evidence that he'd found anything. Each hole was similar in size and shape and depth. Nothing had been abandoned in mid dig, and nothing had been closed over as a precaution.

From a nearby outcropping Felicity looked out over her land and into Sasha's. All she could think was that it made no sense. These holes required major physical effort. Kyle, as she assumed it was, had been digging in only partially thawed ground. This wasn't easy work. What on earth did he think he was going to find in this part of the woods?

———

Felicity hit the brakes and skidded to a stop at the end of the driveway, narrowly avoiding a head-on collision with Lance Gauthier as he turned off the road. Lance jerked to a halt on the verge. Discovering Kyle's foray onto her property had sent adrenaline rushing through her, and she'd bolted without taking the time to think. She wasn't even thinking about driving when she caught sight of Lance's truck at the last minute.

"You okay?" Lance got out and peered into her open driver's side window.

Felicity apologized for her part in the near collision. "I had a shock this morning and I was heading into town without thinking. It's a good thing to have to slow down. You've done me a favor."

"That sounds serious." Lance leaned against the door.

Felicity opened the door and climbed out of her pickup.

"Anything I can help with?" Lance was bundled up for a day in the woods, either hers or someone else's. His work boots had splatters of mud already, and his well-worn green plaid shirt looked soft and warm under his quilted vest and orange overvest. His peaked cap advertised the local hardware store.

"I'm probably overreacting." Felicity relaxed against the pickup. "Sasha Glover, as you may know, was Zeke Bodrun's great granddaughter, and she inherited a piece of land that was once his." As she heard herself describing the situation she wondered how Lance had come to be so pushy about her cutting plan, and whether he was treating other clients in the same way as he was treating her. At first he'd seemed so much more innocent than Kyle, whose blatant foray onto her land left her fuming.

"Around here?"

"It's just off Old Town Road, but it extends up to my boundary." She reminded herself to be cautious about sharing information with a man she no longer felt comfortable trusting. "Anyway, Kyle Morgan, that's Sasha's boyfriend, got the idea that Zeke had buried something valuable on his property, or at least something worth digging up, and I think that's what he's been doing." She paused, surprised at how pale the forester suddenly became. "Lance, you look sick."

"No, I'm fine." He raised his hands as if to stop any further expression of concern. "We both got off to a jolt of a start this morning, that's all. And you have a lot to deal with. You've got some crazy guy tearing up your land." He shook his head. "If I can do anything to help, let me know."

"I saw you at the funeral but we didn't get a chance to speak." Felicity felt better now that she had vented. "Do you know Kyle Morgan?" She wondered if this was the time to bring up the lottery tickets she'd seen him ripping up.

"Not personally. I do know who he is." Lance straightened up, his hands in his pockets. "Listen, I was coming by with the new plan. I simplified it and you can just sign it. I don't want to add anything to your worries. You deal with that guy Kyle, and I'll get on with the cutting, just a straight shot through the area we talked about. Nothing more. And I can get it into the mail for you."

"Lance, that's great." She was enormously relieved. She didn't want to get into an argument with him, and she didn't want to find herself probing him about lottery tickets. She wanted to move ahead, and she was sure he did too.

"Here." He hurried to his truck and pulled out a manila envelope. He drew out a single sheet and held it on the top of the packet. "I have a pen here too." He handed her a pen and held the envelope in front of her so she could sign.

Felicity grabbed the envelope and sheet on top and tossed both onto the passenger seat. She might agree verbally, but she was still going to read every word and double-check every figure. And she would file it herself. "I'll get back to you as soon as I've had a chance to go over it."

"Right, of course, yeah, sure. I'll get right to the rest of the paperwork," he said, his glance lingering on the envelope.

"The notices to abutters?"

"That's about it. Then I can get started." Lance started to back away, then stopped. "Listen, Felicity, if I can do anything to help with the Kyle situation, let me know. I'd hate for it to lead to a lot of police business, and ill feeling and all of that."

"Thanks, Lance, I appreciate that. First Sasha dies in the woods, then Kyle is digging all over the place, and now some guy wants to buy my land at an exorbitant price."

"You have a buyer?"

"Lance! You look even paler." Felicity wondered if she'd missed something even more serious than his gambling. But then, land was his livelihood, and newcomers often had strange ideas about what to do with it. "I turned him down."

"That's a relief."

"So did Jeremy." When she saw how relieved he was, she added, "But I have to be honest, Lance. Someday someone else will own Colson Farm and my place. It's inevitable. And now that I've depressed myself again, I'd better get on to finding Kyle and laying down the law, or at least the boundaries."

Lance gave her a wave that was more of a salute and headed to his truck. As he backed up and drove away, Felicity felt a curious mixture of relief and anxiety. And then she remembered Kyle's new holes and climbed back into her pickup.

———

According to Helena Callahan, Kyle Morgan worked construction erratically and served pizza regularly on the weekend. His most recent job had been on the crew renovating the regional middle school in Durston. Felicity drove out to the middle school, hoping to find him there. Fortunately, she could recognize him by sight in case he was working.

She drove into the dirt parking area, thinking it looked awfully quiet for a construction site, no cranes or large vehicles moving, no groups of men working, and then realized it was break time. She parked and approached the first person she encountered, an older man in a royal blue vest and yellow hard hat.

"Kyle?" He asked the question with a hint of disapproval, and she didn't blame him. No supervisor, which was what his badge indicated, wanted a worker to be interrupted during the workday.

"It's about a piece of land he's been working on," Felicity said.

The supervisor frowned but seemed to think this was allowable. "Okay, five minutes. He's over by the food truck."

Felicity thanked him and headed for the quilted silver truck, its sides open to display sandwiches, snacks, desserts, and drinks. Half a dozen men crowded around the salesman, but one separated himself from the crowd when he saw Felicity. Just as she knew she could recognize Kyle, Kyle could recognize her. He walked quickly to intercept her.

"I saw you at the funeral," he said. "Really sad about Sasha." He glanced over his shoulder, barely concealing his concern over whether any of his coworkers could hear them. "Let's go out here." He led the way to a row of parked Durston city vehicles. "So, what can I do for ya?"

With effort, Felicity stated her business in a calm, nonaccusatory manner. "I noticed that you've been doing some digging on Sasha's piece of land, the piece her mother's cousin gave her, Clarissa Jenkins."

"Yeah, that was Sasha's. She was going to put my name on the deed, so it's okay I'm there." He leaned forward as he spoke, his lips twitching in anger.

"Well, I don't know about that," Felicity said, reminding herself to be calm. "I have no idea what that's all about, but I was out walking yesterday and I could see that your digging has extended onto my land."

"No, no. I'm not on your land." He bent over, one hand on his hip and the other still holding a wrapped sandwich.

"I'm afraid you are. I've done the blazing a number of times through the years. I know where the boundaries are."

"You're wrong."

"Look, Kyle. I'm not wrong. I've never posted my land before but I'm going to post it now, all along that boundary. And once it's posted, if I find you on it, I'm calling in Chief Algren and turning the problem over to him."

"I'm on Sasha's land, which is really my land too." He swaggered as he talked, but he was impressing no one but himself. And Felicity was growing frustrated.

"What do you think you're looking for, anyway?"

And now he smirked. "I know what I'm looking for."

"I would hope so." Felicity took a deep breath and turned to look at the men gathered around the food truck. They'd slowed their business, taking time to watch her and Kyle, and she was sure that after she left, they'd quiz him and then tease him for the rest of the afternoon. And unless she'd misjudged Kyle, he'd let them think whatever they wanted about a woman who showed up at a construction site to argue with her man. "I'm going to post the land," she repeated. "I had a survey done only ten years ago. I have GPS guides. I want you to stay off my property. I don't care what you're looking for. You're not going to dig on my land."

Felicity stepped back, ready to walk away, but Kyle surprised her. She had to work to hear what he was saying, so soft had his voice become.

"Look, let's start over, okay?" He tried a friendly laugh as he watched her. "Sasha and me, we meant no harm. We're just digging around, playing with an old map of stuff left by settlers."

Really, Felicity thought, this is even less believable than the story about hunting for buried treasure. "There's only one cellar hole there."

"Yeah, right, we saw that." He glanced over his shoulder again. He was a scrawny fellow, and his royal blue vest flapped loose even over a quilted work coat. "Suppose we have an understanding? You know, sort of like I had with Sasha?"

"What understanding did you have with Sasha?"

"We agreed to split whatever we found."

"I'm not interested in any idea of hidden treasure anywhere, on my property or anyone else's." Felicity again focused on speaking in a calm, measured voice. "I don't want my land dug up for any reason, so I'm going to tell you again, stay off my property. I'm posting the boundary and I'll have you arrested if you come onto my land again." She heard herself saying these words, insistent and unambiguous, and yet at the same time she looked at Kyle and had the horrible feeling that he might have been the one to attack Clarissa and then kill Sasha.

The whole scenario seemed to play out in front of her. Kyle pressed Clarissa for information, or even a share, and she rebuffed him, determined instead to see the land go to Sasha. Then he turned to Sasha, pressing her, and she refused. They fought, and she told him it was over. If she threatened to sell the land or give it to her mother, then Kyle would have been out of luck if he'd found anything. Whoever owned the land would figure out pretty fast that Kyle was looking for something and perhaps find the money to dig more methodically and successfully. If Kyle really believed he was onto something big, he might have thought killing Clarissa and Sasha would be worth it in the end. And here she was, telling him to stay off her land or else.

And that, thought Felicity as she walked back to her pickup, was about as empty a threat as anyone could come up with. She'd have to sit out there twenty-four hours a day, seven days a week, with a weapon to back that up. She could only pray that Kyle took her at her word and stopped digging.

Twenty

The Kimball Hardware Store advertised itself as the one stop for all your farm needs except the animals. That was mostly true, the operative word being *mostly*. Felicity hoped today the ad would be accurate. She rummaged through the back aisles until she found what she was looking for: a box of *Posted* signs, printed on floppy mylar. She knew she needed one approximately every five hundred feet, but she figured for the section that ran along Sasha Glover's lot, a sign every one hundred feet might be better. The box seemed almost full, so she took about half and hoped that would be enough.

She hated the idea of posting her land—it seemed so unneighborly, especially toward people she'd known her entire life—but she felt Kyle had pushed her into it, giving her no choice but to respond to his refusal to acknowledge that he had crossed the line. First he'd been adamant that he wasn't on her land. And then he was smarmy in trying to talk her into going into the treasure hunting business with him. The whole thing made her skin crawl. She felt sick at the thought of it.

She paid for the signs, clutched them to her chest, and crossed the parking lot to her pickup. When she saw Chief Algren coming toward her, she waited by the open truck door.

"I thought I'd tell you, your visiting Zenia Callahan in the nursing home and your friend visiting also was a nice thing to do," Kevin said. "What? What's that look for? I can offer a genuine compliment, can't I? You did visit her, didn't you?"

"Yes, I did. But I didn't take any friends along." Felicity noticed his eyes flicker and recognized the look he got when he was thinking one thought and articulating another. "Why? What did she say?"

"Only that you came by to offer your condolences for Sasha because you found her on your land." He lowered his voice. "She hasn't lost her mental faculties. She was quite clear that your friend came by also."

"I went alone."

"Your friend came by and they chatted about old times." He waited. "You don't recall who that might be?"

Felicity shook her head. "Maybe she has me mixed up with her daughter?"

"Don't think so." Kevin shook his head. "She described him and it sounded like Jeremy Colson. And I thought that would make sense, you and Jeremy being good friends and all."

"Why would Jeremy go out to visit Zenia Callahan?" Felicity shifted the box of signs from one arm to the other. "You're sure about that? It wasn't another relative who came by or a friend of Helena's?"

"She described a man who visited her a few times, but she couldn't remember his name." Kevin began to step around her. "There's no great mystery here, Felicity. She just got mixed up. Can't remember the name. But she enjoyed the visits, and I was going to tell you it was a nice thing to do for her, but if you didn't do anything, nothing more to say."

"I did visit her." Felicity could feel something nagging at her. But she could see in Kevin's expression a hint of warning. "I wanted to ask her about that cabin of her dad's, but it didn't feel right. Who owns that now? You never said if Zenia did."

"She doesn't. I just got the name of the owner in a report from the state detective."

"So who sold her dad's cabin?"

"She did, a few years ago. Before she went into the nursing home, which wasn't all that long ago. She comes from sturdy stock."

"Who bought it? Anyone we know?"

"Don't you pay attention to land sales, Felicity?"

"For a piece of land like that?"

"Some company bought it from Zenia for not much money. Of course, it wasn't worth much. Still isn't." Kevin began to back away. "But since forensics found no evidence that Sasha Glover had ever been in the cabin, I have no interest in it whatsoever."

"Some company bought it?" Felicity wondered why she hadn't heard more about this. "And it's a company paying the taxes on it?"

"Such as they are."

"Maybe that's why Jeremy went to see Zenia, to buy some of her land." Felicity pulled out her keys. "But Helena said her mother transferred all the land to her, and now she also inherits Sasha's little piece of land."

"Not my concern."

"And nothing new about Clarissa and Sasha's … " Felicity couldn't bring herself to describe their deaths as murder. Every time she tried, the word caught in her throat.

Kevin reached out and squeezed her arm. "Stick to your farm, Felicity. Give my best to your dad." He headed into the hardware store, leaving her standing by her truck. She waited until his figure disappeared into the store and down an aisle, and then climbed into her pickup and headed to Town Hall, his advice forgotten.

Felicity spent less than an hour in the assessor's office. Afterward, she drove straight to Jeremy's current construction site. She parked in front of his trailer office and waited inside it until someone told him that a car had driven up. Jeremy rounded the half-built house and crossed to the trailer, which tipped a bit as he climbed in. He offered her a can of iced tea and took one for himself from the small refrigerator in the kitchen area. He sat down opposite her in the small booth.

The iced tea was cold, but there was not much more Felicity could say for it. Jeremy took two phone calls on his cell before turning to her with a smile. "You're busy, I'm busy. What's up?"

She repeated her conversation with Kevin Algren. "Were you the man visiting Zenia Callahan?"

Jeremy shook his head. "I've no interest in her land. I work with a developer who buys, then I build and move on. I know the Bodrun family, sort of, and I know they don't have anything that a developer would want."

Felicity slouched in the booth. "Some company named Treeline Properties bought the land the old cabin sits on."

Jeremy repeated the name, then shook his head. "Don't know them. Not the kind of name you'd expect from someone around here. We're nowhere near the tree line. We're only about five hundred feet above sea level, and the tree line in New England is about four thousand feet. Maybe up in New Hampshire or Maine it might work, but not around here. It's also too rustic, too woodsy. People who want to develop around here go for things like Pheasant Run and Fox Hollow."

"Do pheasants run?"

Jeremy shrugged. "Have no idea. I've never seen one." He leaned back and reached for his iced tea. "Must be a couple of guys trying to take their camping and hunting site off their taxes, like a business expense."

"The only name I got from the assessors' office was a lawyer in Albany." Felicity twirled the can with her fingers, watching the condensation leave little rivulets on the Formica tabletop.

"You checked?"

"Just now, after talking to Kevin. I never thought much about this until last week, but the list of property owners and the taxes we pay just sits on the counter in that computer printout for all the world to see." Felicity grew thoughtful.

"All the world isn't interested, Lissie." Jeremy smiled.

"I just mean that it makes things easy for people." She twirled the can on the table.

"Including you."

She laughed. "True. But I thought I saw someone going through the book last week, and when I went to look, the assessments were open to a page with my property on it."

"That means nothing, Lissie. Don't start imagining things."

"Well, someone visited Zenia a number of times, because she told Kevin how nice it was to have visitors—me and a man Kevin thought was probably you."

"Only that wasn't me."

Twenty-One

Felicity had a mental list of all she wanted to accomplish the next day and intended to get an early start after her chores. She headed out to post her signs soon after eight o'clock and worked for a couple of hours, mostly along the boundary shared with Sasha Glover's property. Shadow had grown accustomed to following her through the woods and ran parallel with her as she walked, keeping her within sight and never wandering too far away. He seemed to be getting the hang of rural life, and she felt more confident in taking him with her as she worked.

When she felt she'd done enough posting, she put Shadow in the house and headed out to the Berkshire Nursing Home. On the drive she practiced what she'd say and how she'd say it, or try to, to get as much information as possible out of both Zenia Callahan and the nurses and aides. Someone was visiting Zenia, and Felicity wanted to know who it was, especially if that person was leading others to believe that he was associated with her. She found Zenia in the dining room at a table for six with two of her friends.

"Oh, do join us." Zenia patted the chair seat next to her. "Another visitor," she said to her friends. "I've never been so popular." This to Felicity.

She seemed to have joined a conversation, and the flow of words continued. The other women included her in some comments, asking questions about her and her family and her farm, and then veering off into reminiscences. It was like talking to versions of her dad and his friends, only all female.

"And you came without your friend this time?" Zenia looked past Felicity at the doorway opening into the main hall.

"Which friend do you mean?" This was perhaps the only time she'd be able to ask the question that was the whole point of the trip without it seeming obvious. If Zenia understood there was some concern about one of her visitors, she could easily fall into a tizzy or grow suspicious and attract the attention of the nurses and aides, who hovered not far away.

"The tall one." Despite her age, Zenia had a lovely youthful smile and the kind of looks that suggested what she might have been like as a young woman, sweet, lively, and pretty. But Felicity knew she might have been none of those things.

"The tall one? I have lots of tall male friends."

One of the other women seemed to think this was just wonderful and launched into a tale of her partying days, as she called them. Zenia and the others listened patiently. When she finished, Zenia said, "The one who likes to hunt."

That was no help at all, since almost everyone Felicity knew in West Woodbury did some hunting at some point in their lives. She decided to try something different. "The one with the beard?"

Zenia frowned. "No, I don't think he had a beard. Did he have a beard, Melanie?" She turned to one of her friends.

"Just the mustache," Melanie said. "Very trim and neat." She turned to Felicity. "I like a man to be neat. None of this raggedy stuff. So popular once but I don't care for it. My grandson has a ponytail almost as long as yours, but what can you do?"

Felicity knew a number of men with hair longer than hers, but at least she was getting more detail on the unnamed friend. Tall with a mustache, trim and neat.

"And such a sweet accent," another woman tittered.

"And an accent?" Felicity didn't think she knew anyone with an accent.

"A Pennsylvania accent." This from Melanie.

Good god, thought Felicity. What is a Pennsylvania accent?

"I'm from Pennsylvania so I recognized it right away."

"Oh, so he didn't tell you he was from Pennsylvania?"

"Oh, no, dear, he lives around here," Zenia said. "Maybe he was from there once but not now. He isn't from there now, is he, Melanie?"

"No, no, he lives here. But you know who I mean, don't you?" Melanie asked.

"Gee, that sounds like Jimmie," Felicity said, grasping at the first name that came to mind.

"No, no, not Jimmie," Zenia said. She looked confused and turned from one woman to the other for help. Maybe, Felicity thought, she wasn't as mentally sound as Kevin thought.

"Francis?" Zenia said. "Was his name Francis, Melanie?"

Felicity could see the doubt spreading from woman to woman like a virus, creeping into their eyes and spreading down through their limbs. Hands pulled away from the table and crossed over laps, shoulders stiffened, and legs were uncrossed and feet pulled under chairs. If she didn't do something at once, she might never have an open conversation with any of them again.

"Oh, Francis! Of course. I know who you mean," she said, wondering if the name they really meant was Franklin. "I never think about his mustache. You know how you see someone day in and day out and you forget they wear glasses or they have a scar or something."

"My cousin used to do exactly the same thing," Melanie said. And the spell of suspicion was broken. Felicity gave a sigh of relief and settled in to listen to another hour of chatter and reminiscences. It wouldn't do to bolt for home too soon.

———

After she left the dining room, Felicity stopped at the nurses' station. Nearby was a wall of photographs of events and daily activities at the Berkshire Nursing Home. The photos included young children and pets, adult children of the guests, visiting performers, and others. They were colorful and numerous, overlapping and crowded onto the corkboard. Felicity began to examine each one.

A nurse approached and rested her index finger on a group photo. "Zenia's right here. That was a fun afternoon. We had a group of student magicians here, and of course they could do no wrong, even when cards fell out of their shirtsleeves or little bunnies escaped down the hallway."

Felicity murmured appreciation. "I was looking for my friend, Francis. Zenia said he's visited a number of times."

"Oh, Francis," the nurse said. "He's a dear. I haven't seen him lately, but my shift changes every three weeks." She withdrew into her professional persona. "I hope nothing's happened to him. The guests enjoy him so much."

"No, no, he's fine," Felicity was quick to reassure her.

"I'm glad to hear that. He's always a delight."

"I love that Melanie picked up on his Pennsylvania accent." Felicity continued to inspect the photos, looking for a tall man with a mustache who was about the right age to be her friend, or anyone who looked familiar. She was getting the uncomfortable feeling that she might have seen the elusive Francis in the West Woodbury Town Hall perusing the printed list of property valuations.

"She's originally from Pennsylvania, so she would."

"I guess I don't see Francis here," Felicity said, stepping back. "I don't know him terribly well, but I'm glad he took the time to visit Zenia. I didn't realize he knew her."

"It's her son he knows. Helena visits often, and Sasha did too." The nurse turned to the photos. "But Francis came in one day as a courtesy because he knew the family, at least the son. The son lives out of state, I think. Anyway, they hit it off and he kept on dropping by when he was in the area. He told the ladies he travels for work so he can't always get here."

"So his first visit would have been last year, maybe?"

"No, longer ago than that. Maybe two years ago." The nurse gave her a sharp look. "Is there some question about him?"

"I don't know," Felicity said. "Zenia seems to think he came with me. At least that's what she told Chief Algren when he talked to her."

"Yes." The nurse nodded. "I spoke to the chief before I took him in to speak to her. If there's some question here, we should know. I'll check with her daughter about him. The guests love having visitors, but if this man isn't who he says he is, then we need to know that."

"I was hoping to find a picture of him," Felicity said.

The nurse frowned and grew thoughtful, stepping away from Felicity. She moved to stand in front of the cork board and began scanning the photographs. "I thought he was in a few pictures, but I don't seem to see him here. Sorry."

Felicity thanked her and headed out to the parking lot. She had a lot to think about—a strange man called Francis who claimed to be a friend of the family, who had been visiting for two years. Apparently a friend of hers, although not someone who came with her. Felicity began to feel extremely uneasy.

She drove straight back to Tall Tree Farm. She went through her afternoon chores with only half of her attention. She liked Zenia and didn't want to think the woman was being misled by a stranger who seemed to avoid the family, as well as Zenia's other acquaintances, while giving others the impression that he was a friend of the family. She pondered this as she poured grain into a water pail. The jostling of the sheep told her she'd made a mistake. That brought her back to reality and she kicked herself for making extra work.

Making things worse, she turned on the television to distract herself later in the evening while heating up some leftover stew. Rumbling across her thoughts came the voice of the weatherman alerting viewers to a light snow overnight.

Damn, she whispered. She'd forgotten about the forecast.

She turned off the stove and went out to cover up the early crop of overwintered vegetables. She was so excited at the prospect of having something to deliver in April that the earlier reports of a chance of snow had slipped her mind. She pulled pine boughs over the rows of vegetables, working by the light of the barn motion detectors. The only comfort was knowing that she wasn't the only farmer covering up early crops.

By the time she was ready for supper, close to midnight, Felicity had worked herself into a state of frustration and anxiety. She hurriedly heated a bowl of the stew, pacing the kitchen floor while she waited, and then rummaged in the cutlery drawer for a spoon. She leaned against the counter, fretting over the missteps she'd made during the last few days and eating carelessly with the bowl held close to her chest, when she realized that both the dog and cat were staring at her. Miss Anthropy pretended not to, opening one eye to peek at her every few seconds, but Shadow gaped blatantly, watching her and that bowl.

Twenty-Two

Early the following morning, Felicity took the last of her *Posted* signs and headed out to finish the job. Even though the late-night storm had left a small coating of snow throughout the area, she knew someone as determined as Kyle Morgan might have shown up to dig late at night, after his second job at the pizza joint. She wanted to make sure he hadn't torn down any signs and had honored the boundary between the properties.

The frozen leaves crunched under her boots, and the clean cold air made her feel it was December again. Winter could be hard, but there were always moments of beauty and delight. She followed the deer tracks, noting a few prints here and there. Even though humans might jump at the first signs of spring, most other animals knew that nature was fickle and winter could return at any moment, even into May, with a freak spring snowstorm.

Felicity began walking the boundary along Sasha Glover's plot, relaxing in the quiet and planning the rest of the day. She came over a small hill, scuffing the leaves beneath the light snow. And there her goodwill left her. Crossing in front of her was a single line of footprints.

She felt a rush of anger. She'd been as clear as she could possibly have been when telling Kyle to stay off her land. And he had ignored her. And thanks to the late snow, the evidence was right in front of her. She walked back a few feet, then crossed diagonally onto Sasha's property. She could see the prints in the light snow leading back toward the entrance along the road. Walking parallel to the tracks, she eventually noticed a second set going into Sasha's plot. Determined to know exactly what Kyle had been up to, she followed the track onto her property. The trail of footprints circled around and eventually turned uphill and headed northeast. She followed this until the walker turned back and headed southwest, back into Sasha's lot.

The only good result was the absence of any more digging. Perhaps Kyle had decided it was too cold, or perhaps he wanted to scope out where he would work next. In any event, he'd circled a part of her property that seemed to interest him, and then left.

Felicity didn't need to know what his plans were. She would get to him before he could lift another shovel. And this time he would know she meant business. She pulled out her cell and took a few photos.

———

She parked in the municipal lot across from Town Hall, right next to Jeremy's truck. He rapped on her window before she could climb out of her pickup and held the door for her.

"This seems to be our life right now," he said. "You're coming in just as I'm going out." He gazed at her and she knew they were thinking the same thing. He missed her and she missed him.

"I'm a bit wound up this morning," she said. "I need comfort."

"I'm your man." He reached for her hand and rubbed her fingers between his. "So, what's up?"

She told him about the footsteps on her land.

"You're sure they're Kyle's?"

"When I confronted him he admitted he'd been digging, and then he tried to get me to go in on the search with him. He was willing to share the treasure when he found it."

"Nice of him." Jeremy laughed softly. "And I'm sure you agreed."

"Oh, for sure. Anyway, this has to stop, so I'm here to see Kevin."

"And you know what Kevin will say?"

Felicity rolled her eyes and relaxed against the pickup. "If I jumped to conclusions as often as Kevin thinks I do, I'd have a gold medal from the Olympics. Anyway, I need down time."

"Tonight?"

"Definitely." She brushed his hand with hers and headed into the police station.

Before she could greet Padma, she heard Kevin's voice calling her into the office. She closed the door behind her and took a chair in front of his desk.

"I want to report a trespasser." Felicity sat up on the edge of the chair to signal to Kevin that this was all business, serious business. "Aren't you going to take notes?" she asked when he showed no signs of picking up a pen or turning on his computer.

"Just tell me what happened."

"On Monday, I told Kyle Morgan to stay off my land. He was not to go digging on my property." She waited for Kevin to ask a question.

"So?"

"So, he admitted he was digging and then he offered to share the treasure he found." Felicity could feel herself getting worked up again. She was still furious beneath her natural reserve and calm. For some reason, tearing up the countryside was as bad as anything else she could think of. "And I told him to stay off my land in no uncertain terms."

"Is your land posted?"

"It is now, along that boundary."

Kevin shut his eyes, as if to gather strength.

"But this morning I went out there to make sure he hadn't torn down the signs or simply ignored them, and I found his footprints walking onto my property and up part of a hill and over and back again. I specifically told him not to do that."

"Were the prints fresh?"

"They were in the snow that fell last night. And I took a photo this morning." She reached for her cell.

"You can't be sure they were Kyle's."

"Kevin, come on. Whose else could they be? Kyle has been digging there and he admitted it."

"The snow came down around three or four this morning."

"Well, that makes sense. He was in there checking out where he was going to be digging before he went to work."

"It wasn't Kyle."

"I know you think I'm jumping to conclusions because I didn't actually see him, but he admitted he was doing it. And now I've caught him red-handed, or red-footed, if there is such a thing."

"It wasn't Kyle."

"How can you know that?"

"Because Kyle Morgan died in a car accident last night, around two in the morning."

"Oh. Jeez." Felicity's mouth fell open. "Oh, Kevin."

"Exactly."

———

Felicity sat in her pickup staring down into the center of West Woodbury, such as it was. Kevin's news that Kyle was dead had sent her reeling. She'd somehow blamed the poor guy for all the ills that had befallen her, and now he was dead, one more victim of a murderer who cared nothing for people in search of she knew not what.

Kyle Morgan, the man who had been digging illegally on her property, the man she'd considered not good enough for Sasha Glover and whom Sasha's mother had disliked and mistrusted, and the man Felicity suspected of poisoning Sasha, was dead. In a car crash.

She hadn't said the obvious to the police chief, nor did Kevin even hint there was anything suspicious in the accident, but still, it was hard not to wonder at the coincidence. One plot of land passed down in a family and the last two owners had died unnatural deaths. Now the man who considered himself to be the third owner was also dead. Had he been telling people he was the owner now? Had he bragged about this to the wrong person? Had he offered someone else a partnership, just as he had offered one to her?

For most of the time since Clarissa's death, Felicity had assumed this was a simple matter of poaching. She'd put Kyle down as another version of the treasure hunters who went after frigates sunk during the Revolutionary War, or galleons laden with gold from the New World lost on their way back to Spain. These men and women were fantasists, and perhaps one in a thousand actually found something. And a rare find might include a few old weapons encrusted with barnacles or old coins. But most rational people considered such seeking akin to the proverbial beachcombing, a way to have a fun life without doing any real work. There was nothing wrong with chasing moonbeams, as long as you knew that's what you were doing and that the odds of catching anything were very bad. But on her land? On Tall Tree Farm?

Kyle was a fool, but if he was killed for the land, or something on it, then perhaps he wasn't a fool. Lance only wanted the best timber, even when he was told to back off. But what did that outside buyer want? Who was Franklin M. Gentile, really?

Felicity started up her truck and turned onto High Street. Just as she prepared to head back to her farm she spotted Marilyn Kvorak standing outside the Morning Glory Cafe, chatting with a tall man with a mustache. Felicity swung her steering wheel and headed downhill, parking several cars behind Marilyn's Jeep. But before she could get out of the pickup and stop the real estate agent, Marilyn climbed into her Jeep and drove away. The man she'd been talking with walked to his car and also drove off. Felicity scribbled down the license plate number on a scrap of paper and then glanced up as the car rounded a corner and traveled out of sight. Something about the car seemed familiar.

She headed into the cafe and hopped onto a stool at the counter. "I just saw Marilyn outside."

"Yup. Lunch with a client." Bettes filled a mug with coffee.

"Tall with a mustache?"

"Yup, that's the one."

"Francis something?"

"Francis?" Bettes frowned and lowered the coffee pot. "I don't think she called him that. Gill?" She walked to the door into the kitchen and stepped a foot or so into the back. "What's the name of that client Marilyn's been showing around?" She listened. "Yeah, that's the one."

"Who is it?" Felicity asked when Bettes returned to the counter.

"Frank Gentile."

"Frank with a Pennsylvania accent." Felicity left her coffee sitting on the counter.

"How did you know he had a Pennsylvania accent?"

"Someone told me." Felicity turned slightly toward the door, then resettled herself on the stool.

"I'm getting the feeling that's not good." Bettes waited.

"Does he live around here?"

"That guy?" Bettes looked through the large front windows as though he were standing outside. "I don't believe so."

"He's driving a car I think I've seen before."

"Oh, that." Bettes waved her hand. "I think that's one of Hogie's cars." She turned around and again called to Gill, who appeared in the kitchen doorway. "Didn't Hogie tell you he rented a car to some guy looking at property with Marilyn?" Gill nodded.

"He's taken it for a few weeks, Hogie said. And he keeps it at Hogie's place when he's not around and has to go back to wherever," Gill said.

"Pennsylvania," Felicity said absently.

"Yeah." Gill and Bettes glanced at each other. Gill shrugged and went back into the kitchen. Bettes said, "He doesn't want to drive his own car and put mileage on it, so he flies in and rents."

"So he's not local." Felicity leaned over her mug and addressed the single swirl and thread of steam. "And he doesn't look familiar."

"Why would he look familiar if you don't know him?"

"No reason." Felicity tried to tell herself she was overreacting, that the few photographs she'd seen of the man listed on the internet as Franklin M. Gentile, the science teacher, were too fuzzy to use to identify anyone, and she'd barely gotten a glimpse of this Frank Gentile at

Town Hall. "By the way, do you know if Clarissa Jenkins ever mentioned her fiancé's name?"

Once again Bettes walked to the kitchen door and leaned in, calling out her question. She turned to Felicity. "Gill says he heard her talking to him on her cell once and she called him Frank something. Hey, you don't look so good, Felicity. You all right?"

Felicity gave herself a little shake. "I'm fine, Bettes."

"Is this Frank the same guy?"

"I don't know." She ordered a grilled cheese sandwich to give herself time to think. She needed the comfort of other people, and a hot sandwich was a small price to pay for that.

"Have you seen Frank Gentile in here before?" she asked.

"Once or twice, with Marilyn." Bettes grew interested. "He's good-looking, isn't he?"

Felicity nodded. Con men usually are, she wanted to add, but she still didn't know what Frank was trying to get out of Zenia or Marilyn or any of the landowners in the area. And if he was also Clarissa's fiancé, then perhaps he and Kyle were after the same thing, or even in fact working together. "What's he like?"

Bettes shrugged. "Charming, good-looking, but once or twice he seemed impatient with Marilyn, like he was pushing her and she wasn't willing to be pushed."

"I see." Felicity frowned, trying to put these pieces together.

"You could ask Marilyn about him, but I guess you got other things on your mind, like all the extra money you'll be making out of town, huh?"

"Huh? What money?" Felicity jerked her head back.

"That was snarky. I shouldn't have said that." Bettes headed to the cash register, to take the money from a couple who had been seated at a booth by the window.

"What are you getting at, Bettes?" Felicity asked when she returned.

"I shouldn't have said anything. I just meant that you seem to have found a better sawmill for your cutting, the one Lance has decided to use, that's all."

"Where did you get that idea? Who told you that?"

"Dingel Mantell." Bettes folded her arms across her chest. "I mean, it's not really something you can expect to keep secret, at least not for very long. And there's nothing wrong with wanting to get the best price you can. We all get that." She waved her right hand, as though dismissing any expected criticism.

"Secret? Dingel told you that?"

"He was in here this morning and mentioned how tough things are getting with sawmills farther out offering better prices, so he has to think about other work. He was just sad at losing someone whose family has been his customer for his entire life."

"But he's not losing me as a customer." Felicity stood up, her sandwich order forgotten. "Are you sure you didn't misunderstand him?"

"Gill was here. He heard it too." She turned around and called for her husband in the nearly empty cafe. Gill came to the kitchen door, and Bettes repeated Dingel's statement.

"That's what he said," Gill confirmed. "Dingel figures this cutting will be especially good and Lance got a sawmill lined up with a buyer overseas. That's usually what's going on when something like this happens."

"I don't understand," Felicity said, pulling out a five-dollar bill and slipping it under the edge of her plate. "Lance and I didn't talk about anything like that. I never heard of changing sawmills because you want an overseas buyer. And I don't know anything about buyers except Dingel. I always go to Dingel."

"It's more common than you think," Gill said. "A few years ago all the best plywood was going overseas to Asia for their building boom.

233

Now I hear some mills in New York state are exporting high-grade logs to Europe and Asia. They're getting good prices."

"And then one guy told me all the best meat was going to Japan." Bettes pursed her lips. "I hear they pay upwards of six hundred dollars a pound for Angus beef."

"Now wait a minute." Felicity held up both hands. "I don't know about any of that, and I don't care about it, but if Lance told Dingel we were going to someone else, then Lance made a mistake." She pulled out her cell and began looking for Lance's telephone number. "I need to talk to him and get this straightened out."

This couldn't be happening, she muttered as she punched in Lance's cell number. It was the same as someone stealing the old coin silver spoons right out of her house. If Lance had lined up a sawmill and buyers out of town, he was already way ahead of her, way ahead of anything she'd suspected.

By the time she reached her pickup, she'd left two messages for Lance that no one could misunderstand: there would be no more cutting until she talked to him face to face. Still, she felt totally exposed, as though all her reasoning and planning and protecting had been nothing more than child's play. He was expecting to walk off with her timber while she watched with no idea of what she was seeing.

Twenty-Three

With a few hours of daylight left before Jeremy was expected, and feeling the need for strenuous physical work to calm herself down, Felicity decided to tackle the failing barn roof. The erratic weather that had meant snow last night meant bright sun today, so ice and snow had melted and it now felt like spring again. If the roof was clear, she could at least assess how much needed to be done, and then plan to work on it when she had more daylight. She carried out a ladder from the barn, propped it against the side, and steadied it.

Climbing on roofs wasn't her favorite activity. When the barn had needed a major repair some thirty years ago, her parents had decided to replace the roof with one that was less steep. But instead of the expected metal roof, Walter chose shingles because he could do it himself. Of course, this meant less cost when it came to repairs because everyone could get up on the roof and work on it, even Felicity's mother, who insisted her work was inside and she would stay there. No one had been able to persuade Walter O'Brien to use a tin roof.

Once on the roof, Felicity tested each step. She kept her cell phone with her whenever she went down cellar or onto the roof, in case something happened. She knew she would be missed eventually, but eventually could be days, and she could die in a matter of hours from a serious fall.

Although this barn roof was not as high as the previous one, she nevertheless had an unsettling sensation every time she found herself looking out over her property from on high. Her few cultivated acres, the straggly fencing, and the dirt drive were transformed into a painting of rural life.

She found the damaged shingles and estimated what she'd need for repairs. The culprit for some of the damage was a low-hanging branch from a tree that had been nothing but a weed fifteen years ago, and now was threatening to take down the barn. She added the tree to the list of those she had to remove sooner rather than later.

She worked her way to the peak, testing torn and curled shingles, tossing away the loose and damaged ones, watching them fly off into the sky before they wheeled around and fell to earth. When she'd reached the peak she stood, straddling it, and looked out over the countryside. She turned to the west and saw barely a glimmer of the sun sinking behind the trees.

The barn had been built close to the house, as barns usually were. In earlier centuries, animals were often kept on the first floor of a home, the body heat of a single cow capable of providing enough warmth to comfort a family through a cold winter night. When animals were moved into separate structures, the barn was often linked to the house by an open walkway, allowing the heat to travel into the home. But as living arrangements changed, barns became separated, and Felicity's grandparents had built their new barn near to but not attached to the farmhouse.

Felicity did prefer some distance between house and barn, if only for sanitary and olfactory reasons. But as she stood up there she thought about location—location of barns and hunting blinds and camps. Someone had built a blind very near Zeke Bodrun's old cabin. He might have built it, but as a hunter he would have known it wasn't an ideal location. Deer would smell humans in the blind, but also from the cabin. She began to wonder just how much a hunter could see from that spot. Could he see enough to make it worthwhile, even though it might not draw enough sport? Had someone built the blind after Zeke died, someone new to the area who didn't understand hunting, and then just left it after having little success? Had someone built the blind before the cabin, before Zeke, and Zeke just left the structure to fall apart? Felicity sat on the edge of the roof, her legs dangling over the open door.

The blind on Zeke's old land sat at least as far off the ground as the roof of the barn, Felicity estimated. But the ground where it sat was higher than the land her barn sat on. She imagined the landscape between here and the cabin, the rise and fall of terrain, the sections timbered recently or years ago. Somewhere in the back of her mind she recalled her dad timbering the northwest corner of the farm, in the direction of Zeke's cabin.

Her dad's insistence on no logging in one section near the bobcat den made her wonder if perhaps he and Zeke Bodrun had agreed not to upset the growth near Zeke's parcel, to give the old man a place of peace and solitude, a refuge during his final years. But the O'Brien land didn't extend far enough for that. The plot in question sat almost in the center of her property now, the second piece her dad had purchased serving as a link to his more valuable plots to the north. Moreover, if Zeke had wanted that much solitude, why had he set off on his personal odysseys?

The sound of Jeremy's Ford pickup coming down the drive brought Felicity back to the present. She watched him drive up, park, and climb out. He spotted her at once, and waved before reaching into the truck for a sack of groceries.

"How's the view up there?" He walked to the front of the barn, looking up at her. "Contemplating the philosophy of farming?"

"I love it up here." She pulled off her canvas tool bag and held it over him, waited, and then let it go. He grabbed it. "So what's for dinner?"

"Quail. From Loretta's freezer."

———

After taking a shower and changing into clean jeans and a green sweater, Felicity set the table and made a salad. She poured wine and settled in a chair to watch Jeremy cook. He'd changed out of his work clothes into a clean, well-pressed pair of khaki slacks and a flannel shirt. She appreciated that in him. Despite their multiyear relationship, and his devotion to raising his daughter and maintaining his farm along with his construction business, he'd never treated her like she was third on his list. He never took her for granted. She loved him for that, and other things.

"I had a thought while I was up on the barn roof."

"Thoughts are good." Jeremy glanced over his shoulder at her and went on sauteing onions.

"What are you planning on doing with those?"

"Topping for the rice pilaf."

"Who shot the quail?"

"Loretta. It's her specialty. She pretends birds are ruining her vegetable garden and goes at it."

"She hasn't had a vegetable garden in years."

"But she has a long memory. So tell me about your epiphany on the barn roof."

"That sounds like the title of a book. Epiphany on a Barn Roof." Felicity sipped her wine. "It was about the blind over near Zeke Bodrun's cabin."

"What about it?"

"Don't you think it's awful close to the cabin?"

Jeremy turned around, holding the wooden spoon poised over the saucepan, and studied her. He turned back to the stove. "Could be. Could be it was built before the cabin, or while the cabin was empty."

"Hmm. I suppose so." But Felicity wasn't satisfied and continued to sip her wine. "There was something else."

"There's always something else with you."

"Now, Jeremy."

"That sounds like Loretta."

"Well, hear me out." Felicity sat up straighter in her chair. "When I went into the cabin with you and Pat, I thought it looked lived in. Recently lived in."

"Yeah, it did."

"But Kevin said the forensics guys found no evidence that Sasha Glover was ever in that cabin." She rested her elbow on the table, holding up the wine glass. The evening light shimmered through the red liquid and turned the white napkins and tablecloth pink. She played with the light and the glass until she noticed the silence. She looked up to see Jeremy staring at her.

"You're stuck on this idea that Sasha was in that cabin just because her great-granddad once owned it."

"That's not the only reason. There was that smell of vomit."

"Lissie, it was a freak accident that she happened to die on your land. Whoever poisoned her, and it may have been an accident, isn't part of your land problems with Kyle or whoever was walking on your land after the snowstorm."

"You've been talking to Kevin."

Jeremy turned back to the stove, which Felicity thought was probably a good idea because she guessed she would have been irritated by his expression. "I often talk to Kevin."

"You know what I mean." She put down the glass. "Listen, Jeremy, I told Kyle Morgan to stay off my land, to stop digging. I was adamant about it. He gave me some lip and I told him I was posting the land. Two days later he was dead. But—"

"There are no buts here, Lissie."

"Just hear me out. The morning after he died I went out to check that he hadn't torn down any of the *Posted* signs, and they were still there, but so were footprints in the snow. I followed them and they went onto my property, up a hill and turned back and went out through Sasha's lot."

"Just someone out walking," he said. "This is going to be perfect."

"Maybe."

He turned around. "Maybe perfect?"

"No, I mean someone out walking. I'm sure the meal will be perfect. It always is."

"What a great pair we make. I can cook and you can fix a roof."

———

Felicity sat crosslegged on the bed and rested her hands on Jeremy's naked back. Out of the corner of her eye she could see him watching her, but then he closed his eyes and she did too, sinking deep inside until the only reality was heat. After a while—she couldn't have said how long—she felt her fingers slacken and her knuckles rise. She drew her hands into her lap and let her breathing return to normal. Jeremy shifted and turned onto his side before sitting up. She could feel him watching her but he didn't touch her. She appreciated that. He let her return at her own pace.

"How do you feel?" she asked.

"You tell me." He leaned over and kissed her. "Your lips are burning."

She shrugged. "It is what it is." She uncrossed her legs and swung around to sit on the edge of the bed, leaving him room to slide off beside her. "You tore something bad but it seems okay now."

"Thanks to you." He pushed himself off the bed and looked around for his clothes.

Felicity leaned back on a pillow and watched Jeremy dress, then glanced at the clock. "It's late. I could be asleep before you get home."

He smiled at her in the mirror as he buttoned his shirt. "How's the fostering going?"

"You mean Shadow?"

"That's the one."

"He's living up to his name. He follows me everywhere if I let him." She slid off the bed and pulled on a pair of sweats and a jersey.

"You mean if I opened the door I'd trip over him?"

"Possibly."

Jeremy reached over to the bedroom doorknob and turned. He pulled open the door and there sat Shadow, staring into the room. "God, that dog looks forlorn."

Felicity called him in and he trotted circumspectly past Jeremy. "I take him with me into the woods sometimes, and he seems okay with it. He's getting the hang of being a farm dog."

"Think you'll keep him?"

"Maybe. He probably should have a family with children, someone to play with. Still, I'm fond of him." She began to coo to the dog.

"Take him with you when you go look at the blind," Jeremy said.

Felicity started.

"You were planning on doing that, weren't you?"

"How did you guess?"

"And you told me he could track."

"I did, didn't I?" She pulled her hair back into a ponytail and smiled. "But what you're really hoping is he'll be a guard dog, just in case I come across someone I shouldn't."

Jeremy picked up his keys and slipped them into his pocket as he turned to her. "I'm never sure about watching you head off to do something that we both know could be dangerous. I don't want to tell you to stop because I know what that sounds like."

"I'm not going to end up dead, Jeremy." She climbed off the bed and walked over to him and reached for his hands. She held them in front of her.

"Three people, Lissie. Three."

"I know." She slipped into his embrace.

Twenty-Four

The next morning Felicity was on the road, driving the short distance to the blind, by nine o'clock. She had decided not to take Shadow with her because she didn't yet trust her ability to control him in unfamiliar environments. She'd left him at home with his muzzle rubbing against the front window.

Although she worried she'd been neglecting her chores ever since Clarissa Jenkins's car crash, she couldn't pull herself away from the questions Clarissa and Sasha's deaths had raised. Now she had it in her head that the hunting blind held an answer to some of those questions. She pushed down the pedal and sped along the old highway, turning off onto a side road and then down the lane to Zeke's cabin. The pickup bumped along and she hoped she wouldn't rip the undercarriage.

The blind was truly a ramshackle affair, and if it had been on her own property she would probably have pulled it down before someone climbed up and fell through the floor. But as it was, she was more curious than circumspect at this moment.

She circled the tree it was built in. Rusted nails held together the well-weathered boards, even those that had split over the years. She tugged on the rungs nailed into the tree. The first one came apart in her hand. The second one slewed to the side and split in two. She didn't bother testing the third one. Instead, she walked back to her pickup and pulled a ladder from the back, which she propped up against the tree, wedging the top against the trunk and floorboards above. As she looked up at the blind, she knew this could turn out to be a great idea or a truly dumb one.

At the top of the ladder she pressed her palm flat against what looked like a trapdoor. With effort, she pushed until it gave way and rose up; then it fell back, twisting to the side and hanging over the floor. The hinges were too rusted to hold the trap in place on one end, but not so rusted that the whole thing came apart. She gripped the floorboards and levered herself up one more rung and into the blind, her shoulders now above the flooring. The place smelled musty, of animal feces and rotting leaves.

In a far corner was the usual sign of a human-abandoned property, an old piece of cloth taken over by rodents, probably squirrels, and used as a nest. The other corner housed a pile of rusty old beer cans. Propped up behind them was a rusty tin tray advertising Coke in glass bottles, a desirable antique even in its current state. The window to the blind was still propped open, which was odd, now that she thought about it. It should have collapsed years ago.

More curious than sensible, Felicity worked her way fully into the blind, making sure to straddle the boards that looked almost rotted through. She heard a board creak, and another sounded like it was ready to crack in two.

A single branch above her served as a brace for part of the roof, and she grasped it with both hands, easing her weight on the floor as she worked her way closer to the window. She looked out through the opening.

Once again she was struck by what being a mere twenty feet above ground level could reveal. The tree with its blind stood on a knoll she hadn't considered much more than a little mound, but from here she could see far into the woods. With the trees still bare of leaves, she felt as if she could see for miles.

But that was foolish. A hill high enough to be named stood between the blind and her farmhouse. And yet she had the sense of looking deep into a forest, of capturing the feeling that drew the early explorers and lured otherwise sensible men and women into climbing inhospitable mountains just to get to the top.

She pulled out her cell and touched the compass app. The blind was oriented to the southeast. She would have thought a different direction would have been better, perhaps to the north or west, instead of a direction that looked just to the right of the cabin. Despite the blind's location so close to the cabin, she was certain Zeke had built it, not only because of the age of the tin tray but also of the wood, which was pine, cut and aged like that in the cabin, the scars of the circular saw visible on both. The structure wasn't old enough to predate the cabin. But perhaps by the time Zeke had built the blind, he was no longer hunting and didn't care as much about orienting it. But that didn't make sense. She doubted if he would really have given up practices he'd followed his entire life. She glanced down at the cabin, to the right.

The blind, she realized, would have been Zeke's real refuge. The cabin served for winter and blustery weather, but the blind was true to its name, a place to sit unknown and unreachable and yet able to see all. Here Zeke must have found everything he was looking for. Felicity rested her head against the rough bark, wrapped her arms around the branch, and thought about that. *Here Zeke must have found everything he was looking for.*

She heard the words in her head, and she knew they meant more than she at first understood. She'd stumbled on a truth she couldn't fully grasp. She repeated the words. She could hear them pushing against her eyes, resting on her tongue. She had discovered something, even if she didn't know exactly what.

———

As soon as she got back to her farm, Felicity collected Shadow and drove to Sasha Glover's piece of land. She let the dog out of the pickup to walk with her. Shadow followed along behind her until she left the path, then moved about ten and later twenty feet to her right, running parallel with her. Every now and then the dog stopped, sat down, and watched her. If she didn't do something interesting, he stood and resumed his tracking among the leaves and saplings. She wished she'd brought him with her the morning of the snowfall. Perhaps he would have caught a scent and tracked it beyond the stone wall at Old Town Road.

She walked among the hills and the gradually sinking mounds, stood at the edge of holes, careful to avoid undermining the walls, and looked for signs that anyone else had continued the search after Kyle Morgan's death. She tramped onto her own land and followed the path as she remembered it from the day before. But today, she couldn't tell if anyone had been on the property since she'd posted it.

She headed uphill onto her own land. The woods were especially quiet here, and this would continue for a while. She'd called Lance several times since talking with Bettes in the cafe, leaving voice messages and sending texts about him leaving Mantell's sawmill, but he still hadn't replied and she guessed he was avoiding her. She had to stop him and whoever he was working with. She didn't want to catch anyone red-handed because then the damage would be done. She had to find another way. If her suspicions were right, she had to act now.

Felicity walked deeper into the trees, watching where she stepped, keeping an eye out for anyone else's footprints or signs of passage. As she walked, the silence thickened, enveloping her like a blanket, shielding her from the rest of the world. She reached the center of the farm, an area never timbered or cleared or farmed to her knowledge. She tried to see what Old Zeke had seen perhaps over a hundred years ago when he was a young man working in this area, and certainly over fifty years ago when her father was a young man and Old Zeke knew he was well past his prime. She thought about Zeke, an old man with a dream, and her dad, a young man with a future.

As she looked around, Felicity thought the stand of trees wasn't particularly attractive. Most of the trees seemed to be hemlock and beech, with a few sugar maples, yellow birch, and oak mixed in. She noted a chestnut and a few white pine. It wasn't pretty, and it wasn't as thick as she sometimes found. But it had mattered. She looked again.

At moments like this she ached to have her parents back again, young and vital, to learn from them all she knew they could still teach. She knew she couldn't ask her dad because his series of strokes had left him vulnerable and suspicious—his fears rose up before his reason could guide him. She'd learn nothing and be trapped for days in his distress. But perhaps she didn't have to talk to him, to probe for the past and his long-forgotten dreams.

The sun filtered through the trees, warming the back of her neck. Straight ahead, well beyond her sight, lay the path Lance planned to take for timbering. He would be coming straight into her property from the other side, and straight on down toward Sasha Glover's property. A breeze swept through the trees, the susurration whispering as it went past her, the leaves at her feet turning restless. She had to stop him no matter what.

Twenty-Five

Felicity opened the door to her pickup and motioned Shadow to hop in. He sat on the passenger seat watching her punch in numbers in her cell. The phone rang but Lance didn't pick up. She left a voice message and sent a text, once again, and then sat there wondering what else she could do. She felt enormous frustration, but at least now she understood better what was going on. She looked back through Sasha's plot at the trees getting ready to leaf out. If Lance was gambling hundreds of dollars a week, he had to get more money out of his timbering. At least that part of her life was beginning to make sense. But Bettes had told her something else equally important.

She recalled Bettes's comment that Marilyn's client had rented a car from Hogie.

Hogie Dubois was an accommodating guy, well into his sixties, who liked to buy and rent cars he could take care of himself. His weekly rental fees were low, and if the car broke down, he showed up and fixed it in your driveway. His business was just right for people who couldn't afford to buy or lease a car but couldn't live without one. In this area, that was just about everyone. He had a variety of cars, including a few that gave a sheen to a man or woman who needed to look smart and prosperous, someone to do business with. He charged extra for those.

Hogie lived in a small cottage across the river from Flat Road Automotive, where he could see his business in the garage parking lot and call out if a customer showed up. He still had to drive through town to cross the bridge to get to Flat Road, but he could keep an eye on everything when he was at home. Felicity parked in front of his house and waited until a bright yellow Chevy with well-cared-for chrome pulled up and parked. Hogie climbed out and took the steps to his front door. Felicity ran up the path behind him. He turned around and looked her over.

"What's got you in a twist?"

She told him what she wanted to know.

"I can't tell you that." He had a canvas sack hanging off his shoulder with oddly wrapped shapes sticking out. Hogie believed down to his toenails that he'd make it big by buying and trading stuff, and so far he'd managed not to lose his life savings. But that was about it.

"Just the name of the man who rented the car." Felicity had come to suspect that Frank Gentile was an alias, and Hogie could confirm that. The more she thought about it, the more she felt the man she'd seen in the Town Hall window was unlikely to be the helmeted teacher on the Internet.

"Can't do that." He took a step back. His thick gray hair curled above the collar of his heavy quilted jacket, which hung open over a blue chamois shirt. He wore jeans with a wide brown leather belt. "Privacy issues."

Felicity wanted to comment on that but thought better of it. In West Woodbury, she sometimes thought, there was no such thing as privacy. "All right, what can you tell me?"

"Ah, Felicity, you make it so hard." He took a half turn, shifting the strap on his shoulder. Then, in a sudden move, he swung back to face her and gave her the name of a company.

"That sounds familiar. What else can you tell me? Anything. It's important, Hogie."

"It always is with you. Well, the man pays cash. How's that?" He ran his hands through his hair, which he wore combed straight back.

"That it? Nothing more?"

"Why would I ask a lot of questions? It's not like he's a bank robber looking for a getaway car. You know, Felicity, you've been getting strange since your dad went into the home."

"He's offering big bucks, Hogie, to the farmers around here for land. If he's so rich, and Marilyn Kvorak says he is, then why is he renting a car from you?"

"You think there's something wrong with my cars?"

But Felicity had gotten what she wanted.

Later that evening she typed in the name Hogie had given her, hit return, and waited. And there it was. A single mention of Treeline Properties listed in several generic sites for tracking individuals or businesses, with no guarantee that any one of them had any more information than name and address. This was a company that didn't want to be known.

But she didn't need anything more.

Frank Gentile, or whoever he was, worked for the company that had bought Zeke Bodrun's cabin, and he was also now trying to buy farmland in West Woodbury. That wasn't illegal, as Kevin would quickly point out, but it was odd. The spit of land he'd bought was next to worthless except as a wood lot or a blind for hunters. There wasn't enough acreage for a private home, and the land around it was too restricted, unless the buyer was willing to pay the back taxes on land taken out of Chapter 61, the law regulating farmland and tax relief for farmers.

But that piece of land, with its cabin, was valuable to both Ezekial Bodrun and Frank Gentile. So what did it contain? Felicity understood what it had meant to Old Zeke, and she'd come to believe that Kyle Morgan was nothing more than someone caught up in treasure fever, thinking Sasha's land was the valuable piece, and Lance looked to be sinking deeper into debt and desperation. But how did the unknown Frank fit in? Had he been using every one of them?

———

Felicity spent a good portion of her evening ignoring Shadow and Miss Anthropy, to their chagrin, uniting them in disdain for their human as she hunched over her computer. She recalled as much as she could of Zenia Callahan's descriptions of her father's travels and her mother's comments. She searched through old commentaries on life in West Woodbury, including farmers who had given up and moved away in search of better land. She read about the timbering business in New England, the rise and demise of small farms, the mechanization of farming, and the expansion of the Rust Belt. By the time her old clock twanged its way to eleven thirty and the electricity flickered in a gust of wind, she was ready to confront Franklin M. Gentile with what she knew. He would either confirm her suspicions or slam the door in her face.

Twenty-Six

Early on Friday morning, Felicity tossed a New England road atlas into her pickup, a picnic lunch, and photographs of Clarissa and Sasha she'd taken off the internet from online obituaries. She figured she had a four-and-a-half hour drive ahead of her, a straight shot up I-95 to Bangor, Maine, to the school where the retired Franklin M. Gentile now worked as a tutor. She changed the radio station half a dozen times, too restless to listen to anything for very long. When she reached a small private high school, a secretary buzzed her in and a security guard escorted her to the office. Another secretary led her down to Mr. Gentile's office.

"He's very popular with the students," she said over her shoulder. "He has parents visiting all the time. You'll be a nice change of pace this morning."

Felicity glanced up at the clock at the end of the hall. It was just closing in on eleven. The secretary knocked on the door, and the man Felicity had only seen wearing a helmet in photographs opened the door and smiled at her, a broad, cheerful, unself-conscious greeting.

Felicity introduced herself and apologized for showing up unexpectedly, and then explained herself.

"Hmm. Someone with my name?" He ushered her to a seat and took another at the desk.

Just as she expected, this man was not the one Marilyn was driving around the county looking at property. This Frank Gentile stood a few inches shorter than Felicity's five foot eight inches, and considerably wider. He wore plain gray slacks belted tightly at his waist, the belt pushing his pudgy body into soft bulges above and below. His gray sweater was buttoned to the waist and strained against his torso. The tails flared out over the pleats in his pants. He wore no tie but buttoned the top button on his gray shirt.

Determined not to make a terrible mistake, Felicity forced herself to speak slowly and calmly. When she was finished, she stopped. And waited.

"Hmm," Mr. Gentile said. "That's quite a story, Miss O'Brien." She showed him her driver's license, which he inspected, staring at it over his nose. Then she invited him to address her as Felicity. He didn't immediately return the courtesy.

"Well," he began, drawing out each sound as though she were hard of hearing, "I can assure you I've never been in your neck of the woods. I'm not tall with a mustache, as you can see." He patted his midriff and then resettled himself in his chair. "I'm also not youngish, as you can see, and I'm definitely not a man any woman would look at twice." He gave a wistful sigh. And then he laughed. "I've always wanted to be tall and handsome."

"I had to make sure."

"Quite right. I'm glad you did. Your story is not unexpected." He began stacking papers on his desk and moving them to the side.

"Not unexpected?" Felicity leaned forward. "Is there something you can tell me about this man? I Googled your name and found only three people with it, and of course you were one of them."

"You'd think there'd be hundreds, wouldn't you?" He cleared his throat, as though about to begin a lecture. "It doesn't seem so unusual, and each name by itself isn't rare, but together they seem to make an unusual combination." She could hear in his voice the teacher taking hold of the man, but then his tone of voice changed, and with it the volume. His speech returned to normal, that of casual conversation. "Well, that's another matter. In answer to your question, no, I can't tell you anything about this man in particular. But I can add to your mystery. As I believe I said, your story is not unexpected."

"Oh, dear," Felicity said. "Go ahead."

"It may be nothing, but then again, it may be something." He took a deep breath and began. "About a year ago I received a call from a man in Maryland asking me if I still wanted to purchase the painting I'd left a deposit on."

"Maryland?"

"Yes, Maryland. Oakland, Maryland, to be precise. I'm sure it's a lovely place, but I've never been there."

"I've never heard of it. Should I have?" Felicity pulled out a small notebook and wrote down the name. She knew that in the heat of the moment she was liable to forget something important, a detail that meant nothing to her on first hearing but could turn out to be significant later.

"Not really, unless you're a particular kind of tourist."

"What kind of tourist?"

"Nature tourist. That's where Swallow Falls State Park is. Anyway, the painting was of a particular part of the state park, an area not as

255

much visited. The gallery owner described it to me. He said he'd been holding my deposit check for three months and keeping the painting off the market until I decided, and now he wanted to deposit the check for his services."

"And you had no idea what he was talking about."

"Precisely." He took another deep breath. "I told him I was the wrong Frank Gentile, and he said the same thing you said. There are only two or three of you according to the internet, he told me, so I had to be the one he was looking for. So we went back and forth a few times, and I told him what I looked like, and he gave me the same description you did."

"Did he believe you?"

"He didn't have any choice, because I also told him that at the time of my supposed visit I was in the hospital having cataract surgery. You spend your life teaching under fluorescent lights or staring at a computer and you're guaranteed to have cataracts." He glanced at the laptop sitting open on his desk.

"What did he do about the check?"

"He said he was going to deposit it anyway and see what happened."

"Did you ever hear from him again?"

"Oh, yes, he called me a couple of months later to tell me the check had bounced. He was quite upset, and I commiserated, but that's not what he called to tell me. He said he'd been at a conference soon afterward and complained to a colleague about those sorts of problems, and damned if his colleague hadn't had an encounter with the same fellow. He didn't ask him to hold a painting or give him any money, but he was there, visiting Crab Tree Woods."

"I've never heard of that either." Felicity scribbled the name in her notebook.

"But you strike me as an intelligent young woman." Mr. Gentile was sounding more and more like the teacher he'd been for his entire career. "And I bet you can guess what the areas have in common. Would you care to give it a try?"

Felicity didn't try to conceal her laughter. "I'll take that bet. They both have old-growth forests."

"A+, Felicity, A+."

"And they both have good security, so no one can get in there and harvest any of it without someone noticing or stopping them." Even as she said this, images of Lance, her once-trusted logger, flashed across her mind.

"A++, Felicity, A++." He paused and fingered the stack of papers on his desk. "I suspect that others, less alert than you and the fellow in Maryland, have met my namesake. I shudder to think what damage he's done." He swung his chair to face her. "How did you come across him, if I may ask again?"

Felicity added more details. "The real estate agent who was showing him around is a friend, and she's been following up on his offers to local farmers. He says he wants something quiet and peaceful and out of the way." She felt an unexpected animosity for Marilyn as she wondered just how much the real estate agent knew.

"And? I can tell there's something more."

"He told Marilyn, the agent, that he had plenty of money to spend, and she said she checked and he did. He also seems to be part of something called Treeline Properties."

She waited as Frank Gentile repeated the name.

"Never heard of it," he said. "But a smart operator could figure out how to make it look like he had plenty of money."

Felicity had no idea how anyone would do that, but she figured he was right. "So he's going through all this to buy old forests in several states, from what you've told me?"

"Sounds like it," Frank said.

"How does this affect you?"

"It doesn't," he said. "Unless he tells people he's Franklin Marshall Gentile of Bangor, Maine, I have no reason to complain just because he has the same name." He coughed, as though preparing to make an important statement. "But I think I'll just let our local police department know this is going on. I'll feel better if someone in authority knows. I don't expect anything to come of this as far as I'm concerned, but it's better to have the information recorded somewhere."

Felicity agreed that it was a good idea. They chatted a little longer and then Felicity stood up. Frank stood as well.

"You came all this way to make sure I wasn't the man searching your area? That's a long drive."

Felicity agreed as she slipped on her coat. "But people can say anything over the telephone, and we'd have to Skype for me to be confident about your appearance, and that's more computer skill than I have. I've only seen the man twice, and not up close. I had to be sure you weren't hiding out."

He laughed. "I know it's not funny. What you're up against is serious, but the idea of my being a criminal ... " He grew wistful. "I live a very tame existence."

All the way back to West Woodbury, Felicity replayed the conversation she'd had with Frank Gentile. The Frank Gentile of Treeline Properties was going to an awful lot of trouble to get at forests he might not even be able to harvest—unless he could get in with a logger or a forester. That was the part she found most disturbing: the change in Lance Gauthier from long-time friend to someone who was a partner in a very bold theft. If anyone had asked her if Lance would do such a thing, she would have said no, no way. But then, it seemed there were a lot of things she hadn't known about Lance. Like his gambling.

Twenty-Seven

By 9:30 on Saturday morning, the quadrupeds were munching happily beneath the old apple trees, barely giving a glance to the bipeds passing among them, their arms grappling with easels and canvases, drawing pads, and lunch bags. As soon as she'd returned from Bangor the day before, Felicity had called Jeremy to let him know what she'd learned from the other Franklin M. Gentile. Within a few minutes, she and Jeremy had settled on a plan for Saturday.

Now, as the morning sun warmed the field, she set aside her anxiety, left the sheep and artists in Nola Townsend's capable hands, and drove to Jeremy's farm. She reached it well ahead of Marilyn's expected arrival, which gave her plenty of time to tell Loretta about her visit with Frank Gentile of Bangor, Maine.

"So, you mean the buyer is walking around the country looking for old-growth forests to steal?" Loretta poured herself a second cup of coffee and refilled Felicity's mug. The kitchen in Jeremy's farmhouse had been renovated almost thirty years ago and had the feeling of a comfortable old home.

"That's what it sounds like."

"And Lance is helping him? It sounds crazy." Loretta looked at Jeremy, who shrugged. "Why would he do that? Lance is local."

"You know he gambles a lot," Felicity said. "And I didn't really think about it, but he has a seasonal rental out on a lake and he lives in a campground in the summer. Maybe the reason he lives outside is financial, not because he loves it."

"Jeez," Loretta said, staring at her.

Felicity wrapped her hands around the hot mug. "It explains all that traveling Sasha's mother was telling me about."

"What traveling?" Loretta said.

"After Zeke retired, Helena said he apparently got the traveling bug, and her mother, Zenia, said the same. Zeke and his wife went all over the place, but I looked at the places Zenia talked about and they were all states with old-growth forests."

"So? The man liked to be around trees," Loretta said.

"He didn't have to travel for that," Felicity said. "I think he was getting a look at old-growth forests because he thought that's what he could see growing on Tall Tree Farm. He and my dad suspected that untimbered plot of land was going to be valuable in a historical way if left alone to grow unmolested, and in his retirement Zeke went around to other forests to confirm what he suspected. I thought those trees were old but not true old growth, not yet anyway. Now I know better."

"So he and your dad cooked up a scheme to protect that property," Jeremy said.

"I don't think my dad purchasing that land had anything to do with persuading my grandmother that he was a fit suitor for her daughter," Felicity said. "I think it was a ruse to make sure that land would go where it would be protected. My dad bought up the rest of the odd bits around it. And he never cut a trail through it."

"And you just let it be." Jeremy finished his coffee.

"I didn't think about it till Lance said that if it was in the chapter 61 plan it had to be managed, and he was ready to go in there and timber, but I said no."

"He was okay with that?" Loretta asked.

"He's been trying to get in there," Felicity said. "I think he's sure I still don't know, but now I know what Dad meant when he was talking about something being secret and Tall Tree Farm being special. He was thinking about that untimbered land." She paused. "And when he told me not to visit the Bodruns, I think he was trying to keep me from learning anything. He's confused about what year it is sometimes, but not about what matters to him. He meant to keep that secret he and Old Zeke had."

"And that's why he ran away from Pasquanata," Jeremy said, nodding. "He was checking up on his land."

"Maybe it was the mention of Clarissa Jenkins or something else," Felicity said. "I don't remember, but it was right after that he got so upset and took off. And he went straight to the old cabin, we thought, but really he went to the path he and Zeke probably used to get into that particular plot." Felicity smiled. "And here we thought all those years how romantic he was, giving his future mother-in-law a piece of land to prove his worthiness."

"Crafty guy." Loretta began to chuckle.

"But that doesn't explain why Gentile wants to make me an offer on my property," Jeremy said. "When I called Marilyn, she insisted he could come over yesterday evening, but I thought the morning would be better."

"I'll bet he just wants a legitimate reason to walk the land and see what you've got."

"Because he doesn't know what's up here," Loretta said. "Maybe he's been going around to old forests in this area because he heard about a guy from New England talking about old growth and now he's here and he's looking."

"Cutting down old growth forests wherever they are would be a travesty," Felicity said, looking grim.

"There's money in that timber if you can get it," Loretta said. "That could be why he's up here, tracking down Zeke."

"That's a stretch, Mom. Zeke has been dead for years and I doubt anyone would remember him from his travels."

"She could be right in a way, Jeremy," Felicity said. "He could have heard about Zeke and Pioneer Valley. And it's clear he's the one who bought Zeke Bodrun's cabin."

"So you said." Jeremy had listened quietly but attentively to the entire recitation, perched on a stool while his coffee grew cold on the counter beside him. "Treeline Properties bought the cabin, and Treeline Properties in the form of Frank Gentile rented a car from Hogie."

"A rental from Hogie's? And this is the guy Marilyn said had bundles of money in the bank? That was a seven-figure offer she gave you." Loretta was torn between contempt and disbelief. She looked from her son to Felicity.

"It is strange," Felicity agreed. "When's he due?"

Jeremy glanced up at the clock over the doorway. "Marilyn said eleven. They should be here any minute now." He turned barely an inch to glance out the window as Marilyn's black Jeep pulled up in front of the house. Only then did Felicity realize how rigid Jeremy's body was—how disturbed he was and how determined not to show it.

"Did she ask why you'd changed your mind?" Felicity asked.

"I just told her I was ready to make a change." He spoke softly so only Felicity could hear, but he needn't have bothered. His mother was too caught up in watching the car to pay attention to anything her son was saying.

"Is that them?" Loretta peered out the window, making no effort to conceal her curiosity. "Yup, that's them."

"Okay, ladies. Showtime." Jeremy slid off the stool and pushed it under the island counter.

———

Frank Gentile of no known address had considerable charm, Felicity acknowledged. He had already seduced Marilyn Kvorak into near silent adulation and total agreement with anything he said, disarmed Loretta's sharp tongue, and impressed Jeremy with a firm handshake and astute questions. Felicity felt the tug of attraction when he extended his hand, and her skin tingled under his firm but careful handshake. Perhaps sensing her reservations, he turned away to talk to Jeremy. As she watched the two men establish themselves, the image of Clarissa's car weaving down the road flashed in front of her. She tried to hide a sudden shiver.

Frank Gentile was tall and handsome if not also dark. He had even features, sandy-colored hair with a touch of red, and lovely light brown eyes. His mustache was neat and thin. Tall and limber as well as strong, he seemed ready to smile throughout the encounter. He fit the description of Zenia's visitor, but most importantly he looked like the man Felicity had glimpsed in the Town Hall window.

After the obligatory cup of tea or coffee, Jeremy put everything in the sink. He handed Frank a rough map of the farm, then led the little group across the lawn to the barn, through the barn, and out into the pasture. His cows seemed mildly interested in the strangers passing by—certainly more than Felicity's sheep would have been—but not enough to follow or abandon grazing. A single car passed, and Gentile paused to look up toward the road and listen.

"Not much traffic out here," he said.

"Almost none." Jeremy glanced at the car. "You're not from around here."

"No, no, but I wish I were. You have a lovely spot." Frank Gentile rested his hands on his hips and scanned the woods ahead. In the distance, toward the east, a mountain shaped like an egg rose up, and the midday sun gave a rich deep blue background for the dense green shape reaching into the sky. "It's different from the Berkshires and, of course, the coast. More like New Hampshire and Vermont."

"You know those areas?" Loretta looked like she was trying not to tumble into his arms, so smitten was she. She might have been ready to condemn him as a charlatan, but with his first smile she'd given up her resistance, her cynicism evaporated, and her attraction to the stranger in their midst was palpable.

"Not really," he said, turning to her with a direct look. There was nothing smarmy in his demeanor, and Felicity began to feel she had misjudged him. "Just driving through."

"Have you looked at any other property in the area?" Felicity asked.

He stepped back so he could look at her, and perhaps, she thought, take the time to compose his answer. They had reached the edge of the woods and would have to watch where they stepped from now on. "Nothing significant. There's certainly a lot of property for sale around here, but not many large farms."

"They're slow to come on the market," Marilyn said.

"If people are still working them, I don't expect them to sell," Frank said. He shifted a bit toward Felicity. "I understand you're pretty busy with sheep now. Is this your day off?"

Felicity shook her head. "I never get a day off. When I go home I have a lot of chores to get to, and today is the day we have artists out at the farm. I have to be there later to make sure everything's okay."

"You get tomorrow off," Loretta said. She shifted toward Frank. "Another family get-together tomorrow. My granddaughter's coming home from college again. She's nearby, so you'd think we'd get to see her more often, but she's young and she loves college. But she'll be here tomorrow and we'll have a chance to be together. Felicity's family." She startled Felicity with a megawatt smile.

Really, thought Felicity, I have never heard Loretta babble before.

"Family is everything." Frank pressed his lips together in a polite smile, and to Jeremy he said, "Shall we go?"

Jeremy nodded and they headed into the woods.

For once Marilyn had given up her high heels and wore flat shoes, sneakers, so she could keep up with the others. The group of five straggled along a path, emerging into a small clearing. Frank Gentile stepped into the center and looked around at the trees, the uneven ground, and walked across to an old cellar hole. Marilyn pointed out the natural beauty of the area, named a few trees until she realized she was in danger of sounding like a naturalist giving a tour, and began to talk about the town's attractions.

Loretta was little better. She loved West Woodbury and it showed. Every now and then Frank Gentile looked up from his spot on the edge of the clearing and nodded at something one of the women said before walking on.

The troop entered the woods on the other side of the clearing, and Jeremy led them along the boundary, which was marked by a deteriorating stone wall and a bit of rusted barbed wire, and back to the pasture.

The two men led the way up the hill toward the house. Every few feet Marilyn nudged Felicity and looked nearly manic with glee. The real estate agent didn't dare say anything, perhaps for fear of breaking the spell or perhaps for fear of embarrassing herself. But she couldn't contain her excitement. The entire interaction between Frank Gentile and Jeremy Colson spoke of an agreement on the property.

Twenty-Eight

Jeremy leaned against the lowered tailgate of his white pickup, watching his mother hurry back to her house to get ready for another session at the animal shelter offices. He crossed his heavily booted feet at the ankles and stared at her retreating figure, but he was barely seeing her. Felicity knew that by the way his eyes had glazed over.

"She really took to him," she said.

"So has Marilyn." Jeremy looked down at his feet, studying the tips of the reinforced toes on his boots.

"She thinks she's going to make such a big commission she won't have to work for a couple of years at least." Felicity hopped up on the truck bed and leaned against the sidewall. "Man, that sounds so cynical."

"And what about you? What'd you think of him?"

Felicity was afraid she'd blush when she remembered the heat of attraction she'd felt. She turned to look at the farmhouse to give herself time. But in the end, she wanted to be honest with Jeremy.

"I can see how he gets what he wants." She looked back at him. "He sizes up women very well, and if I hadn't had reason to suspect him, I'd be trotting along behind him just like Marilyn and Loretta."

Jeremy laughed.

"That's so embarrassing," she said. "It's like being a teenager again and a new kid enters the school and all the girls perk up and he's someone your parents think is just so nice and you know he isn't."

"And that's the attraction?"

"No, not for me. This guy is charming and he gives you the sense that he's really noticing you."

Jeremy tipped his head back, closed his eyes, and took a deep breath. "He's a good one for sure." He looked again at the road as Loretta backed her car out of the driveway, waved her hand out the window, and drove away.

"So I guess you're not going to make a bundle, huh?"

"He's not interested in my land." Jeremy hopped up on the tailgate, leaning on the flat of his hands, and nudged her with his shoulder. "And I don't think he's really interested in buying yours either, but he won't tell you that because he'll want to take a walk through it."

"Well, that's what we expected, isn't it?" She leaned on the palms of her hands, swinging her legs.

"Yup. So far it's all going according to plan."

"Guess so. He didn't ask the usual questions about boundaries, rights of way, neighbors, relevant land action, back taxes, all that stuff. When I saw him in Town Hall I thought he was getting information on my property—liens and such. But he didn't seem to care about any of that today."

"Interesting that he went in to look at the printout. He could have done the research online, or gotten Marilyn to do it for him." Jeremy once again looked down the road, now empty. It was supremely quiet today, and Felicity savored this time with him. She worked in quiet all the time, but usually she had less sun and no company. Today she had full warm sun and Jeremy's company before she had to head back to her place.

"You're thinking about something specific." She turned to him and leaned against the wheel. "Tell me."

"First of all, Marilyn surprised me with how much she knew about the area."

"Why would that surprise you?"

"She recognized tree species and other flora and scat and some other things that I didn't think she'd know." He paused. "She likes to come across as an urban sophisticate stuck among the rubes."

Felicity laughed. "That is so true, Jeremy!"

"Now, don't go telling her I said that." Jeremy laughed. "She'll be on my doorstep complaining."

"She's already on Loretta's doorstep complaining about all sorts of things."

"Yeah, I heard."

"Okay, so that was first. What's second?"

"Second, for a man that's supposed to be interested in old growth forests," he said, growing serious, "he didn't look very closely at the trees. He either knew what they were, how old they were, and the last time they were timbered, or he was looking for something else."

"Something else?"

"Something else." He went quiet.

"You don't think he's a scout for the government, looking for land to seize for some kind of highway or something, maybe coming down from Canada or across from Albany? Something the local politicians don't know about?"

Jeremy shook his head. "No, nothing like that. I checked and you checked and Seton checked."

"That was the first thing I thought of when he came sniffing around asking about farmland," Felicity said. "Marilyn pretends to be oblivious to things like that, but she knows what's going on. She wondered, too, but she insisted he was just a man looking for a home."

"I don't think he's looking for a home." Jeremy frowned. "We don't know who he is, and remember, we don't know if Frank Gentile is his real name. Whatever he's doing, he's doing on the quiet."

"Did you think it odd that he didn't own up to buying Zeke Bodrun's cabin? I still think Sasha Glover must have been there."

"The police found no evidence of that, Lissie."

"Still ... And I don't understand why he would want to stay there."

"The cabin gave him a foothold where no one could get to him," Jeremy said. "It gave him a base from which he could go out scouting. He was less likely to run into anyone if he was leaving from the cabin than if he was leaving from a hotel or a B&B. But once the police got interested in it, he couldn't go back there."

"Do you think the timing is significant? Treeline Properties bought that cabin and the land it sits on before Zenia went into the nursing home and before she transferred all her property to her daughter." Felicity paused. "I've been wondering if maybe it took Frank Gentile that long to find a local man who would work with him."

"You're thinking Lance Gauthier is so in debt with gambling that he'd agree to clear out your land without you knowing or agreeing?" Jeremy asked.

"I don't want to believe he'd do something like that, but he's been sneaking into that central plot every time he goes over my plan," she said. "So, yes, I do think he's trying to steal my timber."

"If you're right about Lance working with Gentile, that means he's been speculating on something around here for years," Jeremy said.

"It's like he tracked the rumor of a guy named Zeke all the way back home and bought his cabin to get at what he had. Just like Loretta suggested."

"He's looking for something all right. Maybe he's been trying to get information out of Zenia before she's too far gone to remember."

"Surely you don't think he's like Kyle, looking for some kind of buried treasure?"

Jeremy turned to study her. "Lissie, I wouldn't believe it if someone told me that, but our friend Frank spent more time looking down at his feet than looking up at the trees. And he did that even when we weren't on rough terrain."

———

Felicity took the corner near her farm more slowly than usual when she saw the chief of police parked at the end of her driveway. She drove in and pulled onto the verge, facing in the opposite direction. She lowered her window and said hello to Kevin.

"You had any work done on your truck lately?" Kevin studied the blue Toyota Tacoma, perhaps taking an inventory of the dings and tiny rust spots.

"Is that a hint?" She never thought about the condition of her vehicle except if by some unlucky chance she parked next to Jeremy's shiny white Ford or someone else's shiny new anything.

"No, ma'am, not a hint."

"What's this all about?"

Kevin looked through the windshield, apparently losing interest in the truck's pinged and rusted body. He gripped the steering wheel with both hands. "We lifted a print from Kyle Morgan's car." Felicity thought he looked weary, tired of the world and its lines of little ants trucking along everywhere. "It matches a print we lifted from Zeke Bodrun's old cabin."

"But—"

"But nothing, Felicity. We may not have found evidence of Sasha's being there, but someone was."

"What about Kyle's prints?"

"He wasn't in the cabin as far as I know. But his car was tampered with; we know that. He was in a bar drinking, and anyone who wanted to could have got at his car while he was in there. He died on the drive home. Brakes failing again. Like Clarissa's."

"And Sasha was poisoned."

"Someone wants something real bad."

"What could we possibly have around here that's worth three lives?" Felicity looked toward the woods and then to the right, to the boundary of another farm. Nobody here could have anything worth that, could they?

"I dunno, but I'm thinking of posting a man out here." Kevin shifted in his seat. "I want you to stay close to home while we track down those fingerprints. Is there any way you can lock up your truck?"

Felicity looked through the windshield at the blue hood and shook her head. "If anyone came close to the house—" She stopped.

"What?"

"Nothing, it's nothing. I just thought I heard something near the house last weekend, but when I went out to look there was nothing. It was just a coyote or a bobcat."

"Not a bobcat, Felicity. When was this? What time?"

"Late, maybe one or two … It was nothing, Kevin. I had my shotgun with me."

Kevin shook his head. "Why didn't you call me?"

"The last time I did that, you called Jeremy and I ended up with a dog that needs more protection than I do. Besides, it was nothing, just an animal prowling around the barn." She looked at him, but they both knew she was wrong.

"Felicity, I want you to put your pickup in the barn and lock it. Can you do that? I want to get someone over here to inspect it, make sure you haven't been driving around on borrowed time."

"I'm supposed to spend tomorrow with Jeremy and Taylor. She's coming home again, just for the day."

"Have Jeremy or Loretta give you a ride." He eyed her truck. "You can't watch it all the time, I know, but maybe you can leave it for a while till we get this business taken care of. Tampering with vehicles seems to be this person's MO, and your place is much too easy to get onto. I'm giving you an order." He glanced once more at the truck. "I'm heading over to Jeremy's place now, so I'll let him know."

He put the car in gear and headed off before Felicity could tell him Jeremy wouldn't be there. He'd be at work, at the construction site. She closed her window against the dust Kevin's tires churned up and drove down the driveway.

He had left her feeling doubly frustrated. Just as she and Jeremy were beginning to feel they could figure out Frank Gentile, Kevin shattered her confidence.

Felicity parked in her usual spot by the barn and stood at the back of the pickup. Could she actually get it into the barn without any damage to the truck? And then could she get the sheep in and out? It would be tricky. She put the idea aside and turned her attention to three women standing in front of their easels, brushes in hand. They had picked a scene of old fencing falling down, new growth along the posts, and a birch that had split and grown as though three trees shared a single taproot, as indeed they did. She liked that birch, and knew the beavers in the area would too. If it had grown any closer to a body of water, the tree would be gone by now, but she'd been fortunate and the tree lived on.

The house was quiet, but that wasn't the first thing Felicity noticed when she entered through the kitchen door. Ragged balls of fluff, kapok actually, littered the kitchen floor. She walked through the room and around the staircase to the large open front room. More balls of fluff.

Every pillow had been torn to shreds, its innards thrown wherever they might land. The heavy patterned fabric of the sofa hung in shreds, with scraps scattered over the dining table and chairs, caught on a lamp on the desk, draping over the fire tongs and a stack of firewood. The white tufts of the pillows looked like a gaggle of little fledglings tumbling over the multicolored braided rug, her mother's handiwork made in a craft class at the regional high school one winter. And now edges were frayed and little bits had been pulled up near the center.

Felicity began to back out of the room, toward the kitchen and back door, and then she stopped. She took a closer look at the damage and swung around, peering into corners and behind furniture, before coming to stand in the middle of the living room. The desk sat untouched in the far corner. The shelves by the fireplace remained cluttered and dusty. A few copies of *Farm Journal* lay shredded near the sofa. The answer was obvious.

The rush of adrenaline subsided and she took a deep breath, rubbing her hand over her face. "Shadow? Shadow!" She walked into the kitchen. Miss Anthropy sat curled on her chair beneath the window; she opened one eye, stared at her, and closed it again, flicking her tail as if to say, this has nothing to do with me. He's your dog.

Felicity found Shadow on the second floor, cowering in a corner in the unfinished space at the front used for storage and occasionally for cots and sleeping bags for visiting relatives or friends. The dog hadn't gone after anything upstairs, but he had found a hiding place deep in the eaves over the front porch. This was either the coldest or hottest part of the house, depending on the season. She could hear him whimpering as she came up the old wooden stairs.

"Shadow!" She spoke with a tone of gentle admonition. The whining continued but at a lower level. She approached and knelt down in front of him. He stared at her with fearful, questioning eyes. She extended her hand and petted him along the neck and back, scratching behind the ears. He grew calmer.

After several minutes she managed to draw him out of his corner and down the stairs. At the bottom he began to tremble until she soothed him, pressing her hands against his sides, feeling the heat of her palms move into him. When she withdrew her hands he fell flat on his stomach and stared up at her.

"Well, at least he isn't flat on his back," she said to Miss Anthropy. She looked around the room, assessing the damage. "I suppose this is progress, of a sort. But if this is how you react to a police car coming to the house, I may have to post a sign out front."

Twenty-Nine

Later on Saturday afternoon Shadow trotted along beside Felicity, just five feet away, close enough to feel secure but far enough to escape violence in case his owner decided to punish him for the kapok business. She wondered when he'd finally trust her. She hadn't scolded him over the destruction in the living room, but he'd sensed her disappointment and sat patiently and perhaps even penitently while she cleaned up the mess. She continued to pet him every few minutes as she worked, and he relaxed. But he had months if not years of abuse to overcome. It wouldn't happen overnight.

Nola Townsend met her near the paddock.

"They've been having a great day," she said. She led the way to three painters who'd stepped away from their work to take a break. Felicity guessed they were getting tired and probably cold. They'd been standing and painting since she'd left in the morning.

"I thought it might rain a bit this morning. It looked a little gray, but I guess it moved north of us." Felicity looked up at the blue sky.

"We were fine. The only interruption was some workers," Nola said.

"Workers?"

Nola nodded. "A couple of men said the artists couldn't paint where they were, so they had to move."

Felicity frowned. "How far out did they go?"

Nola called to another woman. Cindy, as she introduced herself, walked over with her drying canvas and propped it on the ground near the fence. She'd focused on leaves and a particular tree, which Felicity recognized.

"You said someone told you to leave?" Felicity asked. Cindy nodded and explained that she had walked farther north, probably onto someone else's property. "Did you see any Posted signs?"

Cindy shook her head. "I tried to stay out of range."

"Out of range? Of what?"

"The men with the machinery." Cindy looked from Felicity to Nola. "Were we not supposed to go up there?"

"I'm not sure where you went," Felicity said.

"Where the tape is?"

"Tape?"

Cindy pulled out two short pieces of plastic tape. "I liked the colors so I pulled off a couple of snippets, to make sure I could match them. I have them in one of my pastels and I wanted to get it right."

Felicity took the two pieces of tape, one orange and the other red. "You got these near where you did that painting?" Cindy nodded and

Felicity felt a sense of dread flood through her. She thanked her and headed into the forest.

―――――

With Shadow bounding along beside her, Felicity took a path leading to the northeast section of her farm. She reached an old fire road that ran along the edge of the property, sometimes veering onto a neighbor's land and sometimes into hers. The stone walls dipped and curved, in some sections falling apart after ice heaves had done their work. She hurried along the dirt road that even in her lifetime could turn into a barely discernible track if it continued to be neglected. Through the trees she could see Lance Gauthier's equipment, but no men. Whoever had been working here had left. She followed the path of his intended cutting, but found no one.

Lance had never answered any of her emails or messages after she'd canceled the last cutting plan. She guessed he wanted to have a new plan to show her that absolved him of whatever she might accuse him of, something that would allow him to claim he'd been misguided, not dishonest. But she knew that was a pipe dream. Now that she'd connected him to Frank Gentile, the evidence of stumps and logs in front of her embodied a real threat.

There was nothing on the ground that shouldn't have been there. And even though she'd rejected the plan, she couldn't deny that this area would have been part of any new plan anyway. He knew that and had gambled by beginning to timber, regardless of her instructions. But it was the rest of the plan that upset her, and his apparent connection with Gentile and a new sawmill. He knew he had to use someone other than Dingel Mantell because Dingel would have recognized the significance of the timber and come straight to her.

Felicity walked on, following the path suggested by the cutting so far, and it led her directly to the central piece, that plot of land that had been so important to Zeke and her dad. She walked into the center of the plot, past the outcropping where the bobcat was thought to be denned, southeast of the spot where Sasha Glover's body had been found. Into the center of what looked like any ordinary stand of trees.

This was where Lance was headed.

And this was where Zeke had fulfilled his lifelong mission and Walter O'Brien had found a legacy to give his daughter—old trees now aging into old growth, one hundred and fifty to two hundred years old now, but perhaps only one hundred years old when Zeke first noticed them. The hemlock and beech wouldn't have impressed him, but he was smart enough to notice what wasn't present—evidence of timbering. And he must have studied and thought and revisited over the years until he was certain. And Lance meant to timber them with his elusive partner.

Felicity stepped through the woods, reaching out a hand to touch and hold the trunks. Above her a low canopy, and above that another, all from tall straight trunks, most small and singular, no suckers, but some robust with branches spreading out over all. She walked and turned, her eyes on the sky glimpsed beyond the bare trees, their branches shimmering pink as they grew ready to leaf out. She'd loved the beauty of this area, but never before had she understood exactly what was here. No wonder her dad and Zeke had been so determined, and so devious, when they worked on a way to save this part of the forest. And no wonder Lance and Frank Gentile were determined to get in here.

West Woodbury could soon have its own old growth forest, but it could be gone forever in a matter of days.

All those problems with drawing up a cutting plan were stalls and obfuscations. Gentile had made Lance Gauthier an offer, and Lance had accepted. Lance only wanted a way to cut straight into the old-growth area and harvest as many of those beautiful straight hardwoods—real hardwoods—as he could without anyone stopping him. The market for real hardwood, not new growth or rapidly grown hardwoods, but real hardwood over one or two hundred years old was booming—overseas. Lance knew exactly what he was doing.

Felicity pulled out her cell phone and punched in Lance's number. Nothing. Wherever Lance was, he wasn't answering his cell. She sent another message, telling him to cease cutting. She cast around for one more way to block him. He might be in money trouble, suckered in by a con artist, but he was basically honest. She was pretty sure he wouldn't cross a line. She went home to make a sign to stop his cutting. And then she called Chief Algren. Nothing wrong with giving the police a heads-up, she told Shadow.

Thirty

On Sunday morning Felicity draped cling wrap over a bowl and then stepped back to admire the color. She'd tried something new this time—orzo salad—partly because she'd discovered she had all the necessary ingredients in her cupboards. She had orzo pasta, sun-dried tomatoes, scallions, black olives, and feta cheese. Making a Greek vinaigrette was easy, and she was relieved not to have to take something Jeremy had already seen a dozen times. It was sometimes embarrassing to partner with a man who was a better cook than she was. She carried the bowl to the kitchen table and ran upstairs to get ready.

A half hour later, in her best casual slacks of navy blue Tencel and a white and blue sweater, she pulled on her jacket. Jeremy would be there any minute to pick her up for the afternoon. She had reluctantly agreed not to drive her pickup again until she and Bruce had time to check it over thoroughly. She'd gotten the truck into the barn the night before and closed and locked the doors, making the farm appear abandoned. She looked out the window, but saw no sign yet of her ride.

"Just enough time to give Minnie and the gals a treat," Felicity said to Shadow. Really, she thought, not only am I talking to the dog, I'm starting to treat the sheep like pets. Still, she reached for the treats she'd bought for the sheep and slipped a few into her pocket. They looked like dog kibble to her, but the package assured her they were full of the good things sheep love, including carrots and maple syrup. And, of course, she gave Shadow a treat for himself. He followed her to the paddock hoping for more and watched longingly while she offered Minnie and the other two sheep their new favorite morsels.

And then she heard it. Someone was starting up a chain saw. It could easily be someone farther down the road. After all, it was a nice afternoon—dry, no wind, mild temperatures. But she knew this land, and she knew that sound wasn't coming from down the road. That was coming from somewhere in her woods. And that meant Lance—or someone else—was ignoring her sign. She shoved the gate shut and began to trot toward the path into the woods. And then she remembered Clarissa and Sasha and Kyle. She ran back to the house for her shotgun.

She hurried through the underbrush. Shadow nipped past her, an eager companion once again. He leapt up the hill, sliding through rotting leaves and squirreling into small caves chasing only he knew what. Felicity tried to keep up, but her eye was on the hill, and then the next one, and then the stone wall. She should have changed her shoes, but all she could think of was that chain saw cutting into a two-hundred-year-old yellow birch. When she reached the old fire road, she brushed herself off and ran to the site where she'd seen evidence of Lance's work the day before. Shadow bounded along nearby.

The chain saw sputtered and died.

She stopped, balanced on a rock outcropping while she listened. Birds had disappeared into their branches. But it wasn't silence filling the space. The longer she stood there, the more certain she was of hearing voices. She climbed down from the boulder, sliding on the loose dirt, and moved laterally. She'd been heading straight into the center of her dad's special plot, but now she moved to the side, trying to approach from an angle that would allow her some concealment.

Shadow sensed her caution and followed closely at her heels, watching her, each paw placed on the ground only after she moved forward. After a while she could see through the trees into the center of the plot. Two men were talking. Or arguing. She wished she'd brought a rifle instead of a shotgun.

"Lance?" Felicity pushed through the underbrush into the clearing.

"He's cutting old trees," the other man said.

"Mr. Gentile? Frank?" He looked embarrassed when Felicity identified him. But why were Frank Gentile and Lance arguing? She thought they were working together. But now they were shouting at each other. Was this a matter of thieves falling out?

"I was out walking and I heard his chain saw, so of course I came in to see who was cutting on a Sunday." Gentile waved a hand at Lance. "He's in here timbering. In here! It's outrageous."

"I was just checking the equipment, Felicity. I saw your sign—I did—I was just going to take my stuff. This man barged down the hill yelling at me. He's a crackpot. He doesn't know what he's talking about." Lance balled his fists and lifted his chin a few times at Frank as he spoke, and he bounced on his toes. They were like two dogs trying to intimidate each other. Felicity was afraid they'd come to blows.

"I thought you two knew each other," she said, looking from one to the other.

"I've never seen him before in my life," Lance said.

"Felicity, if I may, you need to give your attention to this man." Frank seemed determined to remain calm and sound official as he pointed his thumb at Lance. "He was getting ready to cut down all the trees in this area. He dropped this." Frank tossed a small handheld device to her. She caught it with her left hand and held the device against her chest.

"This is a clinometer, Lance. Are you out here measuring trees with this after I canceled?"

"It doesn't mean anything, Felicity. I always carry one."

"But why were you using it here? I told you to cease."

"I was just doing a walk-through, Felicity. So you'd have good information."

"He was timber cruising." Frank shifted on the uneven ground, a man ready to lash out.

"Are you sure you don't know each other?" Felicity waited.

"I don't know this man," Frank said. "Why would I know him?"

Felicity glanced at each one. She'd landed in something different from what she'd expected, but perhaps it was starting to make sense. Just because two criminals showed up in the same place didn't mean they were on the same job. "Lance, were you assessing the value of the trees here? You were hoping to timber in here, weren't you? And after I told you to stop?"

"Come on, Felicity. You know me. We've worked together for years." Lance breathed heavily, backing up with every word.

"You know all about this stand, don't you?" Felicity said.

"What're you talking about?" Frank said, but the other two ignored him.

When Lance turned to Felicity, his brown eyes softening and his stocky frame once again that of the boy she'd known in school, she felt her heart sink. How had he changed in front of her eyes without her even understanding? The sign and orders to cease meant nothing to him. He'd crossed a line a long time ago.

"I came through here a few years ago." Lance looked up, turning as he scanned the canopy above. "Think of what this means. This is real hardwood, Felicity. Not in name but in reality. These trees have been here almost two hundred years. There are no suckers, no new growth. It's all old. Think what you could make with this."

Felicity could barely tolerate listening to him, but she knew she had to speak now, while she could. There were two of them and only one of her. They weren't the team she'd imagined, but she was standing between them, alone. One of them had to go.

"How can you talk like that after Clarissa and Sasha?" she said to Lance.

He looked at her, his face a blank. But he blinked and recovered himself. "Listen to me, Felicity. The land produces something wonderful. We're meant to use it. We're part of nature too." He said the last to her alone, and his brown eyes hardened. "You don't appreciate it. You want to just leave it here to rot. Look at that." He waved at a dead tree that had fallen against a living one. "And that." Again, he waved at a rotting tree trunk.

She looked across to the other side of the clearing, at the fallen tree covered in moss, rotting from the inside out. It had once been, perhaps a few years ago, a stately oak. And now it was insect food. The ground was torn up at its root ball, as though it being wrenched from the earth wasn't enough.

"You wouldn't have missed any of it," he said. "You weren't supposed to be here today."

"But I am here. Lance, is this what Clarissa and Sasha died for?"

"What? What are you talking about? I had nothing to do with those two dying," Lance said. "They didn't know about the old growth, and they probably wouldn't have cared if they did."

"But they did know, Lance." Felicity took a step back, slid on the leaves, and recovered her balance. "And you killed them to make sure they told no one, especially me." She wasn't surprised at the look on his face, a mass of confusion and mounting hysteria.

"No, no. I never did anything to them."

"It was you, Lance. And I'm going to go back to my farm and call Chief Algren and Jeremy. I'm going to get them up here to arrest you." She lifted her shotgun. "You won't get away, Lance."

"No, no, I didn't, Felicity. I never..." He stared up at the trees, at Felicity, at the shotgun. He had so much trouble breathing he began to choke and cough. With one last look at her, he turned and bolted up the slope, sliding on the damp leaves, a rotting branch skidding out beneath his feet. She watched him as he scrambled with his bare hands up the hill, slipping and crabbing upwards till he was out of sight.

Felicity looked up at the canopy, at the tall straight hemlock, at the early spring light filtering through. By the outcropping where she'd slid down, the ground had been churned up. At the far end of the clearing, leaves had been swept aside. Unconsciously she reached into her pocket for her cell phone, but it wasn't there.

"Damn. I don't have my cell." She stepped farther down the slope.

"You should go after him." Frank began to move to her left, a small step and then another. "You don't want him to get away."

"He won't get far. He can't do any cutting in here now, and he can't run away." She shifted the shotgun. Kevin was right, she thought. *I don't think things through far enough.*

"It's beautiful, isn't it?" Frank sounded as if the previous conversation had never happened as he pointed deeper into the woods, to the edge of the old-growth area. "Over there, those are black birch, and farther out are a number of old sugar maples. You've got yellow birch and sweet birch, and none of these are young. Lance had a good eye. Look over here." He led her away from the center of the plot, pointing out trees with signs of extreme age, two hundred years, he thought. "The rocky terrain has protected them."

Felicity agreed. "No one could farm in here. They couldn't even pasture here."

"The old-growth part is probably not more than twenty acres, but it's special territory."

He led her in a southerly direction, away from the area where Lance had begun timbering. She looked back up the slope where Lance had gone. She couldn't hear him crashing through the trees anymore.

"Shouldn't you go after him?" Frank Gentile relaxed, his hands open at his side. He ran his right hand through his hair and smiled. "I mean, you're lucky you caught him, but really, you don't want him to get away."

"He won't get away. If I hadn't been feeding the sheep treats while waiting for my ride, I might never have known what was happening until it was too late." She forced herself to smile. "It was lucky you heard him too."

"I happened to be out for a walk and just came down here out of curiosity." He shrugged, lifting his hands as if it was nothing at all.

"Still, I'm so grateful to have saved my trees."

"Not at all. A deed well done today. And you still have time to enjoy your friends."

"I should get back to the farm and call the police. Get them onto Lance right away, before he can disappear."

Frank leaned over her, his face contorted by worry. "He's obsessed, Felicity. You should hurry. He murdered three people. Get to Chief Algren as fast as you can."

"Yes, it was three people, wasn't it?" she said. His eyebrows came together and his brown eyes glistened. She wondered if he even saw her anymore, or if she was just one more person in his way. "Listen, Frank, why don't you come back with me?"

"Not necessary, really." He began to walk backward up the hill, shaking his head and waving his right hand as though a fly were buzzing around his fingers and he was leading the creature on a loopy ride.

"But you heard what Lance had to say. It'd be good for me to have a witness." She'd managed to position herself so she was facing him, standing about ten feet away, her shotgun firmly in her hands.

"It's not necessary, but I'll go in to see the police later if you want. I'm glad to help." He continued to walk uphill, quickly recovering from a stumble, looking to left and right as though he'd lost something.

"I guess you were just out for a walk, is that right?" She held the shotgun a little higher, the barrel pointed at his feet. Frank Gentile listened, but she could see in his eyes the effort of calculating what his next move had to be.

"I'm sure I told Marilyn I enjoy being out in the forest, being in the clean air." He took a step backward, his arms stretched out at his sides to keep his balance. She could see the dirt-encrusted knees of his heavy green work pants.

Felicity lifted the shotgun a fraction. "Let's go back to my place, Frank. I want the police chief to hear what happened. Don't you want to make sure Lance is caught?"

"You seemed pretty sure he would be."

"Yes, but I don't yet know what all the digging is about. I thought maybe you could help me with that." She stepped back, lifting the shotgun another fraction of an inch. "Frank?"

"I can't tell you what those folks were up to, all those holes over there." He nodded in the direction of Sasha's plot.

"So you saw them? You know about that. I suppose it was your footprints I saw in the snow a few days ago, after that freak snowstorm. The night Kyle died in that car accident."

He began to breathe heavily, as though he'd been running through the woods. He watched her with assessing eyes, his hands falling to his sides and his pockets. Before she could say anything else, he withdrew his hand and the light sparkled on a knife.

"Frank, I'm not afraid to shoot."

"No? You've had plenty of chances and you haven't yet."

"That was you all those nights out back of my house?"

"Did you really think someone was trying to get into your cellar through the foundation? I saw the repair work you did. Why would anyone be trying to get into your cellar from the back?"

"Okay. You tell me."

"You don't deserve what you have." He spit out the words, little sprays of saliva collecting light. "You have all these trees, old growth, and you didn't even know it. You're trampling rare plants under your laundry line. All over your farm you're letting these plants die. They're being crushed by people like Lance and those Saturday painters." His face twisted in contempt. His finger arched on the knife. A blade swung out so fast she only saw it after it happened, glittering in his hand. "You're destroying what is worth ten of you." She heard a sound like a growl low in his throat, but he wasn't looking at her now. He was staring at something behind her. Rage contorted his face. She turned to see what had taken over his sanity.

Minnie trudged over a pile of twigs, her muzzle shifting little piles of dead leaves as she snuffled her way over the ground. She pushed her snout into a balsa wood container half-hidden under a pile of leaves and began nibbling at the plants it held.

"Oh no! She must have followed me."

Frank spun on the leaves as he tried to get his footing, his hand outstretched and the blade pointed at the animal. He lunged.

Felicity lifted the shotgun and fired.

Shadow leapt into the clearing, jumping up and down like he had springs on his feet and yapping hysterically. But over the din she heard someone calling her name, and a moment later Kevin and Jeremy and Lance came thrashing up the hill.

"Stop it. Stop that animal! It's eating the orchids," Frank yelled as soon as he got his wind back. He crawled on his stomach, dragging his bloody leg, throwing rocks and sticks and anything else he could get his hands on at Minnie. Felicity handed off her shotgun to Jeremy and used treats meant for Shadow to tempt Minnie away from the box of plants. Shadow remained hysterical.

Kevin hoisted Frank to his feet and arrested him. Lance stumbled from one grouping to the other. He babbled incoherently about having nothing to do with digging holes or killing people. It was only about the trees.

Thirty-One

"Orchids? He was digging up orchids?" Felicity stood in the middle of the kitchen while Kevin stood by the table reading a message on his cell. Through the kitchen window she could see the state police vehicles backing down the drive and then speeding away on the old road.

"That's what he was doing," the chief grumbled, then punched off his cell. "I feel like I'm turning into a pin cushion." He glanced at Jeremy. "Three doctors' appointments next week," he said before turning away.

Felicity took two glasses from the cupboard and put them on the kitchen table. Jeremy pulled a bottle of Johnny Walker out of a cupboard and held it up.

"None for me. Doctor's orders." Kevin looked longingly at the bottle and turned away.

Felicity poured hot water over a tea bag and took her mug to the table. Jeremy added a splash of Scotch in her mug and poured a glass for himself. "I don't get it. Orchids?" she asked again.

"And a bunch of plants I never heard of." Kevin wiped a hand over his face. Felicity noticed his complexion seemed to have returned to normal, the violent pink receding to his more familiar ruddy look.

"Frank Gentile isn't his real name," Kevin added. He rested his regulation hat on an empty chair and looked surprisingly pleased with himself. "He's a Mr. Ralph Parr."

"How did you figure that out?" Felicity asked.

"It was the fingerprints from that coffee mug Mr. Parr used yesterday at Jeremy's place." He nodded to Jeremy.

"It was your friends at the state lab and the state police barracks who helped put it all together," Jeremy said.

Felicity listened to this exchange as the two men went back and forth arguing over who should get the credit. When she couldn't stand it a moment longer, she interrupted. "Why was he digging up my plants?"

"That's simple, Felicity. They're valuable." Kevin leaned back in the wooden chair. It creaked, and the sound felt like a gentle reminder of the Sunday afternoon when a farmer could look around at his week's work and feel all was well. And at least now that it was quiet, Felicity could too. Shadow slept on the floor nearby, Minnie was back with her flock, Miss Anthropy slept in her chair, and no one was running any machinery.

"Is this what Kyle was after?"

"Only Kyle knows what he thought he was digging up, more likely some kind of valuable artifact. Not plants. Maybe old coins. He had a literal mind."

"Are you telling me this man, Parr or Gentile, killed three people to get at some plants?"

"That's exactly what he did," Jeremy said. "Mr. Parr scouts for rare and valuable plants. He either buys up land and depletes it, or he does what he did with yours. He buys a piece nearby, scouts your property, and takes everything he can get."

"And no one ever knows?"

"No one ever knows," Jeremy said.

"That's why he bought Zeke Bodrun's cabin a few years ago," Kevin said.

"Zeke became some sort of legend, this old guy traveling around looking at old-growth forests and talking about how important they were. He went to so many places and talked so openly that people remembered him and he entered into local folklore. Parr heard the stories about this guy from the Pioneer Valley and it got him thinking there might be something up here," Jeremy said. "Old growth and rare plants often go together."

"Zeke was long dead and only his reputation remained, but Parr came up here to check it out," Kevin said. "He's been in this area a lot longer than we knew about."

"He sure kept a low profile," Jeremy said. "At least until recently. The business with Marilyn was just a ruse, like we thought. He wasn't going to buy anything."

"But why kill three people?" Felicity asked. "Why kill Clarissa and Sasha and Kyle?"

"Kyle is easy to figure out," Kevin said. "He was digging all over the place, and very determined. Parr was worried he'd destroy the plants he was after. In the beginning, Parr got engaged to Clarissa thinking he'd be able to use her land to come and go as he pleased, and get what he wanted from your land without anyone noticing."

"But Clarissa gave the land to Sasha," Felicity said.

"Exactly. Clarissa and Parr were engaged, but something went wrong. We're not sure, but we think Clarissa figured out he wasn't on the up and up. Maybe the question of a marriage license came up, or he refused to have his photograph taken, or something small like that, but she heard the warning bells. He tampered with her brakes while her car was at Bruce's. And she was coming to see you, perhaps to tell you there was something about your land you should figure out."

"And Sasha?"

"He approached Sasha, trying to get her to sell him the piece of land, but she and Clarissa were close and she knew she shouldn't." Kevin paused to look at the bare trees outside the window. "It seems Parr met her at the cabin and poisoned her when he realized she wasn't going to sell. That was right after she talked to you. Anyway, it must have started to hit her outside Zeke's cabin. Maybe she caught on to what was happening and ran into the woods. She may have been trying to get to you. We'll never know. She vomited in the woods and Parr tried to clean her up. You're right about that. Good guess, Felicity. We don't know all the details yet. It's early days."

"Three people dead, and all for a few plants. What was he going to do with them?" Felicity asked.

"He sells them. He's got big money behind him. His backers want rare plants. Collectors can be real fanatics, Felicity. And those plants he was digging up? Rare and endangered."

"My plants? I knew we had one or two unusual ones but so what? I mean, I like orchids too, but still…"

"There are all kinds of orchids," Jeremy said. "And you have some unusual ones, endangered too. You have some that only grow in old-growth forests."

"He had a lot of containers there," Felicity said. "I saw something by an uprooted tree but it didn't register just then. Was he planning on taking everything and cleaning out the area?"

"He wanted all he could get," Kevin said.

"And that's why all the pressure on Marilyn to get us to sell, or at least let him walk through our property." Jeremy looked disgusted.

"Was he in my back yard looking for plants?" Felicity asked.

"Yup," Kevin said. "I got a look at his list and it included a kind of purple clematis."

"That's on the list?" Felicity looked at Kevin. "Then I won't tell you how I trample it whenever I hang out laundry, or the time I tried to rip it out."

"No, Felicity, don't tell me that." Kevin cast another look at the Johnny Walker.

"I don't see how he could expect to find the plants now," she said. "None of them are in bloom."

"He marked the spots from earlier visits," Kevin said, "and when Lance started timbering, Frank must have figured he had to move fast before the area was destroyed."

"And Lance was so scared at the idea of being accused of murder that he came flying down the road looking for Kevin." Jeremy began to laugh. "What a confession!"

"I wasn't sure Lance would take the hint," Felicity said. "I'd thought he was in on it with Parr, but then I heard them arguing and they didn't seem to even know each other."

"Lance said he never saw the guy before," Kevin said.

"When he took off, I prayed he would go straight to find you."

"Good one, Lissie." Jeremy nodded approvingly.

"Without Lance, we wouldn't have known where you were," Kevin said. "But we would have heard you. Tell me you won't load up that thing again."

"He told me I would never shoot." Felicity shook her head. "He practically dared me. I had no choice. I was defending my sheep."

"That's not the right answer, Lissie." Jeremy groaned. "The correct answer is self-defense. He was coming at you with a knife. Fortunately, his leg's going to be okay."

"Oh that." Felicity waved away the comment. "Right now I'm more worried about the timbering. I have to find a new logger. I can never trust Lance again."

———

Felicity and Jeremy watched Kevin reach the end of the driveway, turn onto the road, and drive out of sight, but it was a while before either one spoke.

"Do you think there's anything left of that potluck you invited me to?" Felicity asked.

"I'd bet Loretta and Taylor are still sitting at the table gossiping."

"I'm hungry." Felicity walked toward Jeremy's pickup, then stopped. "Do sheep get traumatized?"

Jeremy looked down at her. "You're joking, right?"

"I was just wondering how I'd feel if someone came charging at me with a knife." She rested her hands in her jacket pockets and turned to look at the barn where the sheep had been settled for the night. "I don't know what Minnie thought she was doing."

"If you give her treats, Lissie, she's going to come looking for you."

"You think I'm getting too attached to them, don't you?" Felicity looked wistfully at the barn. A tree branch lifted in a soft breeze and a spotlight came on, lighting up the front of the yard. "Maybe I am, but it feels right."

Jeremy put an arm around her and pulled her closer and Felicity wrapped her arms around his waist.

"I hope there won't be any more flora thieves in my life." She looked up at Jeremy. "Do you realize he could have gotten away with it and I'd never have known? If Lance hadn't tried to cut all the way through to that section, Parr could have lifted every single rare or endangered or valuable plant, and I would never have guessed anything was missing. Unless he took the lady's slippers, of course."

"The tragedy is, they probably wouldn't have survived," Jeremy said.

"He seemed to think he could do it, since apparently he's been doing it for years." Felicity leaned her head against Jeremy's shoulder. "What a way to make a living."

"You mean the farm or the thief?"

Felicity gave him a gentle poke in the arm. "A botanist stopped by a few years ago to buy vegetables, and he admired the farm, what he could see of it. He said it must be a special place. Dad was working the stand and the guy told him he could see some rare and endangered plants just from the road." Felicity looked across the field to the marshy area hidden by trees and to the small pond beyond.

"Did he tell your dad which plants were valuable?"

"He did, and ever since then I haven't wanted to know any more."

"Why?"

"Do you remember that bulrush I said was so ugly when we were pulling out old barbed wire last summer? The one I wanted to rip out and use for compost?"

"Sure, and it was."

"Well, it's protected, so I couldn't pull it out. It's a relict."

"Which is?"

"A relict is a remnant of an otherwise extinct flora, according to our passing botanist." She frowned. "It looks like I'm stuck with that northeastern bulrush, and I tell you that plant is plug ugly. Beautiful orchids hidden in the forest and that hideous bulrush filling up the marsh."

Jeremy opened the passenger-side door of his truck.

"Before we go, Jeremy, there's one thing I want to do." She turned back to the house, picked up a shovel leaning against the porch, and led the way around to the back. Late afternoon light warmed the ground and whitened the straw covering a small garden. "Let's move the laundry pole and give that rare clematis a chance to survive. I've been pretty rough on it all these years."

"You're lucky it's lasted." Jeremy reached for the shovel.

"We're all lucky we survived. That man could have done a lot of damage." She stepped back to give him room. He pushed the tip of the shovel into the ground and put his foot on the edge, leaning on it, then turned to look at her.

"Lissie, I meant what I said when we were waiting for Parr to show up to walk my farm. I'm ready to make a change. We almost lost something more valuable than land. We've been drifting along for fifteen years without thinking about it, but it's time to think about it. You've done right by your dad, and I've done all I can for my daughter."

"Are you talking about what I think you're talking about?"

"Lissie, I told you I'm ready to turn the whole farm over to Taylor when she's out of school in a year. For the first time in my life I'll have nothing holding me. But this is the only place I want to be. I think it's time for you and me to have our own life."

Felicity could feel the heat growing inside her. She knew it wasn't the sun warming her head to toe. She hadn't expected this, but it was right; she could feel it. "I suppose you'll need a place for those cows of yours." She smiled and unhooked the clothesline. She rolled up the rope, then stepped back while Jeremy dug around the pole, loosening it from the thawing ground.

The End

Acknowledgments

Special thanks are due my agent, Paula Munier, whom I first met at a writers' group she held in her home some years ago. She has supported me through more rewrites than I care to remember, and has the gift of saying something won't work without hurting my feelings while directing me to something that will. My thanks go also to Terri Bischoff, my editor at Midnight Ink, for valuable suggestions that gave the Pioneer Valley series a strong start. Sandy Sullivan and Melissa Mierva made a meticulous review of the manuscript, saving me from many blunders.

Over the years my family and I have worked with a number of foresters and loggers on our property, and each one has taught me something valuable about forestry and land management. Their dedication and stewardship always proved invaluable, and I'm grateful to them for their willingness to share their expertise.

Every writer has at least one friend who faithfully listens to sometimes incomprehensible ruminations on plot or character or methods of murder. I'm fortunate to have several who listened and also read earlier versions of this book. Skye Alexander, Danuta Borchardt, Elenita Lodge, and Leslie Wheeler read some or all of the manuscript and offered suggestions as well as insightful criticisms. I'm grateful for their feedback as well as their friendship.

Every day I'm aware of how fortunate I am to have the love and support of my husband, Michael, who has encouraged my forays into fiction from the beginning.

As always, despite all the assistance I have received over the years, any errors or omissions are entirely mine.

About the Author

Susan Oleksiw is the author of three mystery series. *Below the Tree Line* is the first in the Pioneer Valley series, featuring farmer and healer Felicity O'Brien. The Anita Ray series features Indian American Anita Ray, photographer, who lives in her aunt's tourist hotel. Anita's adventures take the reader into the little-known world of life in India beyond the tourist hotel and main streets. The Mellingham series of crime novels feature Chief of Police Joe Silva in the small town of Mellingham, with its quirky residents living along the New England coast.

Susan has also written extensively on crime fiction. Find her essays in *The Oxford Companion to Crime and Mystery Writing* and her favorite books in *A Reader's Guide to the Classic British Mystery*.